Bolan watched water seep from the seal of the hatch

"If we stay down here we either drown or get cracked like an egg!"

The sub's turbine howled up into emergency war power. "The captain says hold on!" Jukka called.

"Up periscope!" The shaft slid down from the sail, and Bolan grabbed it and held on. The dark, tree-lined shore loomed into view. "Tell him five more degrees to starboard!"

The captain threw a valve and the hull groaned as compressed air shoved all the water out of the ballast tanks. The sub rose like a cork. "Twenty-five meters!" The hull shuddered as the captain pushed more levers, and groans and clanks reverberated as gears engaged. "Fifteen meters!"

The sound of hail pounded the hull as the sub breached the water and began taking bullet strikes. "Ten!"

"Five meters!" Jukka's knuckles went white on his panel. "Impact!"

MACK BOLAN ®
The Executioner

The Executioner
Don Pendleton's®

BLAST
RADIUS

A GOLD EAGLE BOOK FROM

WORLDWIDE®

TORONTO • NEW YORK • LONDON
AMSTERDAM • PARIS • SYDNEY • HAMBURG
STOCKHOLM • ATHENS • TOKYO • MILAN
MADRID • WARSAW • BUDAPEST • AUCKLAND

First edition December 2003
ISBN 0-373-64301-2

Special thanks and acknowledgment to
Chuck Rogers for his contribution to this work.

BLAST RADIUS

Printed in U.S.A.

There is no calamity greater than lavish desires.
There is no greater guilt than discontentment.
And there is no greater disaster than greed.
—Lao-tzu
c.604–c.531 B.C.

A nuclear attack and its fallout are too
horrific to contemplate. No one really wins.
I'll take my chances with a preemptive strike,
and send the bastards to hell.
—Mack Bolan

Finno-Russian Border

The Executioner slid silently through the trees.

Nothing good was happening in the forests of Finland this night.

His skis were little more than a rustling hiss in the snow. The whip and moan of the wind through the pines covered their slight sound. The massive storms building out in the cold gray caldron of the North Sea hadn't begun to hammer Scandinavia, but they had sent their outriders on the wind. Dark clouds scudded across the moonlit night sky like black rags. Snow fell upon the pines in eddying pockets and the windchill brought the temperature to just above zero. The strange conditions left parts of the forest brightly lit under full moon and starry sky, and others patches of impenetrable darkness. In Bolan's night-vision goggles the night was painted in black and green.

The Executioner made for the canal.

The Saimaa Canal linked the Russian coastal city of Vyborg with the Finnish Lake Saimaa. On this exact same ground in 1940 the Finns had drawn a line in the snow and waged vicious guerrilla war against the invading army of the Soviet Union. Skiborne Finnish submachine gunners had spit fire into the trudging columns of Red Army riflemen and then faded back into the forest, ghostlike, inflicting casualties against the Soviets out of all proportion to their numbers. The Soviet Union claimed victory.

They had sought to conquer all of Finland. They had taken and held a bare strip of the Karelian Peninsula. The Russian marshall who had led the invasion had bitterly remarked they had conquered just enough territory to bury their own dead.

Bolan clicked out of his skis and unslung his rifle.

What Russian black market nuclear weapons were doing traveling up the Saimaa Canal from Russia into the Finnish Lake Districts at 2:00 a.m. in the morning was a very good question indeed.

The Executioner fitted the .308 M-1-A scout rifle's sling into a rifleman's loop and unclipped his infrared beacon from his web gear. The beacon was barely the size of a mini-flashlight. Bolan stood in a break in the tree canopy and activated the beacon. To the visible eye, nothing happened.

In the infrared spectrum, a quick series of pulses lit up the night.

One of the thousand visible stars above Bolan was an NRO communications and observation satellite. Aaron Kurtzman spoke in Bolan's ear. "We have you in sight, Striker. We have a thirty-minute window on you. After that we'll have to switch horses. Estimate a two- to five-minute blackout if satellite switch is required. We have a ninety-minute window once Satellite Two comes over the horizon."

"Affirmative. Understood." Bolan moved at a good pace for the canal. The snow was several days old and hard-packed; the treads of his raid boots gave him good traction. "Have you acquired the target?"

"Affirmative, Striker. The barge has tied up on the west side of the canal, two klicks due east of your position. Low level of heat emission from the engine. The barge has been docked for a while."

"How many hostiles do you count?"

"We count four figures on the deck of the barge. Two appear to be human. Two more are slightly smaller and moving randomly around the deck. We believe they are dogs. Large ones."

"How many hostiles on shore?"

"We have four standing around. Thermal imaging shows an active, high-intensity heat source in their midst, possibly some kind of mobile stove. Small, moving thermal signatures on the figures indicate they are smoking and drinking coffee or tea. Posture, dispersion and activities indicate a low level of alert."

Good. The enemy wasn't expecting company. But Bolan wasn't betting on their being totally lax, either. Nuclear materials tended to make people very nervous. "Scan a wider area. Any sign of sentries?"

"Negative."

Bolan didn't like the sound of it. "You got Gummer in sight?"

"Gummer confirmed."

Bolan checked his watch. "You got all that, Gummer?"

Gary Manning spoke from his position half a kilometer parallel to Bolan's own. "Affirmative, Striker."

"Bear, do we have any more confirmation on the nukes?"

"Nothing new since you and Gummer dropped."

The Executioner considered. All they had was a wild story from a stateside member of the Russian *mafiya* who was desperate to avoid being extradited to Mother Russia where he would be shot. "They're waiting on somebody. Scan up and down the canal."

"Scanning." There was a long pause while the satellite panned its lens up and down the length of the Saimaa Canal. "Negative, Striker."

"Scan wider. They didn't stop to smoke cigarettes."

"Scanning."

Bolan waited with the patience of a stone.

"I have nothing within a twenty-mile radius."

"No vehicles? No heat signatures of any kind?"

"There's only one road anywhere near your position. Traffic is extremely light. We detect one car on the roadway about twenty-two miles from your position. Traveling at approximately fifty miles per hour. It isn't stopping."

Bolan frowned. "I need something, Bear. Reindeer sledges, anything."

"Striker, I have nothing." Kurtzman's voice was tight. "They haven't broken any law. They've traveled through the first five canal locks without a hitch. This could be a bum tip and an international, incident-level goat screw if we've got bad intel."

"Yeah, and they stopped just after they crossed the Finnish border."

"Engine trouble?" Kurtzman "the Bear" offered.

"I don't buy it."

"Striker, other than some possible dogs on the barge, we have about a zero level of preparedness. No sentries."

Bolan grimaced. "How long have they been docked?"

"Estimate a half hour, perhaps forty-five minutes."

The Executioner's instincts spoke along his spine. "Bear, the transaction is going down. It's going down right now. Gummer, close to fifty yards and maintain position." The Executioner glanced at the illuminated compass dial of his watch. "Bear, vector us in."

"Affirmative, Striker, your call. Change your heading to seven degrees south and maintain course."

"Affirmative." The wind moaned through the trees as the Executioner closed on the canal. Through his night-vision goggles he began to detect the ghostly glimmer of light sources ahead.

Manning's voice spoke in Bolan's earpiece. "Striker."

"What is it, Gummer?"

"I've got a feeling."

Bolan knelt and remained motionless. The big Canadian had spent more time creeping through ice forests than anyone Bolan could think of besides himself. When Manning wasn't creeping through frozen forests or steaming jungles, he was creeping through blast-furnace deserts and the concrete hells of cities shattered by war. Manning was a born hunter.

The man's instincts were money in the bank.

"You think we got a goat screw on our hands?"

"Oh, yeah."

Bolan paused at the tone in Manning's voice. "You don't think we got bad intel."

"I think the intel was right on." Manning's voice dropped. "I think we just stepped in serious shit."

The Executioner crouched motionless in the snow. The wind whipped at his poncho. It's camouflage pattern and that of his raid suit were designed to disrupt his body outline in the viewers of light-amplification devices. The poncho, raid suit and armor were chemically treated to help break up his infrared signature. The satellite above couldn't detect him unless he used the beacon.

An observation post on the ground stood a much better chance, particularly when he was moving, and light amplification and infrared were only two possible tools available to someone who was afraid of company.

Bolan slung his rifle and drew his Heckler & Koch MK-23 from his thigh holster. The .45-caliber was an offensive pistol, made more so by the sound-suppressor tube threaded to the end of the barrel and the infrared laser sight slaved beneath the slide. "Gummer, come on up."

"Affirmative, Striker."

Bolan scanned the trees. Something was wrong. People didn't tie up barges by the side of a canal in the middle of nowhere in the middle of the night for no reason. Kurtzman could be right. The barge seemed to be at a very low state of alert. They could just be having some sort of engine difficulty and were waiting for a tugboat to come and get them.

Or Manning was right and there was something funny going on.

People smuggling nukes wouldn't sit motionless in plain sight, but Bolan was betting on his comrade in arms.

The Executioner raised his beacon. The cone around the lens funneled all of the light upward to the satellite above without spilling it out to ground observers. Kurtzman spoke as he observed the flash. "Gummer, adjust course two degrees south. Striker is one hundred yards from your present position."

"Affirmative."

Manning appeared like a wraith out of the wind and snow and knelt at the Executioner's side. His rifle matched Bolan's. Both weapons had optical sights mounted forward of the breech, which let the shooter keep both eyes open. The arrangement was ideal for precision snapshooting at close quarters.

"Gummer, I'm going to take a look. Cover me."

"You got it."

Bolan moved forward, the big .45 pistol preceding him in both hands. "Bear?"

"No suspicious movement. No sentries are visible."

Bolan could see the lights of the barge through the trees. The glow of the field stove and the men's cigarettes were like flares in his night-vision goggles. Bolan crept up to the edge of the light and crouched by a tree.

The men were speaking Russian. Bolan could only catch snatches, but most of the conversation centered around things like "taking too long." None of the four men appeared to be armed, but their bulky winter jackets could conceal a great deal of hardware. Bolan examined the barge. Running lights lit fore and aft, and there was a small light in the pilothouse. Two more men walked on the deck. A pair of dogs was on the deck and off leash.

Bolan was glad he was downwind.

In the gray-green world of his night-vision gear the dogs had the shape and build of German shepherds, except that they were uniformly light-colored and stood taller. Bolan had been on the wrong end of more animals than he cared to think about. Belgian Malinois were strong-willed dogs and difficult to control. Pound for pound they were some of the heaviest hitters in the realm of guard dogs.

"Jesus, what the hell is taking so long!"

Bolan snapped his gaze to the men around the stove at the sound of English spoken with an American accent. The man who had spoken was tall. He threw his cigar into the snow. It sizzled as he crushed it beneath his snow boot and muttered, "Goddamn Euro trash..."

The other three men looked away and smoked their cigarettes. Bolan noted their posture. The man who had spoken was in a position of command.

Kurtzman spoke hurriedly in Bolan's ear. "Striker, we have movement."

"What kind of movement?"

"A heat source. Kind of flaky, dispersed, flickering in and out, but definitely there, seventy-five yards due east of you, and moving slowly in your direction."

"Bear, I just came from there."

"I know."

"Gummer, someone got past you."

"No." Manning's voice was adamant. "No one got past me." Bolan glanced behind him. "Bear, where did it come from?"

"Out of nowhere. We had a momentary heat flash, and then we picked up this ghost."

"Striker," Manning said very quietly, "you want me to investigate?"

"Negative, Gummer. Hold position."

Bolan rose from his crouch. "Bear, give me a heading."

"Sixty yards, due west and closing."

Bolan began to slowly circle south through the trees. "Heading."

"Holding course, forty yards from your last position."

The Executioner checked his compass dial and plotted his intercept.

"Thirty yards from your original position and closing."

Bolan stood as still and silent as a gravestone. He held the MK-23 extended in both hands. A figure, wearing a hooded poncho much like his own, detached itself from the dark bulk of a tree ten yards away. For a moment, starlight reflected off the lenses of his night-vision gear. The figure had been an absolute part of the tree until he had moved. Bolan knew the killer wore night-vision and heat-disruptive camouflage like his own. As the wind ruffled his poncho, Bolan the soldier could see the dark bulk of armor beneath his camouflage.

The killer carried a Russian-made AS silent-assault rifle fitted with an optical sight.

The Executioner knew the fat .45-caliber subsonic rounds in his MK-23 wouldn't penetrate Russian titanium-reinforced body armor or helmet. He raised his pistol slightly. His thumb flicked the slide lock so that the pistol wouldn't cycle and eject when he fired. The infrared laser sight beneath the slide blinked to life. In his night-vision goggles, a bright white dot appeared within the hood of the killer's poncho. The killer's head whipped around at the tiny intense glare that suddenly manifested itself in his own night-vision goggles.

The sound of the killer's right optical lens shattering was louder than the cough of the MK-23 in Bolan's hands.

The man fell face-first into the snow.

"Hostile down." Bolan released the slide-lock lever and manually worked the action of his pistol to chamber a fresh round. He smothered the hot brass of the spent shell in his glove as it fell into his hand. "Gummer, we only have seconds before this guy is officially MIA. We hit them now. Securing the nukes is priority one."

"Affirmative, Striker. I'm coming in."

Bolan moved for the canal. As he approached the lights, one of the men stood straight and put his hand to his ear. He was wearing a radio beneath the hood of his parka. His head whipped toward the trees as his right hand slid beneath his jacket.

His head snapped back as a .45-caliber hollowpoint round shattered his face.

Bolan tracked the infrared laser dot to the next man who drew a pistol from beneath his coat. The man rubbernecked as the bullet took him in the forehead. Shouts sounded from the barge and the dogs barked furiously. The soldier double-tapped the third man in the throat and tracked for the fourth.

The man who had spoken English dived cleanly into the frigid waters of the Saimaa Canal.

Kurtzman's voice spoke in alarm. "Striker! We have vehicles! One hundred yards from your position!"

Bolan could hear the snarl of engines as he ran toward the prow of the barge. "How many!"

"I count four! Three appear to be small. High probability they're snowmobiles! Fourth vehicle is much larger, tracked, probably some kind of snow tractor! Armor or armament unknown!"

Bolan tore off his night-vision goggles as searchlights swept out of the trees. He leaped to the prow of the barge. He ignored the two dogs and put a bullet through the window glass of the tiny pilothouse cubicle. A man with a Krinkov assault carbine fell through the shattered glass, with his throat torn open.

The lead Malinois leaped for Bolan's throat. He stepped into the dog's attack and turned in what was essentially a Judo hip throw.

Fangs tore at the ripstop material of his raid suit. Bolan's flesh tore beneath it, but the dog's momentum did his work for him. The Malinois rotored sideways through the air and plummeted to the water below the prow.

Bolan barely had time to bring up his pistol as the second animal leaped an open hatch and hit.

Fangs sank into the aluminum of the MK-23's suppressor

tube. Bolan put his boot into the dog's chest while the dog yanked furiously on the pistol. Bolan let the dog have the gun and shoved out his foot with all of his might. The dog yipped around the pistol as it toppled backward down the open hatch cover.

Bolan spun his M-1-A rifle on its sling.

Gunfire erupted out in the trees. Bolan recognized the trip-hammer sounds of Manning's M-1-A firing on full-auto. A riderless snowmobile came snarling out of the trees and flew full-throttle into the canal. The whine of a tracked vehicle overcame all other sounds and the swiveling searchlights swept the barge.

Bolan flicked the M-1-A's selector to full-auto and sprayed between the oncoming searchlights. Sparks shrieked as the five rounds of .308-caliber rifle bullets broke apart against the vehicle's armor-glass windows as it burst out of the trees. A six-foot jet of flame roared in revenge. The smoking green line of a Russian tracer ripped past Bolan's head. He grimaced at the sonic crack of the massive projectile, then touched off another burst and rolled behind the pilothouse.

The four-foot barrel of a weapon atop the snow tractor swiveled to follow. Three rounds fired on rapid semiautomatic struck the pilothouse and shrieked right through. Bolan flinched as yellow flame flared, then flared again. Intense heat singed his eyebrows. He went prone as blinding flame began to crawl up his cover. The pilothouse was welded aluminum, and it was burning like a torch. Whatever the enemy was firing at him had depleted uranium armor-piercing ammunition.

The entire length of the iron barge from fore to aft wouldn't be enough cover.

The pilothouse shuddered and began to burn in earnest as the armor-piercing rounds walked a path downward and sought Bolan's life. He hunkered low and reached for the twin pouch carrier mounted on his fanny pack. The M-I-A rifles he and Manning carried had been modified far beyond the shortened barrel and the forward-mounted optic sights. The barrel of each rifle had been machined with NATO-standard rifle-grenade mounting rings. The soldier slid the finned 40 mm antiarmor rifle grenade over the muzzle of his rifle and clicked it into place.

The barrel atop the tractor thundered at point-blank range.

Bolan rolled as the pilothouse sagged and gave way. As flame whooshed upward like wood settling in a fireplace, the Executioner raised his rifle and stared down the smoking muzzle of the giant rifle in front of him.

The snow tractor was an armored box sitting atop the wide caterpillar tracks. The range was less than twenty-five meters. Bolan put his scope's crosshairs between the tractor's headlights and fired. The short-barreled rifle recoiled brutally against his shoulder. The headlights of the tractor winked out as superheated gas and molten metal lit the interior of the cabin in orange fire and shattered the windows. The man behind the roof-mounted rifle screamed as his lower body was engulfed in flame. The tractor swerved, and the beleaguered box of the cabin buckled as it rammed to a tree and came to a violent halt.

Bolan could feel vibration through his boots as running feet hammered against the deck below him.

Another snowmobile came hurtling out of the trees. One man drove as the man seated behind him fired his AK blindly at the barge. Bolan flicked his selector switch to semiauto and walked three quick rounds up the windshield of the snowmobile. The driver jerked and the gunman behind him flailed as the heavy full-metal-jacketed bullets tore through them both. The gunman fell off the back of the speeding snowmobile as the driver fell across the handlebars. Embers and sparks flew like a fireworks display as the out of control snowmobile plowed into the field stove and spun out-of-control.

"Gummer! Sitrep!"

Manning's voice came back. "Six hostiles accounted for! Third snowmobile taken intact!"

"I need you! Now!"

"Inbound!"

Bolan kept his muzzle on the open hatch. "Bear! What have you got?"

"I have multiple fires! We detect no more vehicles or new heat signatures in the trees!"

Manning came loping out of the trees. The burning tractor and shattered stove lit him up in lurid orange. The big Canadian vaulted aboard the burning barge. "What have we got— Jesus!"

The Malinois streaked up from the open hatch like a fanged lightning bolt.

Manning thrust out his rifle and rolled backward, putting his boot into the dog's belly as it sailed over him.

The dog flew yelping over the rail and plunged into the canal.

Manning continued his backward roll and came up in a crouch with his rifle ready. "Any other loose ends I should know about?"

"Unknown number of hostiles belowdecks. I have one guy who pulled a Houdini in the canal. He..."

Bolan glanced quickly up and down the canal. Great gray shards of ice floated slowly toward the sea. The first dog had swum across the canal and climbed atop some pilings and sat shivering and whining. The other dog was paddling miserably toward its pack mate. Other than that, there was nothing to be seen. Except for the pilings of the walls of the canal, which were concrete and stone. The man who had spoken English and leaped into the freezing waters was nowhere to be seen. Bolan glanced at his watch. The sides of the barge were shear with nothing to cling to. It had been more than two minutes. The man had either succumbed to the cold and drowned or—

"They have a submersible!"

Manning bolted upright.

"That's why they haven't come above deck. The transfer is happening now!" Bolan pulled a hand grenade from his web gear. "Bear! Keep the satellite watching the canal for anything moving north! If they're using propellers you should pick it up!"

"Affirmative, Striker!"

Bolan opened his fist. "Fire in the hole!"

The safety lever of the grenade pinged away as Bolan dropped the grenade down the hatch. Orange fire strobed up out of the hatch and fragments of shrapnel shrieked against the welded steel of the barge. Down below, a man screamed.

The soldier dropped through the hatch with his rifle in the hip-assault fire position, its selector switch set on full-auto. A man lay thrashing on the deck, holding his face. His AK-74 rifle lay a few feet away with its bayonet fixed. Bolan put his boot into the man's temple and his struggles ceased. The door beyond him was locked. Voices were audible below them.

"Gummer, the deck! Breach it!"

Manning uncoiled a length of flexible-shaped charge and pulled the adhesive strip from one side of the triangular hose. He pressed the charge into a three-foot circle in the deck and shoved in a detonator pin. "Step back."

Manning took out his remote and pressed the button.

The circle of flexible charge detonated. The triangular charge funneled its explosive force downward with a hiss. Orange fire made a whip-crack noise as the explosive cut the metal deck and a three-foot section fell away, leaving a smoking hole in its wake.

Russian-issue green tracers streamed up out of the hole and up through the open hatch above. Bolan sidearmed a concussion grenade and threw it down the hole as Manning did the same. The two bombs detonated. The lights in the deck below shattered and the concussion washed up out of the hole, pushing powder smoke and burned high explosive with it in an acrid cloud.

Bolan pulled his night-vision goggles over his eyes and dropped down the hole. His boots thudded into the steel deck. Three men lay on the ground overcome by the stunning blast. A fourth reeled on his feet like a drunk, waving his pistol blindly in the dark.

Bolan whipped the butt of his rifle into the man's jaw and he dropped as if he had been shot. The compartment they were in was large and roughly half the length of the barge. It was empty except for the stunned men lying on the deck. A bulkhead with another door partitioned the lower deck at midpoint.

Manning patted his pouch containing the flexible charges. "Breach it?"

"Get it ready!" Bolan clicked his last rifle grenade onto his weapon while Manning pressed the flexible charge around the frame of the steel door.

"Ready!"

"Fire!" Bolan triggered his rifle. The grenade shot across the room and hit the bulkhead three yards from the door. A small circle of fire blew out around the detonation point. Its warhead was a shaped charge, as well. The 40 mm HEAT round burned a hole through the bulkhead and sent a jet of superheated gas and molten metal into the compartment beyond.

Manning pressed his detonator, and fire and smoke outlined the frame of the door. As the steel door sagged in its frame and fell away with a clang, the big Canadian hurled a hand grenade through the breech.

Bolan leaped through the smoldering doorway with his rifle snarling on full auto.

Two severely burned men lay moaning on the floor. Large wooden crates were strewed all over the compartment, most of them opened and emptied, some of them on fire. A three-foot-tall rectangular docking ring dominated the interior of the compartment, a metal tube sticking from its center.

The lens of the periscope was staring straight at Bolan.

The Executioner shouldered his rifle and shot out the lens. Glass shattered, and the periscope swiftly descended. Air blasted upward and turned the cargo bay into a wind tunnel as the submersible vented air and took on ballast. The hull shuddered as the vehicle broke its seal and water suddenly began to well up out of the docking ring to flood the compartment floor.

Bolan and Manning ran to the docking ring. They pointed their rifles down and churned cold black water into foam as they emptied them on full-auto. Bolan's rifle clacked open on a smoking empty chamber, and he pulled his last concussion grenade. He pulled the pin and the bomb disappeared into the frigid water. Diffused orange light lit the dark depths and water geysered back up through the docking ring.

The freezing water was already ankle-deep in the cargo hold. The enemy was scuttling the barge behind them.

"Bear! Submersible confirmed! Heading north! Track it!"

"Contact confirmed! Moving northward! Approximately six miles per hour!"

Bolan ran up the steel companionway with Manning on his heels. They took the second set and burst onto the top deck. The snow tractor continued to burn, throwing orange light and long black shadows over everything. Bolan clicked on the infrared beacon clipped to his vest.

Kurtzman spoke in his earpiece. "We have you, Striker! And Gummer!"

Bolan leaped from the barge. "Gummer! Grenade!"

Manning pulled his two unfired rifle grenades and tossed one of them to his comrade, who clicked it in place over his rifle and scanned the surface of the canal. "Bear! Where are they!"

"Fifty yards from your position! Middle of the canal!"

Bolan sprinted through the snow. "Gummer! Willie Pete!"

Manning pulled the white-phosphorous grenade from his web gear.

Kurtzman spoke rapidly as the two men ran. "Thirty yards! Fifteen! Seven! Striker, you are parallel!"

"Gummer! Light 'em up!"

Manning pulled the pin and hurled the grenade into the canal. The black water roiled and lit up yellow-white. Water couldn't smother burning white phosphorous; it would continue to feed on the oxygen until the burning metal element itself was exhausted.

A cold, distorted gray shape moved through the unearthly glow of the hellish burning metal below the surface. Bolan adjusted for the distortion of the water and estimated the sub at twenty feet down. The M-1-A bucked against his shoulder as the rifle grenade punched into the water with hardly a splash. The rifle grenade left a white wake in its path as it speared for the sub.

Orange light detonated in the depths.

"Striker! I have multiple heat sources! We're losing the sub's wake!"

The flickering light of the burning white phosphorous roiled as air vented violently to the surface. "We're on him!"

"You hit him!" Manning raised his rifle and sighted carefully down the barrel, aiming for the stern of the submersible. The rifle grenade thumped from the muzzle of his rifle. Orange fire detonated below and was almost immediately extinguished.

Manning slung his rifle and filled his hands with his last two hand grenades.

Bolan had three grenades left. He pulled the pins on his last concussion and his last frag. The bizzare yellow-white light blackened and smudged as oil smeared the water.

"Striker!" Kurtzman spoke breathlessly. "We've lost propeller wake!"

Bolan nodded. "Nice shot, Gummer."

The dark shape of the sub seemed to sink lower below the fading white light of the burning phosphorous. Bolan and Manning tossed their grenades like depth charges. Detonations roiled the water and sent the burning phosphorous elements skidding and eddying like slow-motion stars.

The stars began winking out as the burning metal elements floated downstream with the current and consumed themselves. The canal went black as the last pinpoint of light blinked from existence. There was no light except the stars above and the burning tractor behind them.

The two dogs barked forlornly from their piling perch.

Manning reloaded his rifle as Bolan pulled the pin on his last grenade. The safety lever pinged away and the bomb splashed into the canal and sank. Bolan reloaded his rifle and shouldered it as streamers of white light detonated and spread through the canal.

The big Canadian lowered his muzzle slightly. "Uhh... Striker?"

Bolan's face split into silent snarl.

The sub was nowhere to be seen.

"Bear! The submersible is gone! Give a fix!"

"Striker! I have nothing! Repeat! No propeller wake!"

All Kurtzman's satellite needed was a two- or three-degree temperature differential to pick up a target. If the sub was still moving, it would be putting energy into the water and the spy satellite above would detect the smear of its wake in the canal. Bolan had thrown his grenade right where it was sinking. If it was sunk or hiding on the bottom, they should have been able to see the wavering gray mass of its shape in the flaring light of the grenade.

"Goddamn it!" Manning began jogging along the canal. "I hit the son of a bitch! Right in the ass! He has no propellers!"

"You're right." Bolan went cold. "He has no propellers."

Manning stopped. "What?"

"He has tracks." Bolan lowered his rifle. During the cold war, the Russians had put a great deal of work into miniature submarines. One of their innovations had been subs equipped with tracks. They sailed underwater like regular subs and then sank to the bottom and crawled their way along to map NATO shore defenses and waterways. "Bear, track northward from our position. Tell me you see something. Anything. No matter how tenuous."

There was silence over the satcom link for long moments. "Striker, we have nothing."

Bolan glanced down the canal. In his night-vision goggles it was a long black ribbon stretching toward Lake Saimaa. Chunks of unmelted ice flowed slowly downstream. There were three more locks in the canal, but that wouldn't stop the sub. It could lurk underwater for days and then crawl through the lock hidden beneath the mass of the next ship that came through. For that matter it could use the tracks and come up at any small boat landing along the canal and go cross-country. If it reached Saimaa itself, all was lost.

Lake Saimaa was the largest fresh-water lake in Europe. It was roughly the size of Belgium. It had more than fourteen thousand islands, and a maze of waterways that gave it fifteen thousand kilometers of shoreline. There were hundreds of villages and cities along its shores and thousands of waterfront summer homes and cabins.

The sub could come up anywhere.

"Bear."

"Yes, Striker?"

"We've lost him."

Kurtzman was silent.

Bolan glanced back at the barge. The prow was slowly lifting as the stern filled with water. The sub docking ring was a massive, unsealed breach in the barge's belly, and he and Manning had punched holes in the deck and blown several of her watertight doors. The barge was burning and sinking at the same time.

Bolan estimated the barge would be beneath the black water within an hour.

"Gummer."

Manning looked up from scanning the slowly moving water. "Yeah?"

"How many crates did you count in the hold?"

Manning considered. "Well, they weren't my first concern, and some of them were on fire, but I'd estimate about thirty."

"How many were open?"

"About two dozen, maybe more." Manning shrugged. "I saw at least six neatly palleted and unopened."

Bolan nodded. "Bear."

"Yes, Striker?"

"I need a yacht, and I need scuba gear."

"Affirmative, Striker."

"I need it yesterday."

"Affirmative, Striker."

Bolan turned to Manning. "Gummer, you said you took one of the snowmobiles intact?"

"Yeah."

"I suppose you took the keys?"

Manning looked insulted.

Bolan nodded. "We bundle up the live ones and hog-tie them in the woods."

"Then what?"

Bolan glanced at his watch. "Then we' re out of here, and we see what kind of attention we've attracted in the morning."

Lake Saimaa

"God...damn it!"

Roger Neville's impossibly broad shoulders bunched. Muscles like ropes crawled across his bones with tension. His face split into a snarl as he stared at the submersible. The sub sat under the red-painted wooden arches of the boathouse, which was big enough to hold a pair of large yachts in winter storage, their masts stepped, or to pull them up out of the water to accommodate work or repair. The sub had backed itself up into the landing and most of it was now out of the water. One of the twin propellers was blackened and twisted, and holes pocked the diving planes. An ugly black scar of melted slag sat high up on the hull where it had been breached, flooding the central compartment. Dents and scratches scored the top of the hull and the tiny sail from bullets strikes and grenade shrapnel. The generator chugged as the pump siphoned canal water out of the flooded compartments.

"Wow." Ian Neville, the big man's brother, slowly shook his head. "You got your ass kicked."

Roger's face reddened and he slowly turned. The bones in his hands creaked and popped as they closed into fists. His brother took an involuntary step back as they locked eyes. The big man was the younger of the two, but he was also the larger, smarter and more prone to violent rages. His gray eyes burned with hatred. The older brother flinched and broke eye contact. Roger turned his hatred to the sub.

"Someone knew." He took a moment to restrain himself. "Someone talked."

His brother stared at the sub. "How many did we lose?"

"I'm assuming everyone on shore and everyone left on the barge is dead or incarcerated." The big man's eyes swung murderously onto the sub again. "The bastards shot out the periscope before we broke the seal with the barge. Then they hit us with some kind of explosives. We sealed all compartments when we got hit. They were using shaped charges of some kind. The engineer burned up with the aft propeller in the rear compartment. The main cargo bay flooded when it was breached, and two of the Russians drowned. I was in the sail."

Roger considered the two severely burned Russian sailors, clawing and screaming for their lives as he'd sealed them in. He remembered their pounding on the hatch and their muffled sobs as the main compartment flooded with the freezing water. A strange light lit behind his eyes.

His brother's eyes grew wide. "Jesus, we—"

"Fuck 'em." Roger shook his head dissmissively. "The captain and the mate were in the forward compartment and are alive, as you know."

His gaze swung toward the massive lakeside cabin in the trees.

His brother followed his gaze. The Russian captain had been screaming bloody murder when they had surfaced in the boathouse. It had taken an entire bottle of vodka and the sight of one million U.S. dollars being transferred to his offshore account to quiet him.

Roger glared. "I say the leak had to be on the Russian side. I say we cap his ass, tie up loose ends and get out of here."

"All right." Ian gave him a sidelong glance. "Our friends called."

"Really? What the hell do they want?"

"They want to know if the transaction was a success."

There was a moment's pause between them.

"Tell them it was a complete success." Roger smiled suddenly. "Tell them it went off without a hitch."

"But..." His brother stared at him. "Do we have all—"

"Tell them we have all six."

"Six?" His brother blinked in confusion. "But we—"

"Tell them we have six." The big man's grin grew predatory. "*All* six."

His brother opened his mouth and closed it again without speaking. Roger nodded. "What's the situation on the canal?"

"Well, that's the funy thing."

The big man's face fell. "What do you mean, *funny?*"

"Well that's just it. Nothing is happening."

"Nothing?"

"Nothing. We've been monitoring the Finnish police radio band, and I've had my contacts keeping tabs on police movements. Nothing is happening. No police have been to the transfer site on the canal. If the barge had been scuttled like you said, no one has detected it. That's some cold, dark water in that canal. It would be impossible to get a visual on it if it's on the bottom, and it would take a very large ship to have a keel low enough to hit it. Barring that, someone would have to be hitting the canal with sonar or magnetometers to detect it. Nothing has been reported through police channels, and if a sunken barge had been detected by normal traffic on the canal, it sure as hell would have made the news."

Roger considered this strange new information carefully. "Really."

"I'm telling you. There's nothing happening. It's like nothing happened."

"You know, I'm starting to wonder just who the hell hit us."

His brother heaved a heavy sigh. "I've been worrying about that myself."

The big man stared long and hard at the battered submersible. "Let's not kill the captain just yet."

"What are you thinking?"

"I'm thinking whoever hit us did so without the knowledge of the Russian government and without the knowledge or permission of the Finnish government. All we really have confirmed on our end is a couple of guys with rifles loaded down with explosives that came out of nowhere. That makes for a very interesting situation." The big man turned and loomed over his brother. "We're going to need some assistance, ASAP. This is what I want you to do."

Saimaa Canal

MACK BOLAN ZIPPED into his dry suit. "What have you got for me, Bear?"

"Not much." Aaron Kurtzman's face frowned across the real-time video link. The laptop was connected to a secure satellite link on the yacht's bridge. "What have you got for me?"

"Not much. We've run a recon of the surrounding woodlands. The bad guys had prepared hides for their men and vehicles. Entrenched earth-and-timber construction, pretty primitive, but a small force of men could stay there for a couple of days without suffering too much."

Kurtzman's brow furrowed. "Kind of a strange arrangement."

"Yeah, it was." Bolan shrugged into his scuba tanks. "The weapon they were using on top of the snow tractor was pretty interesting, as well. It was a Hungarian Gepard M-3 rifle, which fires a 14.5 millimeter armor-piercing bullet at more than three thousand feet per second. We have it secured on the yacht." Bolan shook his head. "I think Manning's in love."

Kurtzman smiled. The big Canadian was a born rifleman. "The satellite picked up its firing signature and the explosions of its hits. What were they firing at, you? High explosive?"

"No." Bolan reran the firefight in his mind. "They were using projectiles made of depleted uranium. Those weren't explosions. They were violent heat expansions. They set the barge on fire."

Kurtzman sighed. "So what kind of company were they expecting, tanks?"

"I don't think they were expecting company at all. If they were, their defenses would have been directed outward. With depleted-uranium ammo, that Gepard could punch through the entire barge. It could easily cripple its engine. For that matter, it could reach right down to the bottom of the canal and tear a submersible to shreds."

"You don't think they were security."

"I think they were insurance."

"What did you get from the prisoners?"

Bolan considered the four men hog-tied belowdeck. "They're Russians, and they've clammed up. That's about all we know. Short of sodium pentathol or going medieval on them, I don't think they're going to talk, and I don't have the time. Gummer's going to baby-sit them while I go down now to see what exactly we can learn from the wreck. After that, we make an anonymous call to the Finnish police and leave them for pickup."

"Good enough. I'm going to keep the link open. We have ninety minutes left on this satellite window. If you're up and dry before then, I'd like an immediate debriefing on what you found. The President has called twice."

Manning came up from belowdecks. "You ready?"

Bolan checked the seal on the mask of his rebreather and scooped up his fins. "Ready."

The day outside was cold and clear. Bolan slid on his fins and looped the lanyard of his underwater flashlight over his wrist. "I'm going straight for the hold. Then the captain's cabin and the manifest if it's on hard copy." Bolan rechecked his coil of flexible charge. "I want to dump our guests and be out of here in an hour."

"You got it." Manning checked Bolan's harness and mask and gave him the thumbs-up. "I'll keep the link open."

Bolan fell backward over the rail and slid into the canal.

The black water closed over him and almost immediately choked off the sun. Bolan flicked on his flashlight. The dark bulk of the barge loomed like a leviathan in the outskirts of the beam. The soldier kicked down and surveyed the damage. The top deck was a mess. The depleted-uranium projectiles had done their job well. They were the same kind of projectiles American tanks had used in the Gulf War, except on a smaller scale. The depleted uranium was self-igniting. When it struck anything at more than five hundred feet per second the released kinetic energy set it alight. The aluminum-and-fiberglass structures on the barge had gone up like torches. The welded iron of the hull had melted and slagged in spots.

Bolan swam down to the open top hatch and entered the barge.

It was a ghost ship. The water within was still, and the body of a Russian floated suspended in the compartment. The soldier kicked down through the hole Manning had cut through the deck and into the hold. The cavernous compartment was as empty as he had first found it. He swam through the twisted frame of the blown door and entered the sub dock.

Dead men and debris floated in stasis like flies trapped in amber. Small fish flicked away from feeding on the corpses as Bolan played about his beam. The room was full of flotsam and all of it began to slowly turn and move in the eddies caused by his fins. Mud from the bottom had spilled into the compartment from the open docking ring and it swirled up in creeping clouds. He ignored the carnage, swam to an open crate and focused his light inside. Bolan grimaced. The empty plastic moldings were cut to fit a large cylindrical object. He slowly began cruising the circumference of the compartment, counting open crates. He drew his MK-5 diving knife as he came to the pallet of six unopened crates.

The crates themselves were unmarked. Bolan shoved the reinforced clip point of the knife into the top of the crate and leaned on the handle. The crates were cheap pine and came apart easily. He levered off the lid, cut away the plastic molding and stared at the contents of the crate—a dull green object shaped like a bullet.

The conical object was eight inches in diameter and two feet long. Bolan didn't read enough Russian to understand the cramped technical jargon written on the side in Cyrillic. But he did understand the bright yellow sticker with its black trefoil. It was a universal warning symbol that needed no translation. It meant radiation hazard. A brass ring girded the object near its tip with various markings, allowing adjustments for contact, proximity or timed detonations.

It was a 203 mm Russian tactical nuclear artillery shell.

There were six crates on the pallet, counting the one he had opened. Bolan looked around grimly. Twenty-four crates were open, empty and floating about the hold of the compartment. Whoever the enemy was, they weren't buying nuclear materials. They had bought nuclear weapons. Off the shelf and ready to go.

They had two dozen of them, and they had smuggled them into Finland.

"GARY?"

Manning looked up from examining the Gepard rifle and glanced at the fifteen-inch screen of the laptop. "What's up, Bear?"

On the screen Kurtzman was staring at a monitor of his own. "You have a boat coming down the canal toward you—about a mile away."

Manning's hand went to his M-1-A scout rifle. "From which direction?"

"North, from Finland."

"What kind of boat?"

"Looks like a pleasure yacht. A big one."

Seven barges and two yachts had passed them without incident since daybreak. "Thanks, Bear. I'll keep an eye on it." Manning shoved a Heckler & Koch offensive pistol into the back of his waistband and pulled on a coat. He scooped up a pair of binoculars and went above. He raised the binoculars to his eyes and scanned north.

A yacht about the size of their own was moving slowly down the canal under sail.

Manning scanned the yacht's mast. It flew Finnish registry. Storms were brewing out in the North Sea, and it wasn't exactly yachting season, but people said cold weather was the time to buy, and people were always moving their boats up and down for storage or work.

Manning's hand casually went to the grips of the pistol as someone came out on deck. His eyes widened. It was a woman. She wore a parka and snow boots and her legs were bare. Her head was covered by a knit cap, and she wore mirrored sunglasses. She had a pair of binoculars in her hand. Despite it being fall in Finland, her face and legs had maintained a beautiful olive-complected tan. Manning grinned. She had the face of a supermodel and the thighs of a she-cougar.

The woman looked back at him through the binoculars and waved. "Hey!"

Manning waved back.

She lowered the glasses. Manning scanned the yacht's cabin windows. A big man in a bathrobe stood behind the helm and waved. Manning spoke loud enough for the laptop's mike to hear him. "Bear, any other traffic?"

"We've got a pair of barges, three locks down from your position."

The woman shouted across the water as the yachts approached each other. "You okay?"

Manning noted she spoke American English. "Just a little engine trouble!"

"Aw. Poor baby!" The woman looked to one side and then the other mischievously as her hands went to the front of her parka. Manning's finger slid around the MK-23's trigger. The woman gave a happy shriek and pulled open her parka.

She wasn't wearing anything underneath it except her white snow boots.

Manning grinned. Sometimes the gods smiled.

She was definitely supermodel material.

An invisible force smashed Manning down the short flight of steps into the yacht's cabin. He fell badly, the tiny table shattering as it broke his fall. Kurtzman's head rotated through the air as the laptop flew end over end.

"Gary!" Kurtzman shouted in consternation. "Gar—!" He winked out as a bullet punched the laptop. The cords connecting the computer to the satellite link had been yanked from their ports. Battle instincts had taken over. Manning's pistol was already in his hand and his thumb had flicked off the safety. He sat up with a wheeze and blinked at the stars in front of his eyes. A bullet had taken him square in the chest. He'd heard no report. The big Canadian ripped open his jacket and saw the copper base of the bullet protruding squarely from the body armor over his heart.

Someone wanted some serious payback.

Manning shoved his hand up out of the hatch and emptied his pistol blindly in the direction of the other yacht. He ducked as automatic rifles snarled in response. The glass windows of the cabin shattered, and tracers drew smoking lines above Manning's head.

In the hold below, the hog-tied Russians began shouting in consternation.

Manning snarled. The computer was down and he'd lost his real-time god-view of the canal. He seized up his M-1-A and flicked on the yacht's sonar rig. An exceptionally primitive rig by military standards, its sole function was to locate schools of bottom-hugging sturgeon and other big fish that inhabited the massive Saimaa lake system. The massive bulk of the barge at the bottom, however, was easy pickings. So were the seven large objects moving directly beneath the yacht and diving toward the barge.

There were swimmers in the water.

Rifle fire continued to rake the yacht. The Russians belowdecks began screaming and thumping in earnest terror. The big guy was fifty feet down inside the hull of the wreck with no way to phone home. Manning grabbed a pair of frag grenades and pulled the pins. He hurled one bomb up out of the hatch, the second, a moment later. It was all the warning the big guy was going to get.

Fresh rifle fire tore into the yacht. The bad guys would be close enough to board in moments. Manning dropped the M-1-A on the couch and crawled across the floor as incoming fire smashed out bits of glass and woodwork above him. He took one of the three, 10-round magazines they had liberated from the snow tractor and shoved it into the Gepard. He racked the action and chambered a 14.5 mm depleted-uranium, armor-piercing shell.

Manning grunted with effort as he rose with the forty pound rifle in his hands.

BOLAN'S HEAD SNAPPED up at the muffled thump above him. It almost sounded like a—

A second thump followed a moment later. It was a sound Bolan had heard before, the sound of hand grenades detonating underwater. The MK-5 diving knife slid out of the sheath strapped to his calf. He took a moment to orient himself to the mangled doorway, then clicked off his flashlight. When he kicked forward, his outstretched hand met the frame and he shot through. He kicked up until his hand met the ceiling and then worked his way along until he found the hole they'd cut in the deck. He came up into the narrow corridor and made for the hatch. Light suddenly glared down at him in an intense beam that threw the corridor into a harsh collage of light and shadow. Bolan hugged the roof as the light played through the hatch in a narrow cone.

The Executioner reached out and seized the arm of the dead Russian. He put his feet against the floating corpse's back and slowly shoved. Its arms spread like slow-motion wings, and its head and shoulders eased into the light. Bolan winced at the explosive tearing sound shocking through the water. Streams of bubbles ripped down through the hatch and savaged the Russian corpse. Bolan held his position as the intense light played down on the body.

The soldier examined the corpse from his position as the enemy did from above. More than a dozen fresh wounds riddled the already battered corpse. A good half-dozen steel darts poked out of the Russian's skull where they had failed to penetrate bone. Bolan knew of only one weapon that fired on full-auto underwater, and that was the Russian-made APS underwater, assault rifle.

It wasn't Gummer who had come calling.

The cone of light expanded and the yellow plastic body of an underwater searchlight descended through the hatch, followed by the dark length of the weapon in the diver's other hand.

Bolan grabbed the muzzle of the assassin's weapon and punched his knife forward as the assassin's head cleared the hatch. The five-inch blade sank into the killer's throat. The water went crimson as arterial blood leaked from a mortal wound. He yanked the knife free and sliced the man's air hose. A violent cloud of bubbles rose upward and obscured everything in the hatchway. Bolan yanked the rifle free of the killer's failing grasp.

The light fell to the bottom of the corridor, and the man's head and shoulders disappeared. Bolan kicked backward with his plunder as a hundred sizzling streams of bubbles hissed downward. The Russian corpse shuddered under the onslaught, and the fallen light shattered. The corridor went dark, then lit up again as a fresh light shone down the hatch.

Bolan dived down the hole Manning had cut and descended into the dark of the first cargo hold. If his memory served, the APS rifle held twenty-six rounds per magazine. The man he had taken it from had riddled the dead Russian with an amateurishly long burst. Bolan considered the torrent he had witnessed and estimated he could give himself five shots. The rifle controls were pure AK-47 and old friends to Bolan. He switched the APS to semiautomatic fire and locked open the folding stock. Orienting himself by the touching the roof, he swam for the blown door.

He risked shining his flashlight and entered the converted submersible docking bay. The soldier couldn't afford to break out and have God only knew how many enemies swim up after him. He swam to the ceiling of the compartment and clicked off his light as he pressed a circle of flexible charge in the roof. He pushed in the sonic detonator pin and looked back. Light was stabbing down into the cargo hold behind as the enemy carefully followed him compartment by compartment.

Bolan kicked down and sank into the canal mud at the bottom of the docking ring, took out his sonic detonator and waited in the pitch black. He didn't have long to wait. A pair of lights played across the hold, illuminating the drifting debris. Bolan heard the thumping pok-pok-pok! of the underwater assault rifles—High-velocity darts streaked into the floating Russian corpses. The darts that missed streaked on to clang against the far wall.

Holding his sonic detonator and pointing it up at the circle of flexible charge, Bolan pushed the button and a tight beam of coded, pulsed sound hit the detonator pin. A sound like that of a huge wet towel being torn filled the hold and yellow flame formed a circle in the ceiling. A circular plate of decking the size of a manhole cover fell free and sank toward the floor. Bolan rose up from the docking ring with his weapon shouldered. Two men had entered the hold with lights in one hand and weapons in the other. They were staring at the hole that had magically appeared and seemed ready to shoot whatever came out of it.

Bolan put the front sight of his captured weapon on the first man and squeezed off two rounds.

The APS recoiled violently against his shoulder. One dart struck sparks on the swimmer's shoulder. The man dropped his rifle and his light and flailed as the second took him in the throat. The second man turned his attention from the hole, his head jerking as two darts shattered the plastic plate of his diving mask and turned the water in front of his face scarlet.

The hold turned into wild patches of light and dark as the men's lights hit the floor. Bolan fired two more rounds through the doorway and kicked to the ceiling as his weapon clacked open on empty. Below him streams of darts hissed across the hold as the men behind sprayed their weapons through the doorway. The soldier came up into the compartment and suddenly breached the water. He dropped the spent rifle and flicked on his flashlight. Water streamed down his mask as he quickly scanned his surroundings.

Four feet of water had flooded into the sealed compartment

until the interior air pressure had achieved balance. The single bunk was sodden. There was a partially submerged computer on a small desk. Personal photos and mementos were attached to the wall. Only one person would have his own room on a river barge, and that was the captain. Bolan went to a metal locker-cabinet in the corner, which was padlocked. He took his knife in an ice-pick grip and plunged it into the louvered slits, glancing down as he ripped the blade's saw teeth through the sheet steel. Through the hole in the floor he could see the distorted beams of lights scanning the hold below.

Metal screamed and tore as Bolan heaved with all his might.

He ripped the metal panel down to its frame and peeled the jagged metal back, smiling as he played his light on the locker. Inside were a pair of Krinkov shortened AKSU assault rifles, a bandoleer of magazines, three bottles of liquor, cartons of French cigarettes, several well-thumbed issues of *Playboy* and twenty large-bound stacks of United States one-hundred-dollar bills. Bolan seized a rifle and checked its load as a beam of light shot up through the hole in the floor. He glanced up as he flipped the selector to full-auto. The ceiling of the cabin was scorched from the depleted uranium fires that had burned the top deck.

Freedom was a sixteenth of an inch of iron away.

Bolan jerked back as a stream of steel darts erupted up through the hole in the floor to shriek sparks off the ceiling. He aimed downward and squeezed the trigger. Flame shot from the Krinkov's muzzle and chopped the water flooding the compartment to foam as Bolan burned through an entire magazine.

The lights below prudently flicked off, and Bolan turned off his own beam. The sunken barge was once again plunged into darkness. He slowly stepped up onto the soggy bunk and pulled the last of his flexible charge from his demo bag. Stripping the adhesive, he drew a hoop in the low ceiling above him and pushed in the detonator pin. He had about two and a half feet left. Bolan took his knife and cut the flexible charge into six-inch lengths, then pushed a detonator pin in each one.

Bolan pulled his sonic detonator and slipped three of the lengths of flexible charge down the hole. He counted to three and pushed the button. The hold below lit up in whip-crack flashes

of twisting yellow fire. It was unlikely to kill or to wound anyone, but all Bolan needed was a moment's distraction.

He pointed the detonator at the roof and pushed the button.

The yellow circle of fire hissed like a fiery halo above his
head. Bolan flicked on his flashlight and pressed himself against
the bulkhead. Air pressure held the disk of metal in place for a
moment, and then jets of water squirted into the room. The
sheared section of roof skidded with surface tension and suddenly fell. The captain's cabin decompressed violently as the air
trapped within it shot to the surface of the Saimaa canal.

Bolan dropped the last two lengths of charge down the hole
and detonated them. Twin snakes of yellow fire twisted below.
He let his knife and his light fall around his wrists on their lan-
yards and took a Krinkov in each hand. Bolan shoved up through
the hole in the roof as the water closed over his head, leaving the
claustrophobic compartments of the ghost barge behind. He
kicked strongly for the surface, then turned as something growled
and vibrated against the faceplate of his mask. Bolan fumbled
his weapons into one hand and thrust out his light.

The beam revealed a vast dark bulk slowly moving through
the water toward him.

The growling sound came again, and Bolan realized the submersible had detected a swimmer in the water and was signal-
ing with sonar. He had no way to signal back and kicked for the
surface as quickly as he could.

A great hammer of sound rolled over him, and his eardrums
compressed and seemed to meet in the middle of his brain.
Bolan's mask vibrated like a hive of angry hornets and his body
cringed as the second blow hit him. The sound wave came again
in a third, fourth and fifth hammering wave.

Bolan was being pinged at point-blank range. The sub was
hammering him like a sperm whale stunning a squid.

He tasted blood in the back of his mouth and lights danced behind his screwed-shut eyelids. He forced his eyes open and flicked
on his light. The sub was ten yards away. The blasts of sound hit
him like body blows. Bolan dropped the light and took the pistol
grip of a Krinkov in each hand. He extended the muzzles by memory as purple pinpricks of light danced behind his eyelids.

The Krinkovs shuddered and squirmed in his hands as he held the triggers down on full-auto. The amplified sound of the weapons' snarl was almost as bad as the pinging of the sub. The bottom-crawling submersible was a shallow-water craft. The welded aluminum double-hull could stop small-caliber rifle bullets, particularly bullets struggling through thirty feet of water rather than air, but its sonar dome would be made of reinforced plastic.

The hideous hammering suddenly stopped as the Krinkovs ran dry in Bolan's hands. The vault of blackness above slowly turned to dirty gray as Bolan kicked weakly upward. The light above brightened suddenly and he breached the surface. Blinking blindly in the sunlight and yawning against the intense ringing in his ears, Bolan tore off his mask and oriented himself toward the sound of gunfire.

The yacht had been shot to hell. Bullet holes riddled the sails and every exposed inch of deck. Forty feet beyond, black smoke belched into the clear sky as another yacht burned out of control. Gunfire was still being exchanged between both yachts. Bolan swam toward his own craft, keeping the hull between himself and the enemy boat.

He could hear the screams of the bound Russians belowdecks. The harsh bark of a short-barreled M-1-A scout rifle rang out in rapid semiautomatic. Bolan reached for the rail and failed to pull himself up. He gasped wearily, "Gummer!"

The rifle fire stopped. "Striker!" Manning emerged from the hold and slid low over the deck.

Manning pulled Bolan aboard and shoved a pistol in his hand. "What's going on down below?"

"The bad guys came back. They brought their sub and scuba equipment with them." Bolan ran his eye around the carnage. "What happened up here?"

Manning shrugged. "Some superbabe flashed me some skin and then her boyfriend shot me. Then it was divers down below and Armageddon upstairs."

The big Canadian rubbed his head and stared at the blood staining it from where he had met the table. "They shot Bear, and the radio is toast. We're incommunicado. The engine is mangled, the sail is shredded, and we are dead in the water."

Bolan shrugged out of his rebreather and checked the loads in the Heckler & Koch pistol. "So what's the good news?"

Manning grinned. "I nuked their asses."

"The Gepard?"

"I gave 'em all three magazines. Their tub went up like kindling. We—"

The roar of an outboard motor interrupted them. Both men rolled up with the weapons aimed as an inflatable Zodiac tore away from behind the burning yacht. Bolan and Manning opened fire. Their bullets didn't seem to have any effect. The people in the boat stayed low and didn't fire back.

Bolan shook his head and lowered his pistol. "He's made out of Kevlar."

The Zodiac sped up the canal and swiftly moved out of small-arms range.

Bolan sighed as he watched the black smoke fill the sky. "The authorities are probably going to show up on this one. We're abandoning ship. There's still a snowmobile out in the woods from the other night. Gather up whatever food and water we have, and the cash, and then go hotwire it."

Manning nodded. "What about our friends in the water?"

Bolan glanced at the black surface of the Saimaa. They were out of explosives and the enemy held all the cards once they went below. There was nothing they could do.

Manning stood. "What about our friends in the hold?"

"Leave them for the Finnish authorities. Once they're arrested we'll see what we can do with them." Bolan pushed himself to his feet. The enemy above had bugged out. The enemy below was doing the same. He and Manning had no communications equipment and were just about out of ammo. Neither of them spoke Finnish, and Helsinki was a 130 miles away. They needed a car. A helicopter would be better.

Bolan shook his head and wiped the blood from his nose.

They'd been mauled and the enemy was still free, still unknown, and still loaded with two dozen tactical nukes.

3

Secure Communications Room,
U.S. Embassy, Helsinki, Finland

Mack Bolan stretched out on the couch. He and Manning had been debriefed and gotten a shower and an hour's sleep. Bolan's ears were still ringing from being pinged, and it had been a tiring, jaw-rattling ride by snowmobile to the nearest town. The little village had no helicopters or small planes or cell phones, but it did have a car for rent, which had gotten them to a city with an airstrip. They had decided against stealing a plane; their lack of Finnish forcing them to rent both a plane and a pilot. The upshot was it had taken them twenty-eight hours to make 130 miles. They had lost a day getting back to the capital.

It was very likely the enemy had recovered their six nukes. Now they'd have thirty.

"Bear, we got our asses kicked."

Kurtzman's brow wrinkled sympathetically from the screen of the laptop. "Actually, I'd say you held your own both times."

"Thirty loose nukes and no leads."

"Well..." Kurtzman paused. "Manning saw some skin."

"He got his ass tagged."

Kurtzman nodded. "I want him to give a description of the woman to three sketch artists. I have them lined up and he can do it over the link. Once we have that, we can use some software of Akira's to make a composite."

"Do it. I want the composite within twenty-four hours."

Manning grinned. "I'm telling you, she was a hottie. Genuine supermodel material."

Bolan looked at the big Canadian pointedly. "She shot you, Gary."

"No, she called me baby." Manning folded his arms smugly. "Some other asshole shot me."

"Bear, what did you make of the bullet we dug out of Gary's armor?"

"It arrived in Berlin two hours ago. The Germans have the best and closest forensics lab we could access quickly. I was on-line with them twenty minutes ago. You were right. It was .223 NATO round."

Bolan nodded slightly. During the first fight on the canal everyone had been shooting at them with Russian and Eastern European weapons. The second time around it appeared someone had shot Manning with something Western. "Was it Finnish?"

"No, and that's the funny thing. The Finns still officially use the Russian 7.62 mm round for their armed forces, but for every military rifle they've made in the past two decades they've also chambered a NATO .223 version for export. I asked the German ballistics experts to run a check on the Valmet line of Finnish rifles, but they said there was no need. They recognized the rifling on the bullet instantly, which was polygonal."

Bolan sat up slightly. Only one military gun manufacturer in the world used polygonal rifling in their small arms. Bolan had used their small arms extensively, and had carried one on the Saimaa Canal. "Heckler & Koch."

"Exactly. Someone was using German weapons and, according to our friends in Berlin, the weapon was a G-36 rifle. That's their very latest issue assault rifle. The boys in the lab also noticed something else interesting. They say it's an educated guess at best, but by the range Gary estimated and the bullet deformation against the trauma plate of his armor, the bullet was fired from a twelve-inch barrel. That would indicate a G-36-K. That's the shortened, carbine version of the G-36, and that's pretty much Special Forces issue only."

Bolan mentally filed that away for future reference. "What can you tell me about thirty Russian tactical nuclear artillery shells?"

"I ran the serial number you memorized. It's pretty standard. Those are battlefield nukes, with a dial-a-yield of two to ten kilotons. By themselves, no one of them is up to doomsday, but thirty of them...that starts to be an awful lot."

Bolan didn't like the large number, either. "What kind of price tag would you give them on the black market?"

"We're talking nuclear weapons, Striker. We're talking some very long green. There's no bulk discount on nukes. By Pentagon estimates, the Russians still have several thousand tactical nukes in their arsenal. Getting creative with inventory and stealing one or two is possible, but thirty? That's a huge risk, and it's going to jack up the price way beyond just price per weapon. I would say we're talking at least a hundred million, that's base price, not even counting bribes, transportation and security, and, on top of that, our friends seemed to have had a Russian-tracked submersible. You can't just go and pick one of those up at your local army-navy surplus store."

It was adding up to a very anomalous equation. The Executioner didn't like anomalies. "Someone has a plan for those nukes. Something bigger than trying to turn them around for a profit."

Kurtzman nodded soberly. "I don't doubt it."

"Get in touch with the CIA. See if we have any Russian artillery or ordnance officers who are acting like they just won the lottery."

Kurtzman's fingers flew on his own keys. "That's going to be a long shot."

"Run it anyway, we might get lucky." Bolan peered at the sketch of the woman again. "What the story with the Finnish police?"

"They have your four Russians in custody. Your yacht and the hulk of the yacht Gary torched are in dry dock. There's a great deal of consternation and confusion among the Finnish authorities about what is going on."

"What about the barge?"

"They found it. Divers of the Finnish canal authority went down this morning."

"And?"

"Nothing about any nukes." Kurtzman frowned. "Nothing at all."

Bolan looked away as his worst suspicions were confirmed. "Bear, I need to interview those guys we had in the hold."

"I figured you'd say that."

"Where are they now?"

"They're being held by the port authorities, but given the presence of illegal automatic weapons, one roasted yacht and one scuttled barge, they are going to be transferred to national police headquarters in Helsinki."

Bolan considered the two firefights he'd been in within forty-eight hours. "I don't think our boys are going to make it to Helsinki. I'm going to need someone who is fluent in Russian and Finnish."

Manning looked up from the sketch of the woman and nodded. "We're going to need a helicopter."

THE MBB 105 HELICOPTER roared over the snaking roadway and the trees girding it. The CIA-provided Marine Corps pilot wasn't in the same league as Jack Grimaldi, but few men were. His nap-of-the-earth flying wasn't bad, though, and Bolan needed his hands free. He checked his gear. He and Manning had been forced to dump their weapons in the Saimaa for their cross-country trip. They had raided the U.S. Embassy in Helsinki for whatever firepower they could muster. Both of them had M-16 rifles and bayonets liberated from the Marine embassy guardsmen and a pair of 9 mm Beretta service pistols. They had also lifted a pair of 37 mm gas launchers and a crate of CS tear-gas grenades the embassy kept in case protesters came close to storming its gates.

Embassy linguist Nadine Truyen watched wide-eyed as the forest flew by inches below the helicopter's skids. When she wasn't working on Finnish, Russian or Swedish translations, she taught aerobics and swim lessons at the American School in Helsinki. She leaned hesitantly toward Bolan and raised her voice over the roar of the rotors. "So, what is it we're doing again, exactly?"

"Conducting a quick series of on-the-spot interviews."

"Oh." The woman nodded, then shook her head at the collection of weapons. "What does that mean?"

"It means I need someone who speaks fluent Russian, better than mine." Bolan smiled winningly. "Your superior recommended you highly."

Truyen blushed. "Thank you. You know, I—"

"Heads up!" Manning pointed ahead.

Smoke rose above the trees from burning vehicles on the road. Bolan drew his baklava down over his face and slung the grenade launcher over his shoulder. "Nadine, stay with the chopper!" Bolan and Manning simultaneously flicked off the safeties on their M-16 rifles. The chopper swung out over the road. A car was stopped by the side of the road, its front end crumpled against a tree. A little beyond it a Volkswagen van with Finnish police markings was stopped by the side of the road. A pair of unmarked sedans were stopped in front and in back. One of the escort cars was burning. All of the vehicles were pocked with bullet strikes. Three uniformed officers were shooting into the trees with their service pistols. Five more lay strewed across the road where they had been shot down. Bolan's lips skinned back from his teeth. The Finnish police had been baited into stopping with a false car wreck and were now caught in a cross fire.

Bolan dropped his rifle and brought up the 37 mm grenade launcher. "Gummer! You take the north side. I'll take the south!"

"You got it!"

They shouldered their weapons as tracers began to stream up out of the trees, seeking the chopper. The launcher bucked against Bolan's shoulder and he swiftly broke open the action and reloaded. Truyen screamed as bullets struck the helicopter and glass flew from the shattered windscreen. Bolan fired and fired again. The gas grenade launchers were loaded with skip-chaser ammunition. Each grenade broke apart into several bomblets that skipped and spewed the CS irritant gas into a thick screen.

Bolan reloaded and slung the launcher. He and Manning had both put five rounds into either side of the treeline. A nice obscuring gray cloud of tear gas was crawling like fog through the trees. Tracers still reached for the chopper, but Bolan noted they were much more haphazard.

The enemy hadn't thought to bring gas masks to their ambush.

The pilot shouted as a molding snapped apart above his head and sparks flew. "We're still taking hits! This ain't a military bird! We can't take too much more of this!"

Bolan loaded his last gas grenade and slung the launcher around on his back. He took up his M-16 and burned a magazine into the trees. "Drop it down to the road!"

"It's your funeral!" The Marine pilot grinned maniacally. "And mine!"

The Executioner's stomach lurched as the chopper dropped like a stone. The helicopter stopped and hovered two feet above the ground. "Take her up! Gummer, lay fire on anything that moves in the woods!" Bolan leaped out. A pair of beleaguered Finnish police turned their pistols on the man in black descending upon them. Bolan kept his muzzle high and waved his hand. He hoped none of them went for a head shot. He threw himself next to a uniformed policeman hunkered down by the van as the helicopter roared back up into the sky. Beside the policeman, one of the captured Russians shook in his handcuffs.

Bolan yanked up his mask and smiled at the policeman. "You speak English?"

"Ya! Little! I'm Alva! Sergeant Augustus Alva!" The policeman kept his pistol pointed at Bolan's head. "You?"

"Belasko...Interpol!" Bolan kept a straight face. "We got a tip!"

"Interpol?" The Finn looked up at him incredulously. "Interpol?"

"Oh, yeah." Bolan nodded. "Are any of these cars functional?"

"What?"

Bolan waved his arm in a circle. "Cars! Kaput! All?"

"Dunno!" The policeman grimaced and thumped the burning van he leaned against. "Van, gone!" He pointed at the cars bringing up the front and the rear of the caravan. "Autos? Dunno!"

Bolan eyed the Russian. "What about the rest of your prisoners!"

The Finn shook his head grimly. "Kaput!"

Bolan glanced inside the open door of the van. It was riddled with bullets, and its front windshield and bumper were engulfed in flame. There were five men still inside. Those who weren't burning had been butchered with bullet strikes. Bolan leaned away from the intense heat of the flame. The enemy had another Gepard M-3 rifle.

"We're taking heavy fire!" Manning roared in Bolan's earpiece.

The tear gas had diminished the enemy marksmanship, but titanic storms were piling up in the North Sea and all of Scandinavia. The wind would soon disperse the screen, in the meantime they were taking out their aggression on the chopper. "Gummer! Get clear and circle around!"

"Affirmative!" The chopper roared off over the trees as tracers reached up for it.

Bolan turned to Alva. "Sergeant, we have to get out of here!"

The Finn nodded enthusiastically. "Yup!"

"Sergeant! Sergeant!" His two officers held up their smoking empty pistols. Bolan drew his pair of Berettas and handed them to the policeman. He pulled out his spare magazines and distributed them and Finns began firing into the clouds again.

"Listen!" Bolan jerked his thumb back. "I'm going to get the car! Get your men and your prisoner ready to move!"

"Yup!"

Bolan loped from the cover of the van. The window of the police car behind was a lunar surface of bullet craters with spiderwebs of cracked glass between them. The riddled surface was nearly opaque with blood. The engine was running, and smoke drifted upward from bullet holes in the hood. Bolan crouched and ripped open the driver's door. The interior of the sedan looked like the floor of a butcher shop. The two Finnish policemen had never stood a chance against the hail of rifle fire. Only their seat belts held their bodies together. Bolan slashed the seat belt with the bayonet of his M-16 and yanked the dead driver free. He leaped into the blood-soaked seat and gunned the engine.

The car backfired and belched blue smoke. All of the warning lights were on. Acrid fumes and the stink of burning fluids filled the vents as the damaged engine bled internally. Bolan kicked out the shattered windshield, then shoved the car into gear. The gas clouds were thinning. The enemy would have a clear line of sight within moments.

There was little time.

Bolan stepped on the gas and the stricken car jolted forward. "Gummer! I need air support!"

"Inbound!"

The thunder of rotors threshed the air as the chopper appeared over the treetops. Manning stood in the doorway, firing short bursts into the trees. Tracers reached up in retaliation.

The big Canadian's voice came over the hammering of his

rifle. "South side of road is clear of hostiles! Taking heavy fire from the north!"

Bolan knew the man behind the Gepard was waiting. They needed a shield or they would never get out alive. The Executioner pulled the car up beside the burning van and leaped out. "Augustus! Get your men in! Take the prisoner!"

Alva didn't argue. They pulled out the corpse of their comrade and piled in as Bolan ran forward to the second sedan. The police car at the head of the convoy was in even worse shape. Bolan pulled out the driver. The engine howled and clanked as broken and misaligned parts ground against one another. He crouched as bullets struck the passenger side of the car, making the corpse sitting next to him shudder.

Bolan waved Alva forward. "Now! Now! Now!"

The engine howled as the soldier put it into gear. It lurched a bit, and Sergeant Alva pulled alongside. Bolan's vehicle wouldn't go into second gear. He slid out of the seat and crouched in the doorway, spiking the bayonet into the floorboard and pinning the pedal under the hilt. The car jerked and crawled forward. The two vehicles drove side by side. A storm of bullets struck Bolan's car as the enemy tried to shoot through the sedan shielding the police and their prisoner.

The corpse in the passenger seat shook from bullet strikes. Bolan flinched as one bullet and then another hit his armor. Something burned across his ear, and blood flew across his vision.

"Gummer!"

"We're down to one engine! Truyen's hit! We can't take much more of this!"

"Gummer, I need you! Look for the Gepard's muzzle-flash!"

"Affirmative!"

The helicopter roared overhead, rifle fire erupting from its door. Bolan slammed the driver's door shut and snaked his arm through the shattered window to grab the wheel. The two cars limped down the road as rifle fire struck them. Bolan loped at a crouch between the vehicles. Sergeant Alva looked wild-eyed over at Bolan. "Now! Come!"

"Wait!"

Thunder cracked.

The driverless sedan rocked on its chassis with a massive blow. Yellow fire filled the interior, and Bolan yanked his arm out as it singed.

Manning snarled over the radio, "I see him!" The helicopter roared about in a tight circle and the big Canadian let his rifle rip on full-auto. Bolan backed away from the intense heat of the burning car. One of the Finnish policemen threw open his door and Bolan leaped in.

"Go! Go! Go!"

The Russian howled as Bolan landed on him. Alva stepped on the gas and pulled away from the burning hulk of the other car. Thunder cracked again, and every man in the car cringed and waited for engulfing flame. It didn't come, but the thunder shook the sky twice more in rapid succession. Manning shouted in Bolan's ear, "We're burning!"

Bolan looked up into the sky. The tail boom of the chopper was spouting yellow flame where the depleted-uranium bullet had set its metal skin ablaze. The chopper dipped its nose and skidded sideways through the air. The pilot yanked it straight and shoved his throttles forward. The chopper thundered overhead and flew down the road spewing smoke and fire.

"We're going down!"

"Get as far down the road as you can! We'll pick you up!"

"Affirmative, Striker! We—" The chopper slewed across the sky as it lost its tail rotor. The helicopter dropped as it began to turn, its skids screaming on the roadway and throwing sparks. The helicopter slid along the ground, its rotor blades snapping off against the trees as it hit the side of the road. The airframe dipped as it hit a drainage ditch and rested on its nose. It stood suspended for a moment, then fell back heavily and lolled onto its side. The entire tail was burning out of control. The aluminum skin of the airframe was going up like kindling.

Manning leaped out with Truyen across his shoulders in a fireman's carry. The Marine pilot limped badly beside him. Alva stomped on the gas. Bolan shoved out the shattered rear window and trained his rifle on the road behind them. Men were spilling onto the roadway from the side of the road. Two men carried a heavy piece of ordnance between them and set it in the middle of the road. A big man dropped down behind the immense rifle and put his eye to the optical sight. Bolan fired his M-16 on semi-auto through the broken rear windshield. Three hundred yards was limit of a standard M-16's effective range.

The Gepard could reach out and kill well over a mile.

"Get out of the car!" Bolan said as he fired his M-16 dry. The tires screamed as the sergeant stood on the brakes. The door flew open as the policemen piled out. Bolan seized the manacled Russian by the hair and the two of them rolled onto the road.

Behind them the massive antimaterial rifle boomed like judgment.

The rear tires of the police car lifted off the road as the rear bumper and trunk disappeared in yellow fire. Bolan shoved the Russian behind him and clawed his grenade launcher around on its sling. He'd kept one last grenade loaded, and he flipped up the ladder sight.

Behind him the Marine pilot stood wide-legged in the middle of the road. He held his 9 mm service pistol in both hands and methodically fired at the man and the heavy weapon three hundred yards away. Bolan roared. "Down! Get—"

The Marine flew backward with a smoking hole in his chest. Bolan's lips skinned back from his teeth as he stayed prone. The Gepard shot flame and the supersonic crack of the projectile shook Bolan's bones as it passed inches over his head. The soldier took an extra half second to adjust his aim and squeezed the trigger. Pale flame shot from the 37 mm muzzle, and grenade launcher slammed against his shoulder.

The tear-gas grenade looped downrange unerringly. The immense Gepard rifle twisted and its bipod collapsed. The man behind it flipped backward as he was struck by two of the separating bomblets. Man and weapon were instantly engulfed in a dense gray cloud. The nearby gunmen grabbed him and tried to drag him back as they were caught up in the expanding gas cloud.

Bolan stood.

The helicopter was burning out of control and had set fire to several of the trees near it. The police car was burning. The Marine pilot lay unmoving with smoke drifting up out of the immense hole in his chest. One of the Finnish policemen had caught a bullet in the head. Manning rose, supporting Nadine Truyen. The linguist stood with shocked eyes as blood ran down her arm. Alva and his remaining man stood with empty pistols in their hands. The Finnish sergeant seemed to be unaware of the hole in his leg. Bolan felt the burned flesh of his right arm blistering. Blood ran down the side of his face.

The enemy was obscured by the tear gas filling the road.

Manning scowled. "I've got three rounds left."

Bolan raised a weary eyebrow. Manning always counted his shots. How he did this in the middle of a firefight switching back and forth between semi- and full-auto was a mystery between himself and his creator. Bolan had two magazines left and tossed one to his comrade. They had two rifles with a 30-round magazine each, and they had wounded. Bolan could feel the blood running down the side of his face. He turned to Alva.

"Tell me you radioed for help."

"Ya. Radioed. Reinforcements come." He jerked his head at the desolate stretch of woodland road. "Take time."

Bolan nodded. "The enemy has to be monitoring the police radio band. We'll head into the woods and go to ground." He looked down at the quivering, shell-shocked Russian. "We'll do everything in our power to keep this guy alive."

The Russian yelped as Bolan pulled him to his feet by the hair. "Let's go, pal."

4

Headquarters of the State Police,
Helsinki, Finland

Mack Bolan relentlessly held the eyes of the man in front of him. "Thirty minutes. That's all I ask."

Sergeant Augustus Alva squirmed. His arm was bound across his chest in a sling. The bullet wound in his bicep was the least of his discomfort. Alva considered himself a veteran. Finland had a very low crime rate, but that rate had climbed dramatically with the spillover of the criminal chaos in neighboring Russia. He had stared down many a hardened Russian *Mafiya* gangster. The burning blue eyes of the man he faced were implacable. Alva could neither meet them nor look away.

The eyes didn't blink. "I saved your life."

Alva cringed. He knew all too well that he and his surviving officer would be dead in a ditch and without a prisoner were it not for the big stranger. He nodded slowly. "Yup. I owe you life. But my hands..." He opened them and closed them.

Bolan relented. Alva was a sergeant, and a good one. But there had been unexplained gun battles on the Saimaa, and uniformed Finnish police officers had been ambushed and slaughtered. Bolan and his little party of refugees had been picked up by squads of Finnish police officers with rifles. The enemy had disappeared without a trace. The Russian had been taken into custody. Bolan's every attempt to gain access to the prisoner had been rebuffed at the highest levels.

The matter was firmly out of Alva's hands.

Bolan's own cover as an Interpol agent wouldn't stand up to close scrutiny, and Kurtzman had confirmed it was being closely probed by someone highly interested in exactly who Bolan was. The computer wizard was scrambling to lay a paper trail and to call in favors, but Bolan expected his cover to be blown before sunset. He wasn't under arrest, but he had been asked not to leave Helsinki. Sergeant Alva and two officers had been attached to him since noon as both chaperons and guards. Bolan noted Alva now wore a pair of spare magazines beside the leather flap holster of his service pistol. Bolan held out his hand. "Anything you can do."

"You have my thanks." The Finn took Bolan's hand and shook it. "I will try."

Bolan smiled. "That's all I ask."

"I have many...questions. Perhaps we can..." The sergeant struggled with his English. "Exchange infor—"

A woman spoke in English behind them. "Excuse me."

Bolan and Alva turned.

A beautiful woman stood in the hall outside the sergeant's office. Short, boyishly cut brown hair framed her face. Her slightly pointed chin and large eyes almost made her look kittenlike except for a cool sensuality in the set of her lips and cheekbones. An exquisitely tailored pantsuit augmented the authoritative look in her eyes as well as highlighted her sleek physique.

Her smile lit up the hallway. "Are you Sergeant Augustus Alva?"

Alva stood as tall as he could and nodded. "Yup. You?"

"Theresa Parsons." The woman reached into her purse and pulled out a badge. "Interpol."

It took an effort of will for Bolan to keep his mouth shut.

Agent Parsons's brow wrinkled delightfully. "I contacted your superiors about a certain situation on the Saimaa, but I was told there is already an Interpol investigator on the scene. I had no knowledge of this and my superiors—"

Alva nodded his head helpfully at Bolan. "Yup. Him. I owe him my life."

Parsons ran her eyes up and down Bolan. She peered long and

hard into his eyes without flinching. She noted the bloody bandage on his ear and took in the breadth of his shoulders. "Forgive me, but you are...?"

"Belasko." Bolan shrugged. "Interpol."

Parsons stared at him unblinkingly. "Really."

Bolan nodded. "Oh, yeah."

Her eyebrows rose ever so slightly. "Would you like to show me your identification and give me your superior's contact number?"

"Would you like to have dinner with me first?"

Agent Parsons's smile lit up the room as she locked eyes with him. "Oh, you bet I would."

"DON'T GIVE ME any crap." Theresa Parsons's eyes narrowed. "You're not Interpol. Not by a long shot."

"I'm not?" Bolan asked.

The two of them were quiet as the waitress brought the Interpol agent her food. The cold wind outside rattled the glass walls of the restaurant.

"No." Parsons shook her head as the waitress left. "You're not. Interpol is an international cooperative of criminal data investigation. We're not into enforcement. We're not commandos, and we sure as hell don't go leaping out of helicopters with automatic rifles."

"We don't?"

"No." The agent's lips twisted in bemused irritation as she lit a cigarette. She blew blue smoke up at the light overhead. The aroma of Turkish tobacco enfolded their table. "And last I heard, *we* don't engage in naval actions, either."

"Then what am I?"

"Well, you're charming, in a bruised, burned and beat-up kind of way." Her face turned serious. "You're what? CIA?"

"Me? A spook? Heck no."

"I take it back." Parsons gazed at him intently over her open-faced smoked eel sandwich. She shook her head slowly. "You're definitely not CIA."

Bolan raised an eyebrow. "I'm not?"

"No. You're not. You're definitely Special Forces or something."

"Whatever makes you say that?"

"I know the type," Parsons stated.

"And what does that mean?"

Parson's smile turned to a Cheshire grin. "It means I like sleeping with soldiers."

Bolan allowed the ghost of a smile to flit across his face.

Parsons leaned forward. "Listen, Sergeant Alva already unwittingly confirmed your presence at the ambush on the road."

"So?"

"And I'll bet anything you were involved in the incident on the Saimaa. You and I are on the same side, and I really think we should exchange information. Is there any kind of ID or clearance or anything you can give me to show my superiors? You always seem to be on top of the scene. I know you could help me, a lot, and it's just possible I could be of some help to you."

"Let me ask you a question first."

Parson rested her chin on her hands and smiled up at Bolan demurely. "Shoot."

"Why are you in Finland? And why aren't Finnish Interpol affiliate agents handling whatever it is you're here to handle, instead of you?"

Parson lost her smile. "I'll give you two reasons."

"I'm listening."

"I happen to be something of an expert in black market weapons trafficking."

Bolan tossed back his coffee. "I'm sure the Finns have weapons experts of their own who they're very proud of."

"Yeah, but not a specialist in tactical nuclear weapons."

Bolan set down his coffee cup. "And?"

"And with this many nukes crossing the Russian border, we think someone high up in Finnish military intelligence or the national police must be involved, and..." She looked away unhappily. "We don't know if we can trust the local affiliate."

Bolan stared at her over the candle flame. "What do you mean, *this many?*"

"I mean thirty." She peered at Bolan very intently. "That number mean anything to you?"

Bolan eyed the storm clouds darkening to the north. "Tell me why I should trust you."

"Trust me? Buddy, you owe me! I show up and find out there's already an American Interpol agent on the case, except that he's running around playing Special Forces and can't produce any decent identification!" Parsons shook her head ruefully. "You made me look like a total jackass. The Finns like you, and to an extent they're grateful, but they don't trust you, and now because you've been playing mystery cowboy with Interpol's good name, they don't trust me, either."

"All right, let's talk. Tell me everything you know."

Parsons stabbed out her cigarette with a frown. "You've got to give me some kind of clearance, or someone verifiable who will vouch for you. Something my superiors will accept before I release any information." Her face brightened. "By the same token, I'll be happy to provide any references you require in return."

"How about some of those Green Berets you've been sleeping with?"

Parson's eyes blazed in amused outrage. "You're a pig."

"I can arrange something in the way of references." Bolan considered. "It'll be indirect and it will probably take a little time."

Parson's grinned. "My evening's free."

Bolan shrugged. "It will probably take until morning to cut through the red tape."

Parson continued grinning as she locked eyes with Bolan. "My evening is still free."

BOLAN ROLLED off his elbows and sprawled on the bed. He admired the sheen of sweat across Theresa Parsons's torso as she lay gasping and staring up at the ceiling of her hotel room. Bolan lay back and let his own breathing return to normal. Death was Bolan's constant companion, and it had taught him many things about life. The medieval samurai of Japan had an interesting saying that Bolan had taken to heart.

Live your life as if your hair was on fire.

As a sniper in the hellgrounds of war, through the dark, hunted days and nights of his war against the mafia, and in his War Everlasting, Bolan had seen each and every one of the thousand masks that Death wore. In moments of terrible lucidity, shot, stabbed, burned and buried, as his life slipped from his body,

Bolan had seen the masks fall away and he and Death had shown each other their true faces. They knew each other intimately. They understood each other. He had come back from the brink of death more times than any human being had a right to. He had beaten the odds too many times, and he knew his debt to Death was long overdue.

Bolan knew better than any Zen monk how fragile and transitory life was, and he knew Life was owed a debt, as well.

Any bite of food could be his last meal. Each sunrise and sunset, every day above ground, was a gift. The woman who had lain beneath him and what they had done together could be his last act on Earth, and he treated it as such. Every act required total concentration.

Agent Theresa Parsons was glowing.

"So, you still think I'm a soldier?"

"It would take a platoon of Marines to—" Her head lolled over on the pillow as she grinned at him. "Hell, you *are* a platoon of Marines."

Bolan smiled as he looked at the clock on the nightstand. It was 6:00 a.m. Finland time. He thought of Manning and his midnight mission at the U.S. Embassy. He and Kurtzman would have been working feverishly all night to find someone who could drop a dime on Parsons who her superiors would accept and allow her to release information. Cutting through U.S. interdepartmental red tape was bad enough. Interpol was an independent international organization with nearly two hundred member countries, each with its own agenda. Getting information and cooperation from hostile foreign governments was often easier. Bolan wouldn't be surprised if Hal Brognola had been forced to wake up the President.

"I've got a friend who's been doing some legwork for me. I told him to meet me here and he'll arrive in a few minutes."

"I look forward to meeting him."

Bolan's cell phone rang on cue. He clicked it open and Manning's voice spoke. "I'm downstairs."

"Come on up."

Parson rolled out of bed. Her luggage consisted of a large, well-traveled leather suitcase and an aluminum briefcase that Bolan suspected was loaded with communications equipment.

She set her case on the coffee table. "You said you have your own satellite rig?"

Bolan rose. "My friend is bringing it."

There was one knock and then two on the door. "Striker."

The soldier opened the door. Manning stood with a pair of aluminum suitcases much like Agent Parsons's in his hands. "You wouldn't believe what the Bear had to— Shit!"

Manning flung away the cases and his hand went for his gun. Bolan whirled.

Parsons was still naked. Her beautiful face was split into a snarl of rage. Her pupils were pinholes of hatred. She flipped open her aluminum case and both of her hands came up filled with Glock pistols. Bolan dived to the floor as Manning's weapon cleared leather.

Twin halos of flame erupted as the Glock 18 machine pistols tore into life in Parsons's hands.

Manning staggered backward through the doorway, shuddering as the twin tracks of bullet strikes walked up his chest. Bolan hit the carpet and rolled over on his shoulder. He came up and seized the leg of the nightstand. The lamp and the clock-radio went flying as he raised it overhead and flung it. Wood flinders flew as the pistol rounds chopped into the flying furniture. They went momentarily silent as the tabletop struck Parsons in the face.

She staggered backward and shook her head to clear it as she struggled to bring her pistols back in line.

People in other rooms down the hall were screaming and shouting.

Bolan vaulted the bed. He took one long stride to eat distance and then leaped into the air. He pulled his knee into his chest as his flying side-kick drew a line between the muzzles of the Glocks. The knife edge of Bolan's foot struck Parsons's sternum with all of his two-hundred-pounds-plus behind it.

The woman went flying through the glass of the hotel room's sliding balcony door. She slipped over the edge of the third-story rail and fell out of sight. A moment later there was a crash and a short burst of gunfire.

For a moment all was silent. Then the screaming and shouting throughout the hotel began in earnest. Bolan hurried to Manning's side. The big Canadian sat gasping against the far wall with his Browning Hi-Power pistol held limply in his lap. His leather jacket was torn up its front in a railroad track of parallel bullet strikes that walked from his lower ribs to his collarbones. Four more bullet strikes pocked the wall above him. He blinked and yawned against the quadruple cracks the 9 mm bullets had delivered inches from both ears.

Bolan yanked open Manning's jacket and checked his armor. He saw the bright copper bases of ten bullets. The Kevlar had held. "Can you hear me?"

"Jesus, Mack." Manning winced as he shook his head. "Hanging out with loose women, sleeping with the enemy. What the hell happened to you?"

"She was the superbabe you saw on the boat."

"She was wearing sunglasses and a parka last time I saw her, but I'd remember that body anywhere."

"Yeah, well, she remembered you, too." Bolan took Manning's wrist and heaved him to his feet. "We've got to get out of here." The Executioner went back into the room and drew his Beretta 93-R. He flicked the selector switch to 3-round-burst mode and picked his way barefoot through the broken glass of the balcony, then peered over the edge.

The woman was gone.

A linen service delivery truck was parked in the space below. Bolan stared hard at the top of the cargo hold. There was a good-size dent in the top surrounded by shards of broken glass, and a great deal of blood smeared the white-painted aluminum. The edges of the truck top on either side were scored with bullet holes and the black burns of muzzle-blast. Bolan's eyes narrowed as he put together what he was seeing. The woman had been booted through a plate-glass sliding door and fallen onto the top of a truck. In the time it had taken him to check Manning, she had made her escape and taken her weapons with her.

Bolan scanned the surrounding area. The streets were wet. There was no sign of footprints. He lowered his weapon and retreated into the hotel room. They needed to tag and bag every item that the woman had left in the hotel room and get the hell out of Dodge.

He picked up his cell phone and dialed the most recent preset. He didn't look forward to explaining to Sergeant Alva that there was a lacerated, probably grievously injured, highly pissed-off assassin staggering naked through the streets of Helsinki with a Glock pistol in either hand.

5

Secure Communications Room,
U.S. Embassy, Helsinki, Finland

Mack Bolan watched the fax whir. It scrolled off a sheet of paper covered with charcoal sketch. The three drawings it had been compiled from were inset at the top. All three artists had chosen to include Manning's description of the woman pulling her parka open and flashing him. "She-cougar" pretty much summed up the lean lines of the woman's physique. The fax machine scrolled off the sketch made with Bolan's online description of the woman. Bolan sighed as he compared the two.

The two sketches were a perfect match.

He handed the sketches back to Manning. The big Canadian grinned delightedly. "Can I keep these?"

Bolan ignored the man and returned his attention to the screen.

Kurtzman sighed. "Can you guess what I'm going to say next?"

"No Interpol affiliate nation has ever had an agent named Theresa Parsons?"

"None whatsoever. It looks like we've been probed by the enemy."

Manning grinned up from the sketches. "Yeah, but from what I saw, Mack did some probing of the enemy of his own."

Bolan and Kurtzman regarded Gary Manning dryly. Manning shrugged. "Sorry."

"Listen," Bolan began, "all we have on these guys is that they use very expensive equipment from both Eastern and Western Europe and they have thirty nukes. That Russian being held by the state police is the only real clue we have. Bear, I've got to have a heart-to-heart with that Russian. If the President himself has to drop a dime on the Finns to make it happen, so be it. Our enemies have shown us how sophisticated they are. They're well financed and well organized and vindictive as hell. They came back and killed three of his buddies. I don't think our Russian friend is going to live long in custody. Our best chance is that the Russian is having the exact same feelings."

Kurtzman's brow creased. "That could be a problem. The Finnish canal authority pulled him out of our yacht. You had him hog-tied in the bilge. As far as we know, anything illegal with his fingerprints on it are at the bottom of the canal in the barge. Akira managed to hack into Finnish police files. His name is Shota Novikov, and he works for an import-export warehouse in Vyborg. In his statement to the Finnish police, Novikov claimed he was kidnapped, in Russia, by persons unknown, and claims he had no idea he was even in Finland until the canal authorities pulled him out of the bilge."

Bolan raised a speculative eyebrow. "You're saying he could walk?"

"I don't know. It depends on the Finns. Technically I don't know if they really have anything on him. Their laws are a lot different than ours."

Bolan and Manning exchanged glances as they shared the same thought. Manning smiled. "That could be to our advantage."

Kurtzman read Manning's meaning. "You're thinking about a snatch?"

Bolan nodded. "It could be our best shot. I don't like running a sweep around Sergeant Alva, he's a good man, but if we can cross the Finnish authorities out of the equation we'll be free to offer this Novikov a deal he can't refuse."

"Well, I hate to state the obvious, but your playmates are probably thinking the same thing."

"I'm banking on it."

Lake Saimaa

"GODDAMNED son of bitch!"

The woman snarled as the medic stitched one of her many lacerations. Roger Neville smiled as he watched the blood run down her back. It wasn't the medic she was swearing at. He glanced at his own image in the mirror. An immensely powerful-looking man stared back. He tilted his head slightly as he surveyed his own damage. A huge purple bruise lumped and distorted the left side of his face. The white of his left eye was lost in a bloody sea of broken blood vessels. Similar bruises were turning black on his neck and collarbone where the CS tear-gas grenade had broken apart and its individual bomblets had struck him. The bones in his hands creaked and popped as he made a fist. He tracked the veins that suddenly looped and crawled across the peak of his biceps. He smiled at them, then relaxed his fist.

"So what did you learn?"

"Well, he isn't Interpol." She glared up from the stitches in her arm. The back of her torso, buttocks and thighs were whorls of purples, blacks and blues from where she had fallen on top of the truck. She showed her perfect teeth. "And neither is that asshole friend of his I ventilated."

"Our observer noted two men leaving the hotel. They had your suitcase and what appeared to be all of your belongings."

"Goddamn it!"

"Don't feel too bad. I tried to ventilate the asshole on the yacht, and your new boyfriend out on the roadway." He grinned ruefully. "They're proving...resistant."

"So where are the little jerkweeds now?"

"The observer lost them, but it wasn't hard to figure out where they were going. We picked them up again. They're at the U.S. Embassy."

Her eyes held his. "Can we whack them there?"

Roger considered. "I'm not sure. Inserting a spy into the embassy wasn't hard, but putting an assassin in place could be a problem."

Her eyebrow rose slightly. "Yeah, well, what about your brother?"

The big man considered his brother. The word *billionaire* conjured up a rather exclusive club. Of course he had gotten into that lofty club by being careful. Roger's face set. The time for caution was over. The time for boldness was now. "He's worried about our friends."

"Our friends are toast and don't even know it."

He smiled at her bloodlust. Her watched blood run down one of her perfectly turned legs.

The woman ignored his gaze. "What about Shota? What are we going to do about him?"

The big man shrugged his inhumanly broad shoulders. "I say we kill him."

"How? He's in Finnish custody. He..." Her eyes suddenly widened. "You're going to assault the jail."

"I'd considered it, but I have reason to believe that Shota is going to walk. Our contacts say he is sticking with his story, and the Finns can't really figure out what to do with him."

"He's going to walk?"

"I believe so."

Her eyes grew heavy-lidded. "So we take him."

"Yeah, we take him."

Her eyes hardened. "The assholes will know that. They'll try to snatch him from us."

Roger nodded. "They'll try."

"Is it smart to expose ourselves again so soon?"

"No, it's not." The big man grinned as he thought about his brother. Ian's whining gave him an idea. "But my brother is worried about our friends."

The insanity in the big man's eyes matched the bloodlust of the woman's. "I say it's time they got themselves involved."

Roger took out his cell phone and dialed a number.

Police Headquarters, Helsinki, Finland

MACK BOLAN SCANNED the surrounding street with his binoculars. Yesterday's scattered sprinkles had turned into a steady drizzle, which rippled across the windshield of the embassy BMW sedan. The sky continued to darken in the north. One hell of storm was mounting out in the North Sea. "What have you got, Gummer?"

"I've got *nada,* Striker." The big Canadian, behind a silenced Galil sniping rifle, was on a rooftop half a block down. "No suspicious movement."

Bolan frowned as a woman pulled her car in front of their own and parked. It would make a quick getaway harder, but there was no time to reposition. He turned to face Nadine Truyen where she sat low in the back seat. "You ready for this?"

The linguist's arm was a lump beneath her jacket. It had been bandaged from the bullet wound she had received out on the roadway and was now held across her chest in a sling. "I can't believe I'm doing this."

"I can't believe you're doing this, either." Bolan smiled. "But I'm glad you are."

"Just don't get me shot again."

"I'll try." Bolan turned at motion in the corner of his eye. He put down his binoculars and loosened the Desert Eagle pistol in its cross-draw holster. "There's our boy now. Gummer, you see him?"

Manning spoke over the radio. "Affirmative, Striker. Target sighted."

A man stood outside the doors of the police station, flanked by a pair of uniformed Finnish police officers. One of them was Sergeant Alva. The Russian, hunched into his parka against the rain, tossed his head in the negative as the Finnish sergeant spoke to him, and fished a pack of cigarettes out of his pocket. Alva shrugged and nodded at his men. The Finns washed their hands of the Russian and headed back into the headquarters building. The Russian lit his cigarette and began walking down the steps. He looked both ways and started to cross the street.

He was crossing right toward Bolan's car. "Gummer, I'm taking him now."

"Affirmative, Striker. I have you covered."

Bolan turned to Truyen. "Stay low. We're going to take the man for a ride and make him an offer. All I want you to do is make sure we all understand one another." He loosened his rifle in its canvas case and slid it into the back seat with the woman. "Keep the passenger-side window open and the door unlocked. Keep the driver's side closed and locked."

Truyen saluted up from where she crouched in the back seat. "Affirmative, Striker."

Rain fell in Bolan's face as he slid out of the car. The Russian stopped short as the soldier materialized in his path and let his coat fall open to reveal the massive .50-caliber pistol. Bolan's left hand was closed around the grips of his Beretta 93-R in the deep pocket of his rainslicker. "Hey, Shota, I need a word with you."

Novikov gaped at the gun and then regarded Bolan with horror as he recognized him. He stammered in Russian. "Listen, you do not under—"

"No, I don't. But I want to. Get in the car. Let's make a deal."

"They will kill me—"

"Striker!" Manning shouted through the earpiece. "I have movement! Directly behind you!"

Bolan seized Novikov and flung him against the car. He drew the Beretta 93-R from beneath his rainslicker with his left hand and the Desert Eagle cleared leather in his right. The shop behind them was a Chinese restaurant, and a group of Chinese gunners were piling out of it carrying Finnish 9 mm Jatimatic submachine guns.

Truyen screamed as the weapons ripped into life.

Bolan dropped to put the sedan between himself and his attackers. Ostensibly an embassy vehicle, the BMW was also the personal ride of the CIA station chief in Finland. The windows and the car body were bulletproofed up to NATO .308-caliber full-metal-jacketed bullets. Sparks flew and lead spalling smeared the BMW's windows. People on the street began screaming at the sound of gunfire.

Bolan put the front sight of the Desert Eagle on the lead man and squeezed the trigger. The huge .50-caliber round drilled into the man's chest and he fell back into his associates. Bolan chopped down another attacker with a triburst from the Beretta and kicked Novikov in the back of the knee to put him on the ground.

"Get in the car!"

Two of the Chinese jerked and fell soundlessly, and Bolan knew Manning was watching over him. He dropped to keep the car between himself and his attackers. He leaped into the vehicle, shoved Shota across the seat and behind the steering wheel.

"Drive!"

Shota didn't need much encouragement. He shoved the BMW into gear and the tires screamed and spun against the wet pavement. Bolan dropped his pistols and reached into the back seat. The Galil micro assault rifle slid out of its case with the hiss of steel on canvas. He flipped the switch and powered up the Elbit Falcon rifle sight. The car lurched as it slammed into the vehicle parked in front of it. Shota was screaming and gears ground as he threw the car into reverse.

The Falcon sight wasn't a telescope or a laser pointer so much as a heads-up display like that on a fighter jet. The circular reticule was perched right in front of the rifle's front sight and projected a brilliant red dot not on the target but onto the screen in front of it. The Falcon was a millennial update on the Galilean rifle sight developed at the turn of the century. The Israelis had taken the concept and updated it with the latest technological optical advances. There was no parallax effect. The position of the rifleman's head and the perceived position of the 1.3 mm ruby-red dot wasn't a factor. If the rifleman could see the target and align the dot, he would hit.

"Nadine! Roll down your window! Tell Shota to do the same!"

Truyen shouted in Russian. She and Novikov hit the buttons on their door panels.

Bolan roared. "Duck!"

The woman and Novikov ducked below the windows. Both of them screamed as the seven inch barrel of the rifle breathed a stuttering three-foot tongue of flame over their heads. Bolan held the trigger down on full-auto. The report was deafening in the confines of the car and smoking hot brass sprayed and ricocheted around the car interior as Bolan expended the extended 50-round magazine. The Chinese staggered and fell as the armor-piercing, spoon-tip bullets tore into them.

"Gummer, what have you got—"

"Sniper!" Manning's voice rose over the com link. "Sniper!"

A bullet tore through the BMW's roof and ripped into the car door beside Bolan. "Drive, Shota! Drive!"

Novikov piled the Beamer back into another parked car and spun the wheel. Bolan slid a fresh magazine into his rifle. "Gummer! Where is he!"

"Rooftop, half a block down!" Bolan could hear Manning's rifle action cycling as he fired. "Six o' clock!"

Another bullet ripped through the roof and punched a hole in the windshield from the inside. Bolan took half a second to unlock his rifle's folding stock and lock it into place. He squirmed up and out of the window, grimacing against the rain as he twisted around in the window frame. Novikov spun the tires and hydroplaned against the wet street. Bolan nearly fell out of the window as the Russian slammed the car back and forth in a panic. A high-caliber rifle boomed and Bolan spotted the muzzle-flash on a rooftop behind them. Sparks shrieked off the armored roof of the BMW as it was penetrated six inches from Bolan's head. He put the red dot of the sight on his target and fired. The Galil rifle shuddered in his hands. Bits of masonry flew into the air as Bolan held down his trigger and tried to drive the sniper from his hide and into Manning's sights.

The rifle in Bolan's hands clacked open on a smoking empty chamber. He slid back down into the car as Novikov managed to point the bumper out into traffic. Uniformed policemen were piling out of the headquarters building with pistols drawn. Shota shoved the car into gear and pulled out.

A huge Asian man in a straining waiter's coat rose up from behind a parked car in front of them, a Jatimatic submachine gun in both hands.

"Move!" Bolan roared.

The BMW's tires screamed and the car launched forward as the rubber suddenly bit into the pavement. The armored windshield pocked and spalled as the man burned both 40-round magazines on full-auto. The window was nearly opaque as Novikov aimed the roaring vehicle at the gunman. Bolan slid another magazine into his Galil.

The giant threw down both of his weapons and raced toward the speeding vehicle. Bolan slammed the Galil's action home on a fresh round. The killer leaped into the air with inhuman agility. Bolan snaked the Galil out the window as the flying killer's legs scissored.

The man's heel came through the weakened windshield in an eruption of glass and crashed into Bolan's chest.

Truyen and Novikov screamed. Shota screamed. Bolan flew backward as the back of his seat snapped and reclined. The air exploded from his lungs and purple pinpricks danced across his vision. The car fishtailed and screeched to a halt. Battle instincts took over. His rifle was gone, his pistols were somewhere on the floorboards. A pair of immense legs had appeared in the shattered windshield, twisted around Shota's throat. Veins bulged out of the Russian's brow and his face purpled as the legs vised his neck. Bolan reached down and the four inch blade of his Cold Steel push dagger slid free of his boot sheath. The huge legs convulsed and twisted.

Novikov's neck snapped like kindling.

Bolan rammed the blade into the killer's calf.

The blade ripped free as the assassin yanked his legs out of the car, supporting himself on the hood of the BMW with his palms. He lifted an arm and whipped his legs around like a gymnast on a pommel horse. As Bolan lunged up from his seat and thrust at the killer's throat, the man's hand lashed out and caught Bolan's wrist.

The soldier's wrist bones creaked and compressed underneath the killer's inhuman grip. The fingers of Bolan's left hand stiffed into a blunt spear, and he pistoned the spear-hand into the killer throat. The black-eyed killer didn't blink as Bolan's hand stabbed into his neck, though the Executioner felt as if he were ramming his fingers into marble. He spread his fingers and stabbed for the eyes. The killer caught Bolan's left hand, squeezed, the knife falling from Bolan's right hand as his fingers went dead from the pressure. The killer held his adversary implacably. Bolan spit in the assassin's eyes and put his foot against the dash for leverage.

Shoving his opponent's hands against the hood, the attacker reared and drew his knee up into his chest in another inhuman gymnastic motion.

The guy's boots shot forward around both sides of Bolan's neck and suddenly constricted around his throat like twin pythons. Darkness haloed the edges of the soldier's vision as the blood supply to his brain was cut. He couldn't move his hands. The legs around his neck were like two massive stone pillars. Bolan stared into the eyes of his killer as his vision tunneled down. An ugly smile of victory passed across the assassin's face.

"Screw you, asshole!"

Truyen lunged forward over Novikov's shoulder and extended a short black cylinder. She clamped down on the bright red lever and a hissing wedge of pepper gas sprayed into the killer's face. The legs on Bolan's neck loosened and he jammed his chin down to free his throat. He squeezed his eyes shut as Truyen continued to hose down the killer at point-blank range. The assassin freed a leg from Bolan's neck and flicked out his foot. The woman's eyes rolled back in her head as the massive heel slammed between her eyebrows. The linguist slumped unconscious into the back seat.

Bolan flung open his door and rolled out onto the street. His hand reached back to the floorboard of the passenger seat and came up with the Beretta 93-R. The immense assassin flung himself off the BMW's hood into a backflip and landed on his feet. His hands curled into fore-knuckle fists as he advanced.

Bolan pulled a ragged breath into his lungs as he raised the Beretta 93-R and leveled the front sight between the assassin's eyes.

"Stop!" Şergeant Alva roared in English. His men were yelling in Finnish, but their meaning was clear. More than twenty uniformed police officers filled the street behind him. All of them stood, their service pistols drawn.

"Drop your gun!" Alva's pistol was pointed rock-steady at Bolan's head.

"Gummer." Bolan subvocalized into his throat mike. "What have you got?"

"The sniper has disappeared. All of the attackers are down except the big fella facing you."

The "big fella" stood six feet away from Bolan. He had taken so much pepper spray that it ran down his face like hair gel.

He was smiling.

"Your gun!" Alva looked at Bolan imploringly. "Please!"

Bolan spoke low into his mike again. "Gummer, extract. Tell Bear I'm going to need a serious get-out-of-jail-free card."

"Affirmative, Striker. Extracting. We have your back. The cavalry is on the way."

The Executioner was swarmed by uniformed officers as he dropped his pistol.

He and the giant Asian kept their eyes locked. Neither resisted as each had their arms pulled behind their backs and manacled. Bolan measured his opponent. The man was six foot seven and built like a tombstone. His shoulders and hips were the same width. He was a wall of a human with a bullet-shaped head and the neck of a bull. The killer kept his eyes unblinkingly on Bolan. He wasn't coughing. He didn't weep from the pepper spray. There were no bruises on his throat from Bolan's blows, and the stab wound in his leg didn't appear to bother him. Other than reddened eyes, the killer seemed as fresh as a daisy.

The Finnish police ran a shackling chain around Bolan's waist and locked his handcuffs to it. Bolan smiled back at the killer and made a mental note to load his .50-caliber Desert Eagle with high-velocity solids when he had opportunity.

6

Helsinki Police Headquarters, Finland

Mack Bolan grimaced as he rolled his neck on his shoulders. He peered at the stainless-steel mirror bolted into the wall of the cell. The bruising on both sides of his neck was spectacular. He turned as the viewing slot in the door shot open and someone peered in. A voice spoke in heavily accented English.

"Step back from the door or you will be gassed!"

Bolan stepped back from the door. The chains shackling his legs and wrists jingled. Sergeant Alva stepped in and two men followed him. One was a tall man with thinning blond hair. He wore a poorly tailored suit, and smoked. He carried himself with the ease of one accustomed to command. While his suit hung on him like a scarecrow, the suit of the man next to him strained at the seams. He was bald and as tall as his partner but twice as thick. He held himself with an air of casual brutality. The thin man held out a pack of French Gauloises cigarettes. "Smoke?"

"No, thank you."

The man nodded and turned to Alva. "Thank you for your assistance, Sergeant."

Alva nodded back uncertainly. "You are welcome, Inspector."

The inspector smiled thinly. "You may leave, Sergeant."

Alva shot a look at Bolan, then drew himself to attention. "Of course, Inspector." Alva turned and closed the door behind him.

The thin man lit a cigarette, then smiled at Bolan. "I am Inspector Petri Sillaampa of the state police." He nodded at his hulking partner. "This is my assistant, Officer Heikki Suvari. He does not understand much English. However, he does understand disrespect."

Bolan saw Heikki's hand blur into motion. He sank his breath deep into his belly and rooted his feet into the floor as the big man swung. The flat of Heikki's open hand cracked across Bolan's face with the impact of a frying pan.

The soldier neither moved nor blinked.

Heikki's face contorted in pain. He stepped back and shook his hand out from the impact. His eyes measured Bolan, with new wariness.

"Ah." Sillaampa's eyes measured Bolan, as well, and he nodded slightly with respect. "A tough guy."

Bolan felt the side of his face lumping and swelling with the blow. "What can I do for you, Inspector?"

"Well." The inspector shrugged his thin shoulders. "This is just an interview, we have about an hour, so we will keep it simple." All mocking friendliness left his eyes. "You are going to tell me exactly who you are. You are going to tell me exactly who you work for. You are going to tell me exactly how you found out about the nuclear weapons being transported up the Saimaa. You are going to give me the names of all of your contacts. You are going to give me every piece of information you have, and every piece of information or conjecture you may think you have."

"I believe you'll find I have diplomatic immunity." Bolan kept his doubts to himself. He didn't have diplomatic immunity, but hopefully checking his status would give Manning and Kurtzman time to jury-rig something.

"Indeed?" The inspector rubbed his head thoughtfully. "Well, that may be so."

Heikki reached into his coat. He produced a stun gun, two short lengths of loaded rubber hose and a pair of pliers. He flexed his hand and grinned unpleasantly. The inspector shrugged sadly and reached for the stun gun. "However, for the next forty-five minutes I believe you will find your diplomatic status to be...irrelevant."

Bolan leaped.

Manacles chained his hands to his sides and shackles hobbled his feet together with little more than two feet of slack. His vertical leap, however, was unimpeded. Bolan pulled his knees into his chest and rammed both heels into Heikki's solar plexus like a mule.

The big Finn's eyes bugged as his xiphoid process broke off and lacerated his diaphragm. His knees buckled as his lungs deflated. Bolan fell hard to the bare floor and bounced up. Sillaampa stared for a moment in froze horror as blood spilled over Heikki's lips. The inspector lunged at Bolan. Blue voltage arced and sparked between the stun gun's prongs. Bolan couldn't jump again in time, nor could he dodge the weapon. Bolan took the hit. He snarled as the prongs dug into his chest, and his body locked as the voltage coursed through him. He went with the shove of the weapon and fell to the floor to break contact. Bolan hit the linoluem with bone-jarring force and let his eyes roll.

The inspector bent to shock him again, but Bolan rammed both of his feet into the man's knees. The inspector screamed as his knee ligaments snapped from their moorings. The stun gun clattered to the floor as the inspector fell. Bolan rolled to one side along the linoleum.

Despite his agony, the inspector was clawing for the pistol holstered under his jacket.

Bolan rolled beside the man and heaved his heels into the air. He snapped the shackles around his ankles tight and dropped the chain around the inspector's neck. He twisted his body around savagely and cinched the chain tight. The inspector flailed with the weight of both of Bolan's legs on his back. The Executioner cinched down tighter. The inspector's 9 mm pistol came free of its holster. He shoved the pistol awkwardly behind his back. Bolan yanked his head aside from the black eye of the muzzle. The gun fired and sparks flew from the walls of the cell. He flung himself back and yanked the inspector with him as the gun barked again. The policeman's struggles grew weaker as the stainless-steel chain choked off the blood to his brain. The pistol wavered as he could no longer aim behind himself. The gun fired again into the wall off to the side, then fell to the floor as the inspector went down on both hands.

Feet pounded in the hall. The lock of the holding cell turned, and Sergeant Alva stood with his pistol drawn. More officers piled into him from behind. Alva stared at the inspector as he turned purple.

Heikki sat slumped against the wall, turning a brilliant cyanotic blue.

Alva pointed his pistol at Bolan's head. He seemed utterly flabbergasted. "Please! I implore you! Stop…strangling Inspector Sillaampa!"

"All right." Bolan twisted himself back around and extricated his shackles from around his adversary's neck. Sillaampa let out a great, strangled wheeze and began violently coughing as his tortured lungs sucked in air.

"Sergeant," Bolan asked, "may I rise?"

"Um…" The sergeant's pistol didn't waver. "Very well."

Bolan pushed himself up to his feet. He still felt the shudders of the electricity that had been pumped through him. "I think it's time you and I had a talk with your superior."

Alva nodded rapidly at the suggestion. "I think that would be a very good idea."

CAPTAIN JARI NIEMI seemed highly unamused.

He was a short, almost ridiculously fat man with a face like a basset hound. Bolan stood in the captain's office with his hands handcuffed behind his back and looked the man in the eye. The Executioner could see that behind the jowls lurked a highly capable man. He suspected many men had underestimated the captain's abilities to their misfortune.

The captain stared at Bolan coldly. "You have grievously injured an officer of the state police and assaulted a state police inspector."

"They assaulted me." Bolan rolled his shoulders. "I believe they intended to grievously injure me."

"We only have your word for that." The captain's eye glanced at a file in front of him. "And it contradicts both that of the officer and the inspector."

"They had a stun gun."

"The Finnish police have decided that the judicious use of a stun gun is more humane than the use of clubs." He eyed Bolan shrewdly. "Particularly in the case of violent detainees."

Bolan nodded. "Of course, I agree, except for the fact that they had clubs."

"Um...well." The captain stared at the file again unhappily. "Truncheons still are issued in circumstances, however..."

"However, rubber hoses loaded with lead shot are, shall we say—" Bolan raised an eyebrow "—unorthodox in Finnish police service?"

The captain's discomfort grew more visible by the second. He was clearly appalled.

"State police undercover officers are allowed, a certain amount of, leeway."

"Pliers?" Bolan queried.

"Inspector Sillaampa said he had experienced difficulties with his automobile, and the tool was in his pocket by happenstance..." The captain trailed off weakly. The captain's line of reasoning sounded lame even to him.

"You and I have a mutual problem."

Captain Niemi leaned back in his chair. "We have a number of problems that must be sorted out. Which one in particular are you speaking about?"

"Thirty black market nuclear weapons have been smuggled into your country."

The captain turned pale. "The incident on the Saimaa—"

"Was an attempt on my part to interdict them. It failed, and twice now the enemy has counterattacked. The only lead I had was Shota Novikov. He's dead. However, we have two new leads. One is Inspector Sillaampa. He revealed that he knew about the weapons. The second is the Asian man you incarcerated with me. He was the man who killed Shota, presumably to shut him up. Can you tell me his status at the moment?"

The captain looked as if he might be sick. He struggled to regain some composure. "You are not an Interpol agent."

"No."

"Neither was the woman, Theresa Parsons."

"No, she is working with the enemy."

"Yes, so Sergeant Alva informs me." The captain stared at his report again and then back at Bolan. "Who are you?"

"I'm a concerned citizen of the United States." Bolan glanced at the report. "The Finnish state police have been compromised by the enemy. Nuclear weapons have been smuggled onto your soil. I don't believe they are intended to be detonated in your country, but someone bought them for some purpose, and I don't believe it is a humanitarian one. Something terrible is going to happen. I would appreciate any help you might offer."

The captain took a long breath. "I will grant you the point, it does, at least outwardly, appear that Finnish state police officials are involved in an international crime. The nature of which I cannot personally verify at this time." The captain's eyes hardened to match Bolan's. "You must forgive me if trust is a hard commodity to come by, given how little I know for certain in this situation."

Sergeant Alva snapped to attention as he spoke. "Captain, I do not know for certain who this man is, but he saved my life and the life of one of my men. I believe it is clear that he was trying to protect Shota Novikov, while his opponents were clearly trying to kill him. The Parsons woman also made an attempt to kill him. He has expressed a willingness to me to exchange information. If his methods have been unorthodox, well..." Alva suddenly reddened at his own boldness. He stood straighter. "Captain, I am personally inclined to trust him."

The captain's eyes turned on his sergeant. "Are you willing to stake your career on that?"

Alva swallowed and nodded. "Yes."

"Good, because you are." The captain turned his attention back to Bolan. "You are willing to exchange information?"

"I'll tell you everything I know." Bolan stared out the window at the blackening sky. "Approximately seventy-two hours ago we intercepted a barge on the Saimaa coming from Vyborg, and were engaged by an enemy of squad strength armed with heavy weapons, most of whom appeared to be Russians. We defeated them and the barge was sunk. We took prisoners, including Shota Novikov. The next day we attempted an investigation of the wreck, and evidence we found led us to believe that thirty tactical nuclear warheads exchanged hands and were transported by midget submarine into the lake."

Niemi's eyes hardened. "None of which you chose to share with Finnish authorities."

Bolan met his gaze and then glanced meaningfully down at the report on the incident in the holding cell. "You must forgive me if trust is a hard commodity to come by."

The captain stared at the report bitterly. "Yes."

"During our investigation of the wreck, we were counterattacked. The battle was inconclusive, and we left the prisoners for the Finnish authorities. When the canal authority attempted to transport the Russians, their convoy was attacked, and we assisted. I believe you have a detailed account of the firefight. As you have surmised, Theresa Parsons isn't an Interpol agent, and made an attempt on my life and one of my men. She escaped. We then made an attempt to contact Shota Novikov and offer him a deal. This was interrupted by another enemy attack, and Novikov was killed. That, and the incident in the holding cell, brings us to the present. Can you tell me the status of the other man you took into custody?"

Niemi opened a slender folder on his desk. It contained a single page of scant text. "We are informed his name is Yun Chung Shang. He has not spoken since his incarceration. We received a delegation from the Chinese embassy an hour ago. Mr. Shang—"

Bolan shook his head. "Has diplomatic immunity."

"Yes. We are informed his actions had nothing to do with his diplomatic duties. The Chinese inform us he may have had unknown dealings with the Chinese and Russian underworld. We are informed he is being taken back to the People's Republic of China where he will be tried for his crimes."

"What about his accomplices?"

"You killed them all. Though some appeared to have been killed with a high-powered rifle." The captain looked up at Bolan wearily. "I suppose these were the actions of your accomplice."

"We wanted Novikov alive, Captain. We expected some kind of resistance, snipers or a drive-by, perhaps, or at least to detect surveillance by the enemy. We weren't expecting to be attacked by a detachment of Chinese special purpose troops."

"Special purpose troops?"

"Yes."

"You mean special forces operatives?"

"Yes, like your Ranger Warfare and Special Jaeger units."

"Chinese special forces units."

"Yes."

"Operating in Helsinki."

"Yes."

Niemi looked as though he was about to be sick. "And you are?"

"A concerned citizen of the United States. I suppose you photographed Mr. Shang and took his fingerprints."

"Yes, of course."

"May I have access to them?"

Niemi was silent for a long moment.

"Yes."

7

U.S. Embassy, Helsinki, Finland

"The guy was built like a freight train, Bear."

Bolan examined his wrists as storm winds lashed the embassy windows. There was a perfect imprint of the assassin's hands in swollen, blue bruising where he had pinned Bolan's wrists. "And nothing stopped him. He dumped two magazines into the windshield to weaken it and then did a flying drop-kick right through it. Then he snapped the Russian's neck with a leglock. I hit him twice, both spear-hands to the throat, and all he did was smile at me."

"We got nothing on a Yun Chung Shang." Kurtzman suddenly smiled. "But is this your boy?"

Bolan gazed into the face that appeared in a window on the laptop's screen. The photograph wasn't of particularly high quality. It depicted a man sitting in a teahouse, and he seemed to take up his half of the table. He was looking at a man whose back was to the camera. Bolan would never forget the hooded black eyes that had stared unblinkingly into his own. "Yeah, that's him."

"I sent the Finnish police photo along with your report to the CIA. They sent it to assets the Pentagon has in the PRC. Yun Chung Shang may be an alias. We don't know the man's real name. He has another alias that he's known by, though. They call him Stone Monkey."

Bolan stared at the screen. "Cute."

"No, he earned it. According to our resources he was the number-one hatchet man for the triads in Northern China. According to rumor, he was caught up in a drug bust and arrested. The Chinese government made him an offer he couldn't refuse. They took his already considerable talents as an assassin and sent him to the special warfare school, where they added airborne, mountaineering, underwater demolitions and light weapons specialist to his list of accomplishments. He's known to speak Mandarin, Cantonese and some English."

Bolan frowned. "What were his previous considerable talents?"

"He was a highly feared Monkey Kung Fu stylist."

"So is Gadgets. What does he have to say about it?"

Bolan had spent extensive hours sparring with the members of Phoenix Force and Able Team to improve his own close-quarters battle skills. He had taken the bruises and the lumps from each of them and learned the lessons the hard way. Many of the commandos from Stony Man Farm held black belts in numerous martial arts styles. Gadgets Scwharz studied Monkey Kung Fu, and of all the Stony Man operatives he was the most difficult to lay a glove on.

Kurtzman's worry line furrowed his brow. "Gadgets says you better watch your ass with this guy."

"I know. This guy has already had me dead to rights once. What else did Gadgets have to say?"

"He gave me a quick rundown. There are five basic Monkey Kung Fu forms. Drunken, Lost, Wooden and Standing. Can you guess what the fifth is?"

"Stone."

"That's right. Most students specialize in one, generally the one their master thinks is most appropriate for them. Drunken and Lost are deceptive forms. That's where Gadgets comes from. Standing is more of a conventional long-arm Kung Fu form, and Wooden is a highly aggressive form, typically using all-out relentless attacks."

Bolan could see the rub coming. "And Stone?"

"According to Gadgets, the Stone Monkey form is taught only to the largest and most powerful students who can withstand the punishing training regimen. Their techniques are based on brute force and overpowering the opponent. They'll go toe-to-

toe with anyone, of any style, exchange blows, and win. To accomplish this they're trained internally and externally to withstand blows to any part of their body. It's not unknown for students to be injured or killed during this part of the training. They also train a lot in leaping, rolling and falling maneuvers."

"Yeah, well, it fits. What else do we know about him?"

"Well, before the PRC saw fit to train him in automatic weapons and explosives, it's rumored his specialty was the Iron Fist technique, and that's how he usually killed people for the triads. Lots of shattered skulls and ruptured internal organs."

"Swell. Anything else?"

"Yeah, despite being built like a brick wall, he's famous for sneaking up on people."

"That it?"

"No, Gadgets says you see this guy, you shoot him, and you shoot him in the head. You don't consider him done until you've blown out his skull and splattered his brain matter across the wall behind him. That's a direct quote."

"What about the guy punching holes in the embassy car? He wasn't using a Gepard this time."

"Well, there aren't a whole lot of Gepards in Hungarian inventory, much less laying around on the surplus market. We took one of the bullets Gary dug out of the car and routed it to the boys in Berlin. They were happy to have the business. It was a steel cored .338 Lapua round."

Bolan raised an eyebrow. "Let me guess, the rifling indicated an Accuracy International Super Magnum rifle."

"Give the man a cigar."

Short of a Barret .50, the .338 Lapua Super Magnum was about the most powerful, man-portable sniper rifle in the world. Chambered in an Accuracy International rifle, it was also about the world's most accurate handheld weapon in the world.

"Bear, we've got two sets of players here. The Chinese were all using locally acquired Finnish weapons, and the Russians we dealt with on the Saimaa all had AKs." Bolan considered his opponents. "But the other people we are dealing with, whoever they are, seem to have very expensive tastes in weapons. Heckler & Koch G-36s, Underwater Assault rifles, Hungarian Gepards, Accuracy International rifles." Bolan thought about Theresa Parsons. "Glock machine pistols. It's like these guys are in a candy store with a gold card and can buy anything they want."

Kurtzman's eyes narrowed. "You're talking like they're private individuals or mercs on a shopping spree."

"I'm willing to bet that the Chinese team was state sponsored. A PRC special forces team going rogue in Finland is right off the plausibility map." Bolan considered the woman again. "But who they're in cahoots with, and why, that one is wide open. Speaking of which, what have you got on Theresa Parsons?"

"Not much, but we're working on it. Her fingerprints aren't coming up on anyone's files, but Akira swears he's seen her on the Internet someplace."

"Put him on it. Have him go back and check all of them. It's a long shot, but I trust his instincts. If he's seen something, it's out there."

"I already put him on it," Kurtzman told him.

"Good. I also want you to check on any kind of activity at all by the PRC in Finland, whether it's economic, scientific, political or cultural. Actually, make that all of Scandinavia. Get back to me on anything you find interesting."

"You've got it. How are things on your end?"

"Those nukes are still loose and my hunch is they're not going to stay in Lake Saimaa long. Inspector Sillaampa and his pal Heikki are under investigation. Heikki's in hospital and Sillaampa is under house arrest. They've gotten themselves lawyers and have clammed up tight."

"You going to pay them a visit?"

"No." Bolan had given that weighty consideration. "We'd have to go straight up against uniformed Finnish policemen, and both the sergeant and the captain have asked me to step down while their own version of Internal Affairs does their job."

"And what do you think of that?"

"They'll do their best," Bolan stated.

"What does that mean?"

"It means I think Sillaampa and his buddy Heikki are going to wind up dead under mysterious circumstances within the next forty-eight hours, and I don't think there's a damn thing we can do about it."

"What's your current status legally?"

"Captain Niemi is giving us what cooperation he can, but the state police are pissed and asking lots of questions. The next time I get arrested in Helsinki I don't think the captain is going to get me out of it." Bolan sipped his coffee.

"So what are you going to do?"

"I don't know." Bolan let out a long breath. "We need leads. What's the status of our Stone Monkey?"

"He was escorted to the Helsinki airport by Finnish police and several Chinese embassy guards and put on a flight to Beijing."

"Have the CIA pick him up as soon as the plane touches down and trail him as long as they can."

"They can't do that."

Bolan set down his coffee. "Why not?"

"Because half an hour ago his plane made an unscheduled stop in Islamabad. Technical problems, supposedly."

"Pakistan." Bolan stared at the world map that was inset on his screen. "Interesting. The PRC sells a lot of guns and fighter planes there."

"You think the trail might lead there?"

"No, I think it was simply the most convenient port of call. We've already lost him, but I think our boy is coming right back."

"Coming back? To Finland?" Kurtzman pondered the idea. "You mean, he's coming back to finish you off?"

"I think he'd love to snap my neck. The last expression I saw on his face had 'unfinished business' written all over it. But I think he's coming back because the mission demands it."

"What kind of mission are we talking about, Striker, particularly that would still require his kind of services? He's an assassin, and too valuable to use as a baby-sitter. I'm thinking those nukes are in a pretty damn secure place, if they're not out of Finland already. Why come back?"

"Because the mission demands it."

"You said that already. What does that mean?"

"It means I need a scenario."

"What kind of scenario?"

"Most Chinese covert actions we know about lately have been in places like the Philippines, mainland Asia at large, Panama and the Sudan. Pick any of those save the Sudan, and it would be easier just to stage the boy from Beijing and then out into the Pacific. But his superiors wanted quick turnaround. They wouldn't reroute an airliner just to divert him to the Sudan. They want him back, right here, and ASAP."

"Okay, I'll buy it. But the question still remains. Why?"

"That's your job. Bear, I want you to give me a scenario involving the PRC, thirty tactical nukes and Scandinavia."

Kurtzman snorted. "Nukes? Targeted for Scandinavia? I mean, who would want to nuke Finland, much less Norway or Sweden? Take your most freaked-out, insane terrorist and you still have to ask yourself, what's the payoff? The PRC aren't yahoos, and neither are the people they seem to be playing with. Like you said, these guys are heavily armed, highly organized and highly professional. Besides, thirty nukes? That's one hell of a tall order."

"Cross reference it with you, research into all PRC activity in the Scandinavian countries. Go nuts. I don't care how far out it is. Give me something."

"What makes you think Scandinavia is anything more than a waypoint?"

Bolan listened to the wind hammer the windows in their panes. "My instincts. They tell me there's a storm coming."

The computer expert steepled his fingers. There were few things on Earth he enjoyed more than an intellectual challenge, and few things he trusted more than the instincts of Mack Bolan. For a man like Aaron Kurtzman, it was one of the joys of working with the Executioner. The challenges he threw out were Byzantine, often life-threatening, and challenged both the Kurtzman's intellect and his creativity.

"All right. Though the President, the Pentagon, and everyone and their brother is going to say we're nuts. You want a Scandinavian target for thirty tactical nukes? Fine. I'm on it. But it's probably going to come straight from outer space."

8

City of Turku, Waterfront District, Finland

Yun Chung Shang stared at Roger Neville. His shoulders were impossibly broad and tapered down to the tiny waist of a body builder. His physique screamed of immense and useless upper-body strength. Shang suspected the American could bench press well over four hundred pounds. He kept his disdain from his face. He suspected the American couldn't maintain a deep horse-stance for longer than a minute.

Six tactical nuclear weapons lay in a line on the warehouse floor between the two men.

The American smiled. "You ready to take the shipment?"

"The captain is worried about the weather." Shang's eyes flicked to the corrugated roof that hammered under the rain. "He has been paid extra, and deems the risk...acceptable."

Roger eyed measuringly up and down Shang. "I hear he got a piece of you."

Shang stared expressionlessly. It was true he had lost his entire team and been arrested, but he had been extracted and reinserted within twenty-one hours. Shota Novikov was dead and the leak plugged. Money had changed hands and people were in place, and State Police Inspector Petri Sillaampa and Officer Heikki Suvari were both unknowingly within hours of hideous deaths from some very esoteric Chinese herbal poisons. His end of the mission had been a complete success. He took in the smugness on the American's face. Shang's leg was stiff from the knife wound. It bothered him that he had the man in a death grip and yet the blue eyes he had stared into had revealed no fear. It bothered him that the man had shot down his hit team within seconds. It bothered Shang more that the only reason he himself was still alive and standing in the warehouse rather than lying in a morgue with a bullet in his brain was police interference.

Whoever the agent was, he reeked of trouble.

"Shota Novikov is dead." Shang looked past the American and his bodyguards. They were all cut from the same cloth. They were Americans. They were cowboys. Shang didn't trust them. "Where is your brother?"

Roger frowned slightly. "He's taking care of business." He stared pointedly at the row of nukes standing in line like soldiers. "You have your people in place?"

"All is in readiness. Once the weapons are delivered, the plan will proceed."

"What is your timetable?"

Shang considered. "A week to the delivery point. Preparations have already been laid. Placement may take a week, perhaps two, depending upon the weather. What of yourself?"

"The final phase will be in your hands." The man gave his irritating smile again. "However, we will have people in place both on-site and abroad to assist you as needs be."

"Very well." Shang turned and jerked his head at his men. They began packaging the weapons for transport and loading them onto the little Swedish Valp truck. Given the utterly unorthodox nature of the mission, Shang had been given a great deal of leeway in choosing his soldiers. They were all special purpose troops, though some had some very unorthodox backgrounds. All spoke Russian or English. Other specific linguists as well as technicians had been chosen to fulfill the mission requirements, though those capacities were being fulfilled by the team already in place. All was in place. For once, the old men in Beijing had seen fit to spare no expense. Shang had absolute faith in himself and his men.

He didn't trust smiling Americans.

What he had seen in the eyes of his American opponent outside the police station in Helsinki left him deeply disturbed.

Shang put such thoughts from his mind for the moment. He held out his hand to the American. The toothpaste-selling smile lit up the man's face as they pumped hands. It was a Western custom Shang despised. The American squeezed his hand in what he had to have thought was a bone-crushing grip.

Shang allowed a smile to come to his face. He resisted the temptation to grind the man's bones to powder.

"WHAT DO YOU THINK of that?" Ian Neville emerged from the shadows of the warehouse office. Roger folded his arms across his massive chest and smiled as he listened to the truck's engine pulling down the wharf toward the transport boat and phase two to the mission.

"I think they haven't got a goddamn clue."

Ian twitched his shoulders. He was a captain of an empire, and had ruthlessly crushed his opponents in boardrooms and from the tops of the highest financial towers in the world. But his brother was playing a very dangerous game with very different rules. He had looked long and hard at the Chinese through the one-way glass.

Shang scared the hell out of him.

"Are we really prepared to screw these guys over?"

"Most definitely." Roger nodded. "They're going to accomplish their mission. It's just that we're going to help them succeed beyond their wildest dreams."

"You're absolutely sure this is going to work?"

Roger turned and searched his brother's face. He was well aware of his brother's capabilities and his weaknesses. He had started displaying them when the wet work had begun. "You have doubts? Your own people have looked into it, and they say it's more than feasible. Any residual effects we get back home will be minimal, and worth it, particularly compared to what happens to our enemies. We've been over this a million times, Ian." The big man shrugged casually. "What's the matter? You having second thoughts about being the richest man on Earth?"

"I'm saying I don't like the look of that man." Ian couldn't keep his thoughts off of Shang. "And I'm asking if we're really prepared to screw these guys over?"

"They go down." Roger's face was stone. "They all go down, and we go to the top. It's our destiny. There's never been any other path. Not since you and I were born. Not since the second we hit Plymouth Rock."

Ian stared at his brother. He was fairly certain he was insane. But he was insane enough to make it work, and Ian had no second thoughts at all about being the richest man on Earth.

It was, indeed, his destiny.

"No, I'm not having any doubts, Roger, it's just the Chinese delegation was more than I expected."

"This is a game for all the stakes. You didn't think they'd send the baddest of their bad-asses. Our boy Shang is a stone-cold killer, no doubt about it, but I don't care how much Kung Fu crap he knows. When the time comes, he goes down."

"Speaking of going down, where's Theresa?"

Roger snorted. "Well, you don't like loose ends, and I don't like that asshole who keeps popping up at our parties. He moves like a shadow, and then falls out the sky like a hammer. He seems like a real crackerjack operator. I want to do something about him."

Ian's eyes narrowed. "I thought we were in agreement that hitting the embassy was a bad idea. The chances of success are real low unless we use one of our extra firecrackers, and that's just the kind of heat we don't need this close."

"Oh, I agree with you completely. We have to pin him down to hit him, and I want to hit him up close and personal. We don't know who he is, but we know who he's been working with."

"What are you suggesting?"

"I'm not suggesting anything. It's already in motion." Roger grinned at his brother's sudden discomfort. It was always good to remind him who was really in command. "We're going to hit some of his peripherals and see if we can make him jump. I put Theresa and some local help on it."

Helsinki University Central Hospital

"IT'S HIDEOUS."

Nadine Truyen lay on her hospital bed. She regarded the bug-eyed, stuffed reindeer Bolan held out from purple bruising that raccooned both of her eyes. Sergeant Alva held out a bouquet of daisies. "I brought flowers."

Truyen took the animal and the flowers. "Well, thank you. Thank you both."

Bolan sat on the bed. "You're welcome, and thanks again for all your help."

The woman blushed around her bruises. "Oh, help nothing. I didn't translate a single word of Russian for you. All I did was get myself shot and nearly have my brains kicked out."

"You saved my life."

Truyen stared down at the stuffed animal and absently played with its antlers. "Oh, well, Daddy always said carry protection."

Bolan smiled. "You need anything?"

"Well, they say I have a concussion. They want to keep me another day for observation. My arm hurts. I ripped my stitches in the fight in the car. But I guess I don't really need anything. Everyone has been very nice to me, and I have a private room." She suddenly looked up concernedly. "So Shota's dead."

"Yeah."

"What are you going to do now?"

"I don't know," Bolan replied. "Probably bring you another stuffed animal tomorrow. Maybe a bear or something."

Alva finished putting the flowers in a glass beaker he found and motioned to the man he had brought with him. "This is Senior Constable Tuisannen. He will be staying by your side until the doctors clear you to go back to the embassy."

Truyen stared up at the man in awe. Tuisannen was blond and blue-eyed and as tall as tree. He could have passed for the Norse god Thor if he was wearing an iron breastplate and carrying a sledgehammer. He stood at ramrod attention and smiled at her.

His English was atrocious. "Good evening. I am pleased to be making your acquaintance."

Truyen giggled and began speaking to him rapidly in Finnish.

Bolan waved. "I'll check on you tomorrow."

The woman nodded at him absently as Tuisannen sat his mass on the edge of the bed.

Bolan and Alva turned and left the room. The sergeant's face grew concerned again. "What will you do?"

"I don't know. How are the inspector and Heikki doing?"

Alva's face fell. He waited until they had gotten into the elevator and the door had closed. "That is one of the reasons I wished to meet with you."

"They're dead."

"Yes." Alva sighed. "Both appeared to have been poisoned in identical ways. Their deaths were horrific, but so far our coroner is unable to identify the poison. It does not appear to be any known compound in his catalog."

Bolan shook his head as the door pinged open and they exited the elevator. Chinese assassins had gotten about a ten-thousand-year jump on the rest of the world when it came to formulating poisons. Their long history of herbalism and their ancient mapping of the human systems, both physical and esoteric, left no part of a human they couldn't attack. It was a tradition that had survived the Cultural Revolution and was being ever more extensively employed by their secret services.

"I don't know what I'll do next. I'll have to thank your captain for all of the help he's already give—"

Bolan froze.

Alva looked around as the soldier sniffed the air. "What?"

Bolan began walking down the lobby as the scent grew stronger. Alva followed as Bolan pushed open a door and then another. Several uniformed nurses looked up as the Executioner entered the room. There were a few couches in the room and a coffeemaker. It was a nurse's salon. Most of the nurses were smoking.

Bolan smelled the powerful aroma of Turkish tobacco.

He turned on Alva. "Ask them which nurse was smoking Turkish tobacco."

"What?"

"Ask!"

Alva spoke rapidly in his official voice. One of the women answered. Alva frowned. "She says she doesn't know what you m—"

"Ask them which nurse was smoking strong cigarettes!"

The nurse tossed her head and spoke with some disdain.

Alva shrugged. "She says some new one. She didn't even bother to say hi and left when they came in—"

The nurses screamed as Bolan's pistol cleared holster. Alva leaped after him as he tore out the door. The soldier skidded to a halt and scanned the elevators. Both were in midtransit. He sprinted down the hall and ripped open the door to the stairs. His boots thundered on the steel stairs and echoed in the vertical chamber as he took the stairs four at a time.

"W-what!" Alva struggled to keep up as he drew his pistol. "What is happening!"

"She's here!"

"Who?"

"Agent Parsons!" Bolan kicked open the door to the fourth floor. Doctors and nurses scattered as the big American drew a line through them. The Beretta machine pistol brooked no argument. The door to Truyen's room smashed off its hinges beneath Bolan's boot. The muzzle of the 93-R swung to cover the small room. Alva nearly piled into him. The Finnish sergeant stared at the scene in horror.

Constable Tuisannen lay slumped in his seat. His head had lolled onto his shoulder and the cylinder of a long syringe stood out of his ear where the needle had been spiked through his eardrum and into his brain. A small trickle of blood ran down from his ear to his jaw. His eyes were rolled back in his head. He had neither seen nor felt his execution. Bolan turned his gaze to the bed.

Nadine Truyen had.

The bedclothes and the side table showed signs of a struggle. It was a struggle the woman had lost. Her body lay sprawled on her hospital bed. The piano wire around her throat had been cinched so tight it had sliced into her throat. Blood stained the front of her hospital gown and the white sheets in disarray beneath her. The twin handles of the garrote had been twisted around each other so that there had been no hope of Truyen freeing herself from the strangling wire as she thrashed, though her fingers were cut and bloodied from trying

Bolan whipped around and crossed the hall. The duty nurse goggled in horror as he bore down her with the pistol in his hand. He whipped a folded sketch of Theresa Parsons from his jacket. "Have you seen her?"

He barked at Alva. "Sergeant!"

Alva turned from the room, his pistol in one hand, his cell phone in the other. "What?"

"Ask her if she's seen this woman. In a nurse's uniform, in the last five minutes."

Alva stabbed a finger at the sketch and asked Bolan's question. The nurse stared back and forth from the massive muzzle of the 93-R that wasn't quite pointing at her and the sketch and stuttered a response. Alva bolted upright.

"Yes! A new girl! She did not check in but she was carrying a tray! She went into the room and came out a few moments later." Alva grabbed the nurse and shook her. The nurse pointed wildly down the hall.

"She thinks the woman went that way! There are another set of stairs and elevators at the other end."

Bolan went down the hall and smashed out the safety glass covering the emergency firehose mounted on the wall. "A minute to ditch her nurses uniform and wash her hands! She's extracting now! Go down the stairs! Be careful!"

"And you!"

Bolan swung out the red-iron reel of the firehose and yanked the heavy brass nozzle from its bracket. "I'll meet you!"

Alva ran down the hall barking into his cell. Bolan kicked open the door opposite the hose mounting. The woman on the bed inside screamed. The entire floor started screaming as Bolan aimed his pistol over the Helsinki skyline and shot out the window. He tossed the brass nozzle over the balcony rail and kept yanking heavy canvas hose until the reel ran out. Bolan shoved his pistol in his belt and went over the side.

The canvas hose went warm and then hot as it slid between his fingers. Bolan opened his hands and let himself free fall. His shoulders nearly yanked out of their sockets as he seized the nozzle and its throttle ring. Bolan hung dangling between floors with a story and a half to go.

He aimed himself at some ornamental pines and opened his hands. He kicked off the wall as he fell and somersaulted once. Branches snapped between his hands and the treetop suddenly bent violently under his weight. More branches ripped at his face and clothes, and every ounce of air left Bolan's body as he smashed into unyielding mud and tanbark. Bolan rolled over painfully and pushed himself up out of the mud.

A pair of Pomeranians yapped at him in stereo. The elderly Finnish couple attached to the pair by leashes was clearly appalled. They were horrified as Bolan stood and unlimbered his massive .50-caliber pistol. He staggered off across the lawn and stepped onto the concrete of the traffic circle at the main entrance. He raised the Desert Eagle in both hands and put the glowing green tritium dot of his front sight on his target.

"Freeze!"

The woman froze. She had just stepped off the curb. The cigarette she was about to light fell from her lips and her lighter snuffed out.

Theresa Parsons stared down the .50-caliber muzzle of Bolan's gun in slack-jawed astonishment. Her eyes went as wide as dinner plates, and her mouth opened and then closed as she looked in Bolan's eyes. The pistol never wavered from the middle of her face.

"On the ground. Now."

There were certain sounds that had beaten themselves into the survival mode of Bolan's subconscious at the most subliminal levels. One was the sound of helicopter rotors. Another was the telltale klatch! sound of a Kalashnikov assault weapon's selector lever being thrown from safe to full auto.

Bolan threw himself behind a car as rifles opened up.

A pair of men leaped out from the back of an ambulance. They were dressed as paramedics, but the AKM automatic rifles spraying lead and brass belied their true identity. Glass shattered out of the windows of the parked Citroën that Bolan was using for cover, the door panels cratered with hits. Bolan pressed himself into the pavement, extended the Desert Eagle pistol beneath the chassis of the besieged car, and put his front sight on one of a pair of the dazzling white Nike running shoes and squeezed the trigger.

The immense weapon spit flame. The Nike shoe suddenly skidded and rolled across the parking lot trailing its wet, red contents. Bolan tracked his muzzle onto the second target. The other pair of feet disappeared vertically. Bolan saw the tires of the ambulance lurch and knew the other gunman had prudently jumped into the back of the ambulance. Bolan's first target fell into view screaming and clutching the stump of his ankle where the .50-caliber, jacketed-hollowpoint bullet had expanded and made its way through his ankle bones at more than sixteen hundred feet per second. Bolan ignored the first assassin and his agony.

He put his sight on the ambulance's left rear tire and fired again.

Bolan rolled from cover as the tire exploded. In the split second that the chassis lurched, the gunman grabbed the door frame to steady himself. Bolan raised his muzzle as the assassin desperately took his AKM back in two hands. Pavement chips flew as the rifle chopped a line beside the Executioner's head. The rifle fell silent as the Executioner's round hurtled the killer backward into the cabin of the ambulance. Bolan ejected his spent magazine and slapped in his spare as he came to his feet. The Desert Eagle swung to cover the front of the hospital. Sergeant Alva was lying on the steps of the hospital clutching at a knife in his belly.

Theresa Parsons had disappeared, and he didn't speak enough Finnish to ask anyone which way she had gone.

Bolan ran to Alva's side. Blood dribbled over the sergeant's lips as he tried to speak. Parsons had rammed the knife into him low in the belly and ripped upward all the way to his sternum. Alva's abdomen had been opened to the sky.

"I—I didn't see the knife."

"Don't worry about it." Bolan pressed down on the wound with both hands. "You picked the best place in the world to get yourself stabbed."

Alva smiled slightly around the rictus of agony contorting his face. "I..."

Medics were running down the hallway inside the hospital with a gurney.

Alva died before they made it out the door.

9

Helsinki, Finland

Bolan stood in a sea of officers in dress uniform. Rain sleeted down upon the mass of mourners. It seemed as though the entire Finnish police force had turned out. Finland was a peaceful, prosperous and homogenous country. It was rare for a Finnish officer to die in the line of duty. Sergeant Augustus Alva had been a respected and well-liked officer. More than a few officers looked up from the grave to turn hostile eyes on the American who had gotten him killed. Bolan ignored their eyes and mourned a brave man.

The police band struck up the Finnish national anthem as Alva was lowered into the ground.

Captain Niemi edged his way to Bolan's side. "Thank you for coming."

"It was the least I could do. He was a good man."

"Indeed." The casket was draped with the Finnish flag. "He was one of our best."

"Do you have any idea who the gunmen were?"

"Yes. Local street thugs. They both have fairly extensive criminal records. You killed one of them. The other we have in custody."

"Is there any way I could speak with him?"

Niemi squinted up at Bolan. "Personally, if I had my way, yes, I would let you."

Bolan nodded. "But."

"But it is my unpleasant duty to tell you that you are no longer welcome in Finland. I do not know whether you have diplomatic immunity or not, but we have instructions not to cooperate with you further. Were I you, I would get out of Helsinki, or at least get yourself within the walls of the U.S. Embassy before someone above my pay grade sees fit to have you arrested and interrogated. It would not be an interrogation such as the late Inspectors Sillaampa and Suvari had in mind, but it will still not be pleasant, and if you do not have diplomatic immunity, it could go on for many days, perhaps weeks or months."

"I appreciate your candor."

"You must also appreciate our position. You come jumping out of helicopters firing automatic weapons and engaging in firefights in our streets. I can understand why you would not coordinate with the state police. It is clear we have been compromised, but nevertheless, to my superiors, the situation is intolerable. We cannot allow independent American covert operations on our sovereign soil."

"What about the nukes?"

"Salvage teams have investigated the sunken barge and the evidence they have found confirms your story. It is very disturbing."

"What do you intend to do?"

"What we can. We will investigate, but..."

Silence fell between the two men. The enemy was always two steps ahead of them. What little chance they had in pooling their resources was lost.

Niemi took a folder from under his jacket. "This is the police file we have on the two men who attacked you last night, and the files of their known associates. They are gangsters, and they have connections across the border with the Russian *Mafiya*." The captain cleared his throat. "Anything you do with this information could lead to your arrest and incarceration."

Bolan took the folder. "Thank you, Captain."

The little man's eyes went steely. "No one kills one of mine and gets away with it."

Bolan nodded. He knew the code well.

Niemi looked up at Bolan speculatively. "Your grasp of the Finnish language is limited."

"Very limited."

Niemi's eyes slid across the grave to the family of the deceased. A woman with two children was weeping beneath the awning. A burly blond man stood by her side with an arm over her shoulder. "That man is Augustus's brother. His name is Jukka. He is a fireman."

Bolan measured the big Finn. "Oh, yeah?"

"Yes. He also went to high school in the United States in his youth on the foreign exchange program. His English is excellent."

"Really."

"Yes. He is very angry about what has happened." Niemi nodded curtly to Bolan. "Thank you again for coming. You must excuse me while I give my condolences to the widow and the children."

Bolan stood in the rain as Captain Niemi moved to the awning where the family was gathered. Bolan noticed that the first member of the family the Captain Niemi spoke to was Jukka.

"YOU KNOW we're going to be breaking the law."

Thunder rattled the hotel room.

Jukka Alva sat on the bed. The police files Captain Niemi had given Bolan were spread out on a low, rickety table. Jukka met Bolan's gaze unblinkingly. His eyes were red and hard with tears he hadn't shed yet for his brother. Tears he hadn't shed to stay strong for his family. They were tears he wouldn't shed until he had seen justice for his brother's death. "Yup."

"The bad guys are street gangsters. The information your brother's captain gave me says they have a nightclub in a not so nice part of Helsinki. They run drugs, guns and whores. They have connections with the Russian *Mafiya*. They'll be armed, hostile and there's no guarantee that we can connect them with the woman who killed your brother. They're probably just cutouts, but they're the only lead we have at the moment."

Jukka nodded. "Captain Niemi told me your linguist was killed. I studied Russian in school. I can speak it. I can help."

"People may get killed."

Jukka smiled hard. "I hope so."

"Maybe me and you."

Jukka shrugged. "I am a fireman. I risk my life every day I go to work." The big Finn looked back and forth between Bolan and Manning. "Stabbing a police officer is against the law, and people have already been killed. My brother was a policeman. He risked his life every day he went to work, too. He knew it. I do not blame you for his death, and I am willing to assist you in any way I can."

Bolan measured the big man. Finland was a hard country, and it bred brave men. Whatever they were putting in the water, Mrs. Alva's boys seemed to be loaded with it. But there were thirty loose nukes in Finland, and there were Russian and Finnish gangsters, Chinese special purpose troops, and forces unseen dead set on shepherding them to an ugly and unknown final destination. Bravery alone wouldn't be enough. "Can you shoot?"

"I did my required two years military service when I graduated from school." Jukka shrugged. "All Finnish men must."

Bolan nodded. "What was your specialty?"

"I was a radio operator."

Bolan and Manning stared at each other.

"I was with the ski troops. I carried a submachine gun."

"When was the last time you fired one?"

Jukka grimaced. "Sixteen years ago."

"When was the last time you fired any gun?"

Jukka cleared his throat. "Five years ago."

"Have you ever fired a pistol?"

"Once." Jukka broke eye contact. "My brother let me fire a magazine from his service pistol, at a picnic."

"How long ago was that?"

Jukka studied his shoes. "Five years ago."

The Finn was a brave and determined man, but Bolan wasn't quite sure what he could do with Jukka other than get him killed.

Jukka brightened slightly. "I brought this."

The big Finn unbuckled the canvas roll he had brought with him and opened it up on the bed. Bolan and Manning stared at the object Jukka revealed. A three-foot length of well-turned tapering hickory lay on the bed.

The fireman had brought an ax handle.

Manning grinned. "I like him!"

Bolan found himself smiling. "Can you get two more of those?"

"Ya, sure." Jukka's face hardened. "Can you get me a gun?"

"We can get you a gun." Manning turned to Bolan. "We can get Jukka a gun, can't we?"

Bolan shook his head slightly as he looked at the polished length of wood. "Yeah, I think we can get Jukka a gun."

Warf District, Helsinki

JUKKA STARED at the M-44 submachine gun in Bolan's hands. The big Finn was jammed into some loaned CIA body armor that was a size to small for him.

Bitterly cold sleet lashed against the windshield of the rented Volvo. Bolan gestured at the weapon. "That's the model you're used to, right?"

"Yup. A Model 44." Jukka took the weapon. It was crude-looking by modern standards, and made almost entirely of weldings and stampings. It was the Finnish version of the Russian PPS-42 that had been borne during the siege of Leningrad. The stock was folded. "But we were issued 36-round magazines." He glanced at the huge, round metal casing in the magazine well. "Not the drums."

"Well, that holds seventy-one rounds." Manning waggled his eyebrows. "Try not to use them all at once."

"Short bursts. Yup." Jukka took the weapon and checked the safety. "As our sergeant said in basic training."

Bolan peered at a tiny blue neon sign down the street that read "Bjorns." The club was a converted warehouse in a bad part of town. It was 2:00 a.m., and despite the late hour, the sleet and the cruel wind, a bouncer in a parka stood outside beneath a tiny awning. "All right. Stay low." Manning and Jukka hunched down as Bolan drove down the street past the bar and turned right. He turned right and then right again and stopped a block away.

"Jukka, I want you to engage the front man in conversation. Gummer and I will come up from behind. Give us three minutes."

"Three minutes. Yup." Jukka hung his submachine gun over his shoulder and pulled on his parka. He stepped out into the whistling wind without another word. Bolan took the car down the cross street and pulled in behind the bar. The back alley was dark and empty except for some trash bins. Bolan parked the Volvo with its bumper against the back door.

"Let's go." Bolan pulled his jacket around his own submachine gun and took an ax handle in each hand. He and Manning fell into formation as they left the alley and rounded the side of the bar. The bouncer's back was to them, but it was clear he stood well over six and a half feet tall. Jukka stood unsteadily in front of the bouncer and was shouting and waving his arms. Bolan smiled. The big Finn was being faced by an even bigger one, but he held his ground and did a credible job of acting drunk.

The bouncer finally snarled something and gave Jukka a shove. The fireman staggered backward and shouted in outrage. The bouncer raised his hand and took a menacing step forward. Jukka cringed. Bolan tossed one of the ax handles over the bouncer's head. The bouncer whirled at the motion. Jukka caught the club as Bolan drove his own ax handle into the bouncer's solar plexus like a bayonet.

The giant wheezed in pain. Manning chopped his ax handle into the side of the bouncer's neck. His eyes rolled and he collapsed as Jukka cracked him across the kidneys from behind. Bolan stepped over the big man as he fell and kicked open the door. Heat and music washed over Bolan in a wave. The sound of the bass throbbed the walls of the warehouse and someone was rapping badly in French. A man and a woman stood in the little foyer. The woman was a blonde, and she leaned against the register. Her eyes went wide as the wrecking crew entered. The man had one strap of her low-cut dress off her shoulder, and her surgically enhanced breasts had his full attention. He looked up distractedly and gaped at the intruders. He regained his composure and shoved his hand under his coat as ax handles fell upon him like rain.

Bolan broke his collarbone. Manning rammed him in the floating ribs with the cracking of cartilage. The gunman dropped to the floor as Jukka kneecapped him. The woman's mouth opened as she sucked in air for a scream. Bolan's club blurred in his hand. The scream died on her lips as the end of ax handle stopped an inch from her face. The Executioner lifted a finger to his lips.

"Shh."

The woman's mouth worked open and closed in horror, but no sound came out. Jukka took the groaning man's revolver and shoved it into his belt. Bolan strode forward, with Manning and Jukka flanking him. Bolan's boot flung open the double doors to the club.

He quickly scanned the interior. There was a bald man behind the bar, and six others were visible. Four men and three young women sat around a table drinking liquor and snorting coke. Another was at the bar, and the last was at the sound system flipping through a rack of compact discs. The closest man at the table rose and pointed a finger accusingly as Bolan bore down on him. *"Ey! Mika tama on—"*

Bolan whipped his club downward in a short, chopping blow. The man screamed as his pointing finger smashed. He fell spitting teeth as Jukka cracked him across the mouth. A pair of Colt .45 pistols lay on the table among the shot glasses and the coke mirrors. Manning shattered the wrists of the man who reached for them. The women screamed and scattered to the sides. The third man had half risen as Jukka's club whipped under his jaw and cracked it. The fourth man was farthest. He ignored the guns on the table and bolted. Bolan raised his weapon.

Manning shouted in alarm. "Striker!"

The man at the bar had pulled a pistol from his belt. Bolan hurled his ax handle side arm and the three-foot length of hickory scythed through the air. The gunman fell gagging as the wood took him across the throat. The bartender and the man by the sound system froze and put up their hands as Manning freed his submachine gun for all to see.

"Gummer, hold down the fort! Jukka!" Bolan jerked his head toward the hall where the fourth man at the table had bolted. "You're with me!"

Bolan approached the hallway from the side. Down the narrow passage were men's and women's washrooms and an exit. The man was pounding on the exit door against which Bolan had parked the Volvo. "Hey! You!"

The Executioner leaned back from the doorway as a small pistol barked at him and stripped a sliver of wood paneling from the hall. Wood and metal tore as the man began to fire his entire magazine into the wood around the knob of the door that was defeating him. Bolan freed up his M-44., but Jukka was a step ahead of him. The big Finn stepped around the corner.

"Hey!" The M-44 ripped into life with the sound of tearing canvas. Jukka held his trigger down, and the submachine gun began burning its seventy-one round drum at nine hundred rounds per minute. Wood paneling tore, and the door perforated like Swiss cheese under the onslaught as Bolan's weapon joined the barrage. Smoking brass shell casing sprayed against the walls and jingled to the floor underfoot as the two men marched forward.

The Finnish gangster pulled his arms and legs into himself and sat shuddering in the corner as bullets ripped all around him. Both submachine guns clacked open on smoking empty chambers. Bolan let his weapon fall on its sling and drew his Desert Eagle. Jukka drew his commandeered revolver. The sound of him cocking it seemed very loud in the sudden ringing silence.

Bolan frowned at the carnage in the hall. "I thought you agreed to short bursts."

Jukka shrugged as he kept his handgun trained on the man curled up in the corner. The big Finn didn't seem particularly repentant. Bolan cocked his head slightly. The gangster had covered his head with his hands and was stuttering. The man was stuttering in Russian.

"He's speaking in Russian."

"Yup." Jukka nodded. "He is praying."

Bolan knelt and shoved the muzzle of the Desert Eagle into the shivering man's face. "Tell him when he's done talking to God, I'd like a minute of his time."

The gangster flinched and squeezed his eyes shut as the big .50's safety came off with a click. His prayer trailed off to a whimper.

Jukka smiled unpleasantly. "I think he's done now."

10

Lake Saimaa

Bolan scanned through his laser range-finding binoculars. "My Russian isn't great. Ask him if that's the one."

Jukka snarled a few words and prodded the Russian with the muzzle of his M-44. The Russian flinched and mumbled despondently. *"Da."*

"Yup." Jukka flicked the safety off his submachine gun. "That is the one."

Bolan continued to scan the objective. The ceaseless rain and sleet had turned the ground to half-frozen slush. A break in the mounting North Sea storm had left Finland shrouded in dull gray light. The snowmobiles they'd rented had taken a beating in the soupy ground, but they had brought them to their target the back way. The weather had made the lakeside roads almost impassable. It had also taken them twelve hours to get organized. It was a half a day Bolan couldn't afford to burn.

He considered his objective. The massive mansion on the lake rose up like a three-story log cabin. Its entire structure was of massive timbers. Several sheds and outbuildings ringed the main structure separated by lawns, a tennis court, a swimming pool with adjacent hot tub and sauna facilities, and a concrete helicopter pad. A boat shed big enough for a pair of yachts stretched out over the water on pilings. No boats moved out on the water, and the mansion commanded its view of the huge lake system without any neighbors for several miles in either direction.

Smoke was curling up out of one of the chimneys.

"Nice." Gary Manning scanned the mansion through the scope of his M-4 carbine. "Cozy. Looks like Santa's Village."

Bolan spoke into his throat mike. "Do we have any movement?"

"Negative, Striker." Back in Virginia, Aaron Kurtzman was watching the mansion intently from a satellite. "You have a thirty-minute satellite window."

The captured Russian's name was Ulov. He didn't know much, but he had come to Lake Saimaa, to a very large mansion, and acted as security on a truck that had gone to Helsinki. At the house he had met a fellow Russian whom he had heard others refer to as "the captain."

That was all Ulov knew.

Bolan eyed the boat shed and measured it against what he knew about Russian minisubmarines. "Bear, we're going in."

"Affirmative, Striker."

Bolan gave Ulov a hard look and then turned to Jukka. "Tell him he'd better behave himself."

Jukka dropped his submachine gun on its sling. He took up his ax handle, pushed the wood against the Russian's sternum, and held him pinned against a tree. The Russian made unhappy noises as Jukka explained the facts of life to him. Jukka smiled and nodded at Bolan. "He understands."

Manning lowered his binoculars. "How do you want to play it, Striker?"

"That place is a fortress. Every outer beam is at least four feet thick."

Manning glanced back at their snowmobiles. "Okay, so a ramming attack is out of the question."

Bolan raised an eyebrow. "That wasn't quite what I had in mind."

Manning grinned. "You've had a thought."

"I'm thinking it would be nice if someone opened the door for us."

Manning blinked. "That'd be a nice trick."

Bolan glanced back at the snowmobiles. All three had heavy

canvas gear bags strapped on either side to hold their weapons
and equipment. He considered the boat shed again and a very feeble ruse came to mind. "This is what I want to do."

BOLAN, MANNING, Jukka and Ulov walked up the slush of the
gravel drive to the mansion. Most of their weapons, including
their rifles, explosives and communications gear, was stowed in
the canvas snowmobile bags. Each of them carried one or two of
the bags across their shoulders. Each of them, except Ulov, carried their bags yoked across their shoulders with an ax handle.
Bolan, Manning and Jukka each carried a pistol thrust under
their belts and covered by their parkas. Rain sleeted down on
them as they trudged. The weather was working in their favor.
The roads were, indeed, impassable by automobile. The only way
to approach the house on the lake was by water or by air, and the
weather was miserable for both. No one was watching the road.

The Executioner and his team marched right up to the porch
and banged on the door.

Bolan glanced up at the security camera peering at him from
under the eaves. He raised his mittened hand and waved like an
idiot. Voices could be heard inside, speaking in Russian. The fish-
eye lens in the doorway darkened a moment, then an unpleasant
voice snarled. Bolan knew enough Russian to know the voice was
demanding to know who they were and what they wanted.

Bolan spoke very quietly. "Ulov."

Ulov shouted through the door to identify himself. "Ulov!"

The voice paused barely a second and with increasing anger
demanded to know what the hell Ulov was doing here and what
the hell he wanted. Bolan spoke quietly to Jukka. "Tell them
we're the welders. Tell them we're here to repair the submarine."

Jukka grinned delightedly and shouted at the door.

There was a profound silence on the other side of the door as
this information was digested.

Consternation broke out as a man behind the door shouted at
someone deeper inside the house and they shouted back. An intense argument ensued. Bolan took the opportunity to speak low
again to Jukka. "Tell them our car is stuck in the mud and we
had to walk the last six kilometers in the rain. Tell them this is
highly irregular and someone should have helicoptered us in."

Jukka began shouting and pounding.

The door opened and two men with pistols held low by their sides opened the door. They began shouting in Russian, and Jukka shouted back, waving his free hand in the direction they had come. A tall, older man with a beard and a face swiftly turning red with rage was stomping down the hall toward the commotion. He bore down with a definite aura of irritated command.

Bolan whispered at Ulov. *"Kapitan?"*

Ulov answered in a morally devastated whisper. *"Da."*

He pushed past Ulov and tipped his ax handle. The canvas bag slid off of the shaft and clanked to the porch. Jukka was now browbeating the captain and the two gunmen with increasing vehemence. He pointed at the boat shed and thumped his bulging bag. The captain was roaring at the top of his lungs and wanted to know how the hell they knew about the submarine.

Bolan took the opportunity to swing his ax handle like a golf club between the closest gunman's legs.

The man screamed in agony and collapsed clutching himself. Manning chopped the second gunman's pistol out of his grasp, breaking most of the bones in the back of the man's hand doing it. The man's scream cut short as Jukka lashed out with his club and took the gunman in the teeth. The captain suddenly found himself facing three men armed with bloody bludgeons, his bodyguards fallen at his feet. Three ax handles clattered to the porch as Bolan, Manning and Jukka dropped their clubs. The Captain's eyes went wide as the three men pulled back their parkas and drew a Beretta 93-R machine pistol, a Browning Hi-Power, and a .357 Magnum Manhurin revolver respectively.

"Tell the captain we're not welders," Bolan instructed, "but we're definitely here about his submarine."

Jukka cocked his revolver and relayed Bolan's message.

The captain paled.

North Sea,
Aboard the Oil Rig Heather

SHANG HUNCHED into his parka against the biting cold and violent wind. The massive storms that hadn't yet hit Finland were in full effect in the North Sea. He sank his *chi* into the pit of his belly and stood rooted on the oil platform as the wind buffeted him. Platform *Heather* had been abandoned by British Petroleum as unproductive. British Petroleum hadn't been willing to sell the rig, but they had been persuaded to lease it out at an exorbitant sum.

Shang smiled slightly. It was one of the advantages of working with capitalists. With the help of their allies, exorbitant sums didn't really have any meaning. It was also very convenient of the British to be so helpful in their own murder, however unwittingly. The smile died on his lips as his thoughts turned to his allies. He didn't like them. He didn't trust them at all. He suspected that the older brother had no control of the younger, which to Shang was pathetic. Shang was also fairly confident that the younger brother was insane, and would have to be dealt with.

Shang stared out over the heaving gray sea as the storm lashed it. None of that was important at the moment. The mission was succeeding, and succeeding beyond wildest expectations. Shang had no qualms about using capitalists as pawns, but he held strong reservations about working with them directly, much less depending on them. However, despite his reservations, they had come through. The weapons had been secured. The plan would succeed.

It was perhaps the greatest plan ever devised.

Shang checked his watch. It was time. He kept his eyes on the turbulent ocean. He didn't have long to wait. One hundred meters south of the platform, the sea began to boil in opposition to the crashing waves. The long, dark hulk of the submarine rose up in a collar of wave-tossed foam.

The sub was a modified Wuhan class. The Wuhan's had started life as one of China's first ballistic-missile submarines and, nut for bolt, were almost-identical copies of Russian subs. When the next generation of Chinese subs had come on-line, almost the entire class had then been modified. Their vertical missile bays had been replaced with banks of elevating launchers for massive, ship-killing, long-range cruise missiles. This particular Wuhan had undergone a third generation of even more extensive modification. Its function was no longer to deliver weapons of mass destruction. Her function now was to deliver some of the world's most dangerous men to highly sensitive targets undetected.

The immense double cruise missile launchers forward of the sail had been removed. The cruise missile magazine beneath had been removed, as well. This had left significant space forward of the sail open for other activities. The sub rolled gently in the waves as a pair of huge clamshell hatches split and lowered to either side.

Sailors within ran out and released the retaining lines from the cleats that held the helicopter. Another pair of crewmen unfolded the rotors and locked them into place. The helicopter could either deliver or extract an eight-man squad. With stores from below, it could also be changed into gunship configuration with gun and rocket pods and a variety of guided-missile munitions.

This day, the helicopter was being used as a crane.

Its engine roared into life as it rose unsteadily from a heaving flight deck barely wider than itself. The helicopter lifted like a dragonfly. The pilot saluted Shang as he came level with the platform and rose overhead. The helicopter swayed precariously in space as it tried to hover in the howling wind. Two of Shang's men ran to catch the cable that was deployed from the belly of the aircraft. Shang's men took the huge hook and locked it onto the loading ring attached to the strapped-and-palleted load that Shang stood beside.

The pallet contained five tactical thermonuclear weapons.

Shang reached into his pocket and pulled out his phone. He punched a preset and was answered on the first ring. "Yes, Comrade Shang!"

"The submarine is here. The cargo is being loaded. Get the men ready. Make sure all equipment is ready and assembled." Shang watched the pallet and its deadly cargo rise into the air as the helicopter banked out over the North Sea toward the submarine.

"The men are already assembled, Comrade! All weapons and gear are ready for transport. We await your order."

"Good. I want everyone and everything out on the platform in twenty minutes. As soon as the cargo is safely secured, we will transfer onto the sub."

11

Lake Saimaa, The Mansion

"A big American?" Bolan considered the man who had spoken English and dived into the Saimaa canal during the night raid.

Jukka asked the captain again. The man nodded and repeated himself, and then added some embroidery. He and his two bodyguards sat on the couch. The gunman kept their eyes on their shoes. The captain kept his eyes on Bolan even as Jukka asked questions. Jukka listened and nodded. "Yup, he says an American was in charge. A big one. Bigger than you or me. He says the American scared him. He says he had crazy eyes."

"What does he mean, crazy eyes?"

"He says his eyes were crazy. Hot crazy. Like he might do anything that struck him at any moment, without fear of consequences. He says hot crazy."

"What was his name?"

"He says he doesn't know. Some very bad men, Russian *Mafyia,* approached him in Vyborg and produced a minisubmarine and large stacks of American hundred-dollar bills. Captain Volkov took the job to pilot the submarine up the Saimaa Canal, take on cargo from a barge and bring it to this house. After his submarine was attacked, he was instructed to bring it back down the canal and was ordered to help the counterattack the next day."

It all fit so far. Bolan took Captain Volkov's gaze and held it. "What does the captain know about his cargo?"

"He says nothing, except that it must be very valuable. He says he was paid not to ask any questions. He assumes it was weapons or drugs."

Bolan turned to the video link and satcom he had set up on the coffee table. Kurtzman's face filled the laptop's screen as he listened to the interrogation in real time. "Bear, what do we have on this house?"

"It has multiple owners. The first layer is ostensibly Finnish. Your friend Captain Niemi won't like it, but Akira has hacked the Finnish police and government files. There's not much we can prove, at least not yet."

"What have you got that's unproved?"

"I ran a comprehensive search on Lake Saimaa and looked for anything interesting."

"What did you find?"

"Only one thing. The house you're in right now was used by a group of Orbitech executives for a cross-country skiing-team building retreat eight months ago."

"Orbitech." Bolan considered. He knew of Orbitech. They were one of the new young lions of orbital satellite communications. Their technology was on the cutting edge, and it was in use in the satellite link he and Kurtzman were communicating across now. "That's an interesting coincidence."

"I thought so."

"Bear, what have you gotten so far on the homework I gave you?"

"You mean, coming up with a scenario involving thirty tactical nukes, the PRC and Scandinavia?"

"Yeah, what have you got?"

"Well, I've ruled out Sweden."

"Thanks. So had I."

"I know. Sweden is easy. They're an officially neutral country. They have nothing you could consider a strategic target. A nuclear attack has zero payoff. That leaves Finland, Norway, Denmark and Iceland. I'm prepared to rule out Finland. I tend to agree with your first impression. Finland is a waypoint out of

Russia and has little in the way of strategic targets, as well. That leaves Norway, Denmark and Iceland, who are all NATO allies. I think that makes them your most legitimate targets, assuming that we're still on the money and that the target or targets are in Scandinavia."

Bolan read the look on Kurtzman's face. "You don't like it."

The computer expert scowled at one of the screens ringing his wheelchair. "Well, what good does it do you? You nuke Denmark into glass, and what have you accomplished? You reduce Reykjavik and our air bases there to rubble, and what happens? Does Denmark secede from NATO? Does Iceland sink into the sea? The answer is no and no. I can't think of anything worth nuking in Norway, and why the hell do you need thirty weapons to accomplish the task even if you can think of one?"

"Good questions," Bolan agreed. "Keep up the good work. I want you to go up the chain of command at Orbitech. It's a relatively small and specialized tech company. Find out who owns it or has a major piece of it. Follow the money trails. I want ideas on who could afford thirty nukes and midget submarines. I'm looking for someone who doesn't care what the price tag is."

"And wants to nuke something in the Arctic Circle."

"Yeah."

"All right, I'm on it. What are you going to do in the meantime?"

"First off, the captain here is— What's happening, Gummer?"

Gary Manning had risen from the couch and gone to the window. He was peering keenly into the leaden skies. He cocked his head and then put his hand against the window glass. "We've got multiple rotors, coming this way." Manning unzipped his weapons bag. "How the hell did they know, Striker?"

Bolan shoved his Desert Eagle into Volkov's face and gave him a good look at the .50-caliber muzzle. "How did you send a signal?"

"Nyet! Nyet!" Volkov cringed from the gun, babbling denials. Jukka took out his M-44 and checked the drum. "He denies it."

"We've had Ulov under direct supervision the entire time. There's..." Bolan looked around the room carefully and finally raised his gaze to the light fixture above. The Executioner's eyes

The Gold Eagle Reader Service™ — Here's how it works:

Accepting your 2 free books and gift places you under no obligation to buy anything. You may keep the books and gift and return the shipping statement marked "cancel." If you do not cancel, about a month later we'll send you 6 additional books and bill you just $29.94* — that's a saving of 10% off the cover price of all 6 books! And there's no extra charge for shipping! You may cancel at any time, but if you choose to continue, every other month we'll send you 6 more books, which you may either purchase at the discount price or return to us and cancel your subscription.

If offer card is missing write to: Gold Eagle Reader Service, 3010 Walden Ave., P.O. Box 1867, Buffalo NY 14240-1867

NO POSTAGE
NECESSARY
IF MAILED
IN THE
UNITED STATES

BUSINESS REPLY MAIL

FIRST-CLASS MAIL   PERMIT NO. 717-003   BUFFALO, NY

POSTAGE WILL BE PAID BY ADDRESSEE

GOLD EAGLE READER SERVICE
3010 WALDEN AVE
PO BOX 1867
BUFFALO NY 14240-9952

Get FREE BOOKS and a FREE GIFT when you play the...

LAS VEGAS
GAME

Just scratch off the gold box with a coin. Then check below to see the gifts you get!

YES! I have scratched off the gold Box. Please send me my **2 FREE BOOKS** and **gift for which I qualify**. I understand that I am under no obligation to purchase any books as explained on the back of this card.

366 ADL DRSL

166 ADL DRSK
(MB-03/03)

FIRST NAME	LAST NAME

ADDRESS

APT.#	CITY

STATE/PROV.	ZIP/POSTAL CODE

7	**7**	**7**	Worth TWO FREE BOOKS plus a BONUS Mystery Gift!
🍒	🍒	🍒	Worth TWO FREE BOOKS!
🔔	🔔	♣	TRY AGAIN!

Offer limited to one per household and not valid to current Gold Eagle® subscribers. All orders subject to approval.

narrowed. There was a small camera attached to it. He stepped into the kitchen and quickly found another camera. Bolan reached into his bag and unlimbered his M-4 carbine. "The house is bugged. It's rigged for sound and video in every room, and it transmits 24/7. We've been made."

The sound of rotors was becoming clearly audible.

Manning drew his SR-25 rifle and checked the scope. The ten pound .308-caliber battle rifle looked like an M-16 on steroids. Manning drove the butt stock through the window. "Here they come."

Bolan racked a grenade into the M-203 launcher slaved to his rifle. Manning's rifle began to hammer in rapid semiauto. The Russians flinched with every shot.

"We've got three choppers at least!" Manning never took his eyes off of his target. "Make that four! They're not firing back, they're—"

The house shook as the helicopter rotors thundered the air above. Several objects thudded against the roof. Bolan strode over to the laptop. "Bear, I'll get back to you."

"Striker—" Kurtzman's face disappeared as Bolan clicked the laptop shut. He slid it and the satellite link into a bag, which he threw into Ulov's manacled hands. "Carry that!"

Bolan looked up as smoke alarms began going off all around the house. Manning glanced over as he slid a fresh magazine into his smoking rifle. "They're going to burn us out."

"And burn up the evidence at the same time."

Bolan turned on Volkov. "Jukka, ask the captain how sea-worthy his sub is."

Jukka quickly questioned the captain. "He says he would not like to take it out to sea, but it should survive conditions on the lake."

"Good, tell him he's our ride out of here."

Bolan flicked off the safety on his carbine. "Gummer, we're out of here. Pop smoke out the back window, and then we go out the front."

"Affirmative." Manning drew a pair of smoke grenades from his bag and pulled their pins. He threw the first bomb and then the other out the window. The empty ground between the back of the house and the woods began to fill with gray smoke. The helicopters orbiting above could be heard moving to cover the back of the house for the anticipated breakout. The SR-25 Manning carried was a precision rifle that had been modified at Stony Man Farm. One modification was that it was capable of full-auto fire. The second was that John "Cowboy" Kissinger had rebarreled it with NATO-standard grenade-launching rings. The hammering of firing grenades would throw off its tack-driving accuracy, but Manning liked to be as flexible as possible. He clicked on the long blue shape of a French GIAT antiarmor rifle grenade.

Bolan went out the front door firing.

A commercial Russian Mi-34 Hermit helicopter hovered between the house and the boat shed. Bolan hurled himself to the ground as a man leaning out on chicken straps opened up with a light machine gun. The strikes flung up a line of geysering mud and snow and tore into the steps. The gunner adjusted his aim as Bolan rolled away.

Manning stepped onto the porch and took a moment to aim carefully at the hovering helicopter. The pilot spotted him and started to dip his nose to jink. Manning's rifle bucked and the grenade punched through the helicopter's cockpit canopy and detonated. The antiarmor weapon filled the interior of the helicopter with a jet of superheated gas and molten metal. The windows blew out in gouts of orange fire. The helicopter's nose continued to dip as it slewed out of control through the air. Chain link fencing tore and the rotors snapped away as the dying helicopter plunged into the tennis courts.

Bolan was up and running for the boat shed. Manning brought up the rear as Jukka shepherded the four manacled Russians between them. Roaring flames rose from the roof and the top floor of the house. Clouds of thick black smoke filled the sleeting sky.

The masses of smoke roiled and broke apart as three helicopters came plunging through them in an angry wedge. Their door guns opened up.

"Go! Go! Go!" Bolan turned and raised his carbine.

One of the Russians broke formation and ran for the woods. A line of tracers from above walked across the grounds and intercepted his path. The man shuddered and fell in the muck. The

M-203 boomed as Bolan fired. The grenade looped between two of the helicopters and detonated. Sparks flew as metal fragments shrieked against their fuselages, and one of the door gunners sagged in his straps as flying metal tore into him. The two choppers banked sharply away from the detonation. The third helicopter was forced to bank off to avoid being hit by the leader. Bolan tracked the lead aircraft and burned a magazine from the carbine into it. The helicopters roared overhead and flew out over the gray expanse of Lake Saimaa. They would be coming back for a more coordinated gun run and to deploy flanking troops, if they were clever. The formation broke apart in answer and the choppers began to set up a coordinated run.

Bolan ran as Manning kicked in the door of the boat shed. The remaining Russians piled in as Bolan and Jukka brought up the rear. The boat house had two berths; one was dominated by a minisubmarine. The hull was battered and scored where Bolan and Manning had attacked it, and metal patches had been crudely welded over some of the larger holes. More patches covered the rear diving planes. The swollen torpedo shape had two long bulges along its sides where the caterpillar tracks deployed. The hull was on a ramp, wooden blocks holding it up out of the water. Bolan strode over to a tarp stretched across some equipment and yanked it back.

There was a Russian DshK heavy machine and several Krinkov carbines.

Everyone ducked as bullets ripped through the rafters. Bolan scanned the tiny conning sail of the sub. There was a mounting ring for the heavy gun so that the sub could cover the withdrawal of extracting Russian special forces troops. The weapons had obviously been removed from the hold while repairs were effected and the water pumped out. Bolan picked up a carbine and held it out to Volkov. "Jukka, tell the captain he's run out friends."

Jukka spoke and the captain's face hardened as he answered. "He says he understands. He has become a liability to his employers."

"Tell him he won't live to even think about screwing me."

The captain nodded. He didn't need the translation. Bolan tossed him the carbine and gave one to his surviving gunman. "Tell them to mount the machine gun."

Ulov looked at the other Russians and began to speak.

Jukka scowled. "He wants to know if he gets a gun."

Bolan stabbed at the bag Ulov carried. The bag holding the laptop and the satcom link. "You tell him if he drops this or gets it wet, I'll kill him."

Volkov leaped up to the sail and threw open the hatch while his man hoisted up the machine gun. Manning clambered up and helped the gunman lock the heavy weapon into its mounting ring in the sail. More bullets tore through the boat shed. Something thumped on the roof. Bolan glanced up as smoke squirted through the rafters. They were being burned out again.

He pointed at Volkov's man and the chalks holding the sub up on the ramp. The Russian nodded and leaped down. The two of them went to either side of the sub and heaved on the chalking levers. Timbers groaned and the two wedges squirted out from under the sub. Splinters tore on the ramp as the steel hull scraped its way down and hit the water. Volkov had disappeared into the belly of his submarine with Manning and Ulov. Bolan looked up. The boat shed was beginning to burn in earnest. He took up his carbine and jacked an armor-piercing round into the M-203 chamber and aimed it at the crossbar of the boat shed's double door. The weapon shoved back as Bolan pulled the trigger and the grenade detonated against the wooden door. The timbers cracked and charred instantly under the superheated gas and molten metal.

The Executioner ran and leaped to grab the sail as Volkov gunned his engines and the sub lurched forward. Bolan crawled up and spilled into the sail as the sub rammed the sagging double doors. Planks cracked and the doors fell away to either side as the vast metal bulk of the sub pushed through.

A pair of helicopters hovered broadside fifty yards ahead, nearly touching the water. The third covered the rear of the boat house. The door gunners in the helicopters ahead opened up. Blood sprayed over Bolan at the bottom of the sail as Volkov's man was cut to pieces as he tried to bring the heavy machine gun to bear. "Dive! Dive! Dive!" Bolan roared down the open hatch as enemy machine guns burned their belts into the sub.

Air blasted out of the sides of the submarine as Volkov took on ballast. The enemy machine guns suddenly fell silent. Bolan reared up and shoved the dead Russian aside as he took the handles of the DshK. He tracked the front sight of the weapon onto the nose of one of the helicopters and shoved down the firing paddle. The skin of a light helicopter was no defense against armor piercing rounds larger than an American .50-caliber. The weapon shuddered in Bolan's hands as he held down the trigger and kept the tracers streaming into the helicopter's nose. The front windows of the cockpit turned opaque with bullet strikes. He swung the big weapon around on its mounting ring as he sought the other aircraft.

It was already banking away, and he couldn't manually traverse the big gun fast enough to keep up with it. Manning shouted up from the hold as water rose around the sail. "Striker! This elevator is going down!"

Bolan abandoned the DshK and slid down the hatch, pulling it closed behind him as he dropped into the hold and spinning the wheel to lock it. The cramped interior was lit with lurid red light. Volkov sat in a swivel seat at the conn and kept his eyes on his instrument panel. He was snarling something unpleasant in Russian.

Jukka shrugged. "He says he doesn't have a helmsman and only has two hands."

Bolan pointed a the tiny stool beside Volkov. "Take a seat. Do whatever he tells you."

Jukka leaped into the seat, and he and Volkov began a very rapid conversation in Russian. Ulov cringed against the hull, clutching the gear bag. His face was ghost-white with terror. The engine throbbed and clanked and vibrated the hull as Volkov shoved the throttles forward. Bolan reloaded his grenade launcher and slid a fresh clip into the carbine.

Jukka looked up from his position. "The captain wants to know where you wish to go."

"Tell him to pick a random heading. We'll pop up in few hours once we're sure we've shaken—" The hull rocked and a dense thunderclap sounded outside its thin metal walls. A second and a third detonation slapped the sub like a giant hand.

Manning shrugged as he fitted another rifle grenade to the muzzle of his weapon. "I think they came with sinking this sub in mind."

Bolan ignored the big Canadian. "Jukka! What's our depth?"

"Twenty meters!"

Bolan braced himself as another explosion hit closer and tried to turn the sub on its side. The shriek of tearing metal was met by Ulov's scream as a patch tore and a jet of water squirted into the hull. Ulov slid to the floor and Manning nearly lost his feet as something seemed to land right on top of the sub. Two more of the patches failed.

Ulov screamed and screamed as he was doused with water. Warning lights were blinking across Volkov's board. Jukka translated. "We have lost hull integrity! We are taking on water in all compartments!"

Bolan had done his level best to sink the sub a few days ago. What he had succeeded in was seriously compromising it. Twenty meters of water wasn't enough to run and hide in, but it was more than enough to drown in.

The captain shouted in consternation and Jukka translated uncertainly. "The captain says we are being...pinged!"

"Have him ping back! Who's out there?"

The captain began to fire his own damaged sonar. "He says there are no craft in the surrounding water! The sonar is coming from above!"

"Jesus!" Manning shook his head. "These guys brought their own sonobuoys!"

Bolan watched water begin to spray down from around the seal of the hatch. "These guys are a fast-reaction team. They've been on standby and they've been equipped to deal with an incursion or the captain deserting.

"Jukka!" Bolan said, "ask the captain how close the nearest shoreline is! If we stay down here we either drown or get cracked like an egg!"

Jukka scanned the screen in front of him as the captain shouted. "Fifty meters starboard!"

"Tell him to go for it! Wait until the last second and then blow all ballast and deploy the tracks!"

Jukka and the captain shouted at each other in Russian. The sub lurched as the captain turned her as hard as he could. The sub's turbine howled up into emergency war power. "The captain says hold on!"

"Up periscope!" The shaft slid down from the sail and Bolan held on for dear life. The dark, treelined shore loomed into view. The trees were broken by a thorn thicket, leading to a beach of pebbles. "Tell him five more degrees to starboard!"

Jukka shouted and the captain adjusted course. Jukka's eyes were glued to his screen. "Thirty meters!" The captain threw a valve and the hull groaned as compressed air shoved all water out of the ballast tanks. The sub rose like a cork. "Twenty-five meters!" The hull shuddered as the captain hurled more levers, and groans and clanks reverberated as gears engaged. "Fifteen meters!"

The sound of hail pounded the hull as the sub breached the water and began taking bullet strikes. "Ten!"

"Five meters!" Jukka's knuckles went white on his panel. "Impact—!"

Bolan was thrown from his feet. Ulov screamed and thrashed in the water flooding the hold as he broke Bolan's fall. Manning hung from an overhead rack like a monkey and Jukka was thrown from his seat. Supplies broke loose from their racks and cleats and went flying through the compartment. Volkov grimly held on. The entire hull bucked as the caterpillar tracks slammed into the rocks and mud of the shore. Momentum carried the sub forward, and the treads bit into the rocky muck to shove the sub up onto land.

"Eyes!" Volkov shouted what little English he knew. "I need eyes!"

Ulov howled as Bolan stood on him and seized the periscope handles. The thorn thicket loomed only yards away. "Forward! Go! Go! Go!"

The captain threw his gear lever and shoved his throttles forward. The tracks whined and clanked like a clockwork dinosaur. Machine-gun fire continued to rake the top of the hull, the sides screaming and grating as branches and trunks of the thicket scraped and snapped against the lumbering behemoth.

"Gummer! Me and you! Topside!" Manning spun the wheel on the overhead hatch and flung it back. Daylight and rain spilled into the compartment. "Jukka! Take the periscope! Direct the captain! We don't stop for anything!"

"We stop. Now." The submarine heaved to a halt. Ulov had picked up the captain's fallen carbine and had it pointed at the captain's head. He swung the muzzle toward Bolan. "Drop your pistol."

The interior of the sub was silent except for the idling engine. Bolan took the Desert Eagle from his waist with two fingers and dropped it into the water at the bottom of the compartment. Bolan turned. "You heard him, Gummer."

The muzzle of the carbine swung on Manning as he withdrew his Hi-Power. Bolan put his hand in his pocket. Ulov swung his weapon around as Manning dropped his pistol. "You! Stop!"

Bolan froze.

Ulov took a step forward and raised the muzzle level with Bolan's face. He spoke in Russian to Jukka, who frowned. "He says take your hand from your pocket. Very slowly."

"All right." Bolan took his hand from his pocket. He opened his fist halfway to reveal the fragmentation grenade he held. Ulov's eyes went wide. The Executioner opened his hand all the way, and the safety lever pinged away and bounced off of the bulkhead to the engine compartment. Bolan smiled and spoke in his basic Russian. "One."

Ulov lunged for the ladder.

"Two."

Ulov shot up out of the hatch like a castrated ape. The machine guns of the orbiting helicopters opened fire instantly. "Duck!" Bolan tossed the grenade through the hatch and pressed himself against the hull. The bomb detonated with a crack, and shrapnel shrieked down to slash through the water flooding the compartment floor.

"Volkov! Move it! Jukka! Take the periscope!"

Gears ground, and the submarine lurched forward once more. Ulov's riddled body slithered back down the hatch in a rain of blood. Manning yanked his corpse out of the way and picked up his SR-25 rifle. "How do you want to handle it, Striker?"

Bolan checked the loads in his carbine, then retrieved the Desert Eagle. "Jukka, steer Volkov into some trees. We need a second or two free of fire to get topside!"

Jukka stared fixedly into the periscope sight and began barking in Russian to Volkov. The captain yanked gears and the sub spun on one track.

Jukka leaned back from the periscope. "Here come the trees!"

The sub rocked on its chassis as it ran into something and smashed it out of the way. Bolan bounded up the ladder and stuck his head out of the hatch. Trees waved and buckled spastically overhead as the sub smashed its way through the forest. Machine-gun fire was still pounding the hull of the sub. The outer skin of the vessel was a lunar landscape of bullet holes, but the sub was double hulled, and the light machine guns carried by the choppers didn't have enough oomph to punch all the way through.

Bolan's gaze narrowed. The enemy had thought of that. He raised his carbine and held the trigger down at the figure leaning out of the lead chopper trying to get a clear shot with an RPG-7 through the trees. "Port! Port! Port!"

The gears clanked and screamed within the boat as one reversed itself. The boat spun like a whale trapped in molasses and smashed saplings as it lurched left. The RPG-7 rocket-propelled grenade hissed out of its launch tube and sizzled toward the sub. Bolan threw himself to the floor of the sail. "Incoming!"

The rocket struck the sub in the stern and detonated. Black smoke gouted from the rear of the vessel as the intense jet of superheated gas and molten metal flooded the interior. The secondary shrapnel effect sent jagged bits of metal scoring and sparking along the sides of the hull and pinging off the already battered sail. Bolan rose out of the sail and fired another burst from his carbine. The helicopter swerved away to reload in safety. He could hear the second chopper, but he couldn't see it as it orbited somewhere just out of sight over the trees. Probably lying in ambush. "Gummer!"

The diesel screamed and died as its components were melted and fragged. Miraculously the sub lurched on. Manning clambered up the ladder coughing. "We're all right! The engine compartment was sealed, but she's burning and we don't dare open the door. Volkov's gone to electrical power, but he says without buoyancy and running at full land speed, the batteries will bleed dry in minutes!"

Both men ducked as a sapling was smashed apart before the

sub and branches flew like shrapnel. Like a beached leviathan, the sub lurched onward. Bolan listened to the rotors. They were close, and using the forest canopy for cover. He glanced at the SR-25 and the rifle grenade mounted on its muzzle. "We're sitting ducks in this sub and we're meat on foot." Bolan grimaced.

"Gummer, you're on."

"See ya!" Manning threw a leg over the lip of the sail and slid down the side of the lurching sub. The big Canadian was almost instantly invisible as he plunged through a thicket. They were going to have to suck the enemy in. The floundering sub was one hell of a piece of bait. Bolan shouted down the hatch. "Can't this tub go any faster!"

There were outraged snarls in Russian from below.

Jukka shouted back. "We are at emergency war power! Twelve kilometers per hour! Batteries at seventy-percent!"

"All right, keep—" Bolan ducked as machine-gun fire swept the front of the sail. The helicopter was a hundred yards ahead and swinging wide. He took a moment to lead with the ladder sight of the grenade launcher, then squeezed the trigger. The weapon thudded back against him, and pale yellow flame fired from the 40 mm muzzle. Bolan snarled as the white-phosphorous grenade sailed past the nose of the chopper and detonated in white fire another hundred yards farther in the forest. He squeezed the trigger of his carbine. The rifle chattered in his hands and clacked open dry. The helicopter spun on its axis and brought the door gunner armed with the RPG to bear. Bolan dropped the carbine and drew the Desert Eagle. He took it in both hands and began firing as fast as he could pull the trigger. The grenadier ignored and sighted in his weapon. The Desert Eagle racked open on a smoking empty chamber. Bolan swiftly reloaded.

Something thudded under the trees fifty yards away. A thick bullet shape smeared by speed shot up and struck the hovering helicopter in its belly. Flame shot out its side windows as the interior was engulfed in superheated gas. The chopper shuddered and fell burning into the trees. Bolan spoke into his throat mike. "Thank you, Gummer."

"You're welcome. I can't see our other friend. Can you get a fix?"

Bolan scanned the wind- and rain-lashed treetops as the sub

ground on. The sound of rotors seemed to come from all directions and no direction at the same time. "No, but I hear him. He's close."

"Striker, they've lost three aircraft. Why doesn't he just climb the hell out of small-arms range and track us from altitude?"

Jukka shouted from below. "Batteries at fifty percent!"

"He's—" Bolan ducked as the helicopter popped up on the left flank and machine-gun bullets hammered the wall of the sail. Bolan crouched and fired back blindly over the lip. "He's herding us. I think we've got more company. Gummer, can you keep up?"

Manning's voice was amused. "You aren't exactly burning rubber, Striker."

"All right, stay parallel. Keep flanking."

"Affirmative."

Bolan dropped his spent carbine. "Jukka! I need a gun!" The sub clanked on. A moment later the Finn shoved his submachine gun and his revolver up into the sail.

"All we got!"

Bolan stared vainly at the heavy machine gun mounted on the sail. Unless the chopper pilot was stupid enough to stay still for him, he just couldn't traverse it in time. The soldier took up the M-44. Its 7.62 mm pistol ammunition was no guarantee at all against a helicopter. Things were getting grim. He flicked off the safety and scanned the trees. The sub lurched as it hit a hillock and lumbered upward. There was a sudden break in the trees, then the hillock leveled off and dropped.

"Road!"

Gears howled and ground but momentum kept the sub moving as it tipped. The helicopter roared overhead and walked a burst across the hull. Sparks screamed off the sail. Bolan fired a burst after the aircraft, then held on to the rim for dear life as the sub went over the side. The sub's hull slewed in the slush and overcorrected as Jukka screamed and Volkov furiously worked his gears. The sub slid down the hill. Its nose struck hard surface, and Bolan was nearly thrown from the sail as the hull scraped hideously and bottomed out. The sub was on a road.

Cars were coming at it.

"Left! Left! Left!" The sub spun on its tracks to face the new attack.

Three Land Rovers were bearing down at top speed. Their snow tires threw spumes of rain and half-melted snow as they hit their brakes. Gunners leaned out the windows with AK-47 rifles. They gaped at the smoking bloated apparition filling the road in front of them at less than thirty yards. The Land Rovers hydroplaned as their tires spun and lost traction. The studded tires of the lead vehicle gripped and it ground to a halt. The two vehicles piled into it from behind.

Bolan seized the handles of the DshK. A man stood up out of the open sunroof of the lead Land Rover, an RPG-7 across his shoulders. Bolan dropped the muzzle of the heavy machine gun onto the windshield of the vehicle and the two men exchanged fire. The heavy machine gun hammered in Bolan's hands. The windshield of the Land Rover erupted as the machine-gun bullets drilled through effortlessly. The RPG-7 rocket-propelled grenade whooshed out of its tube and sizzled through the air. Bolan had the satisfaction of seeing the rocketeer go down. The rocket struck the sub dead on the nose. Flame and superheated gas shot out of every one of a hundred bullet holes in the prow of the sub and was followed by black smoke.

The sub was burning fore and aft.

Bolan shoved his head down into the smoky interior. "Jukka! Are you all right!"

The Russian and the Finn were still screaming at each other. The bulkhead, between the compartment and the sonar dome was blackened, but the sonar had disrupted the superheated jet and kept it from burning its way into the cabin. Jukka hacked and shouted. "Batteries at twenty-five percent!"

"Forward! Go!" Bolan jumped back up behind the machine gun. The lead vehicle was ten yards away. The heavy machine gun had chewed up everything inside. The second vehicle was desperately spinning its wheels in reverse against the third vehicle behind it.

Manning stood at the top of the hill and was pumping rounds into the third vehicle's engine compartment.

"Go!" Bolan roared.

Jukka shouted back as he looked through the periscope. "But cars are—!"

"Go!"

The submarine clanked forward upon the stalled caravan of cars. The burning prow crushed the hood of the lead Land Rover. The vehicle seemed to disappear beneath it, and the tracks gripped and heaved upward. The submarine crawled over the Land Rover crushing it beneath its tracks like a steamroller, then spitting out the flattened and shredded remains behind it. The prow smashed into the second vehicle and its tracks bit. The Land Rover was sucked down and crushed like a tin can.

The three surviving men in the last vehicle leaped out the driver's-side doors, spraying their rifles on full-auto. They fell, shuddering, into the slush as the heavy machine gun in Bolan's hands drew a line through their ranks. The sub crunched down on the final vehicle and it tracks pulled it beneath its immense mass. The slow-motion destruction suddenly stopped. The starter clicked repeatedly and died. For a moment there was no sound other than the sizzling of the rain hitting the burning compartments fore and aft and the popping and ticking of the sub's tortured hull.

Bolan kept his hands on the heavy machine gun and spoke into his throat mike. "Gummer, you got a fix on the chopper?"

Manning waved from the top of the hillock. "Negative, Striker. Last I saw he was clawing for altitude over the lake."

Bolan nodded. The enemy had lost three helicopters and three Land Rovers, and, all told, at least twenty men. They had also burned the house and any clues that might still have been left within it. Jukka stuck his smoke-blackened face out of the hatch and shrugged unhappily. "The batteries are kaput."

"Yeah." Bolan nodded and handed Jukka back his weapon. "Take this."

"Thanks."

The Executioner stared up into the darkening skies and the falling rain. The afternoon was dying. It was going to be a long, dark, wet walk to get anywhere useful, more hours burned while the enemy continued with whatever they were planning.

Jukka frowned up at Bolan. "What now?"

"Go get Volkov." Bolan shook his head at the black smoke pouring out of the prow. "Tell him we're going to abandon ship."

12

Secure Communications Room,
U.S. Embassy,
Helsinki, Finland

Mack Bolan sank wearily into a chair. Gary Manning leaned back and closed his eyes. They were done in. Their leads were all but dried up and they'd used whatever local cooperation they'd been able to, save Jukka. Captain Volkov's story corroborated what Bolan had already suspected. The nukes were long gone. Finland was becoming untenable.

"Bear." Bolan rolled his head around on his neck. He'd spent the past few days having the hell beaten out him with almost nothing to show for it except the deaths of some good people. "You gotta give me something."

"Well, we have the results from Captain Volkov's online interview with the CIA sketch artist. I had to call in markers to route one out who spoke Russian. But the artist said Volkov had a flair for description. The captain has seen the sketch and says it is a dead likeness of our mysterious American."

Bolan gazed bleerily at the screen. "Send it."

An image downloaded onto the screen. Bolan forgot his weariness as he regarded his foe. Volkov's estimates were printed in the corner. Approximately six foot three. Approximately two hundred, forty-five pounds. Brown hair. Blue eyes. The man's shoulders were inhumanly broad, his waist incredibly small. He had the physique of a superhero, and his anvil jaw and piercing eyes only added to the effect.

Kurtzman's face appeared on smaller window in the corner. "You think he's Special Forces?"

"No. Special Forces guys have to be able to run twenty miles, swim twenty miles and then climb five hundred feet of rope in the rain. They're gnarly-looking all right, and ripped to the bone, but they're lean and mean. They're not built like professional wrestlers." Bolan considered the eyes. "They're not psych jobs, either. Special Forces guys are cool customers. Volkov said this guy's eyes were 'hot crazy,' and as a minisubmarine captain in the Russian navy, he would have been used to working with Spetsnaz and other Russian unconventional forces. He'd know the type."

Bolan's eyes narrowed. "This guy isn't Special Forces. He's a wannabe, and he's built himself up into the image of what he thinks a Special Forces soldier is, or he's overcompensating. He may have been in the military. As a matter of fact, I'd bet on it." Bolan's instincts solidified as he studied the sketch. "I bet he was tiptop in boot and regular service, and went on to Ranger School or BUDs training to be a SEAL, but he washed out. Probably during the more in-depth psychological examinations."

Kurtzman stared at Bolan through the video link for several moments. "That's a very interesting observation."

"It's just a guess. For all I know this guy made SEAL, served, was honorably discharged, and then bulked up to become a professional wrestler." Bolan leaned back again and rubbed his eyes exhaustedly. "It worked for the governor of Minnesota."

"No." Kurtzman shook his head and nodded at the same time. "I mean, yeah, it did. God bless him. But I like your first scenario a lot better. The question is, how did a psych case get involved with the Chinese and thirty nukes?"

"That's the rub. We've butted heads with the PRC on more than one occasion. They're cagey, and wouldn't work with anyone unstable, at least not willingly."

"Not willingly. I think that's a key statement." Kurtzman wrapped his considerable mind around the problem. "So what would make them?"

"He was forced on them, or forced himself upon them. From what little we've learned, he seems to be operating in some sort of command position in whatever group the Chinese are working with." Bolan set down the sketch, punched keys on the laptop and called up a window showing the sketch of the woman. "How's Akira doing with his search?"

"He thinks he has a ringer, but can't be sure it's exactly the same woman based on a charcoal sketch."

"Who does he think she is?"

"A model. A Landau model named Tereza Parzilay."

Manning looked up from the printed sketch of the woman with the alias "Theresa Parsons" written on the top. He was grinning delightedly. "Well, now, there's a hell of a coincidence."

"Landau models are some of the top in the world. Landau gives the Ford Models Inc. a run for its money when it comes to producing supermodels. Akira says that the Parzilay woman did some pretty spicy stuff in Europe before she became semifamous as a Landau model, and he says there are lots of websites devoted to the sordid pasts of the rich and famous."

Bolan grinned. "I'm sure he's been to all of them."

Kurtzman nodded. "He's pretty sure that's where he saw her."

"Pretty sure isn't good enough. I want every single thing you can find on Tereza Parzilay, and I want it ASAP."

Kurtzman punched a key. "I'm transmitting everything I have now. More will follow."

Bolan rose. "The Landau Modeling Agency, that's in New York City, right?"

"I believe so."

"Tell Barbara to get Gary and me transportation to New York from Helsinki, and I don't care what kind, as long was we are stateside within twelve hours. Tell her to arrange some kind of way into the agency, I want to go in soft and then get harder with them as the situation warrants."

Kurtzman stared out of the scene dryly. "So, you and Gary are going undercover as male models?"

Bolan shrugged. "Cops, male models, Santa Claus and one of his helpers. I don't care as long as it's in place when we hit the big city."

Kurtzman began hammering keys. "This should be good."

New York City, New York

"BEAUTIFUL, BROTHER." Roger gazed lovingly upon the twenty-four tactical nuclear weapons. "Absolutely Fuckin'-A beautiful."

Ian stared at the row of tactical nuclear artillery warheads and a Chinese proverb from his daily calendar of Taoist aphorisms came to mind.

A sword begs to be used.

Ian stared at his brother, who was practically salivating. Roger turned as he felt his brother's stare. "Do you know what the Europeans are, Ian?"

"Pussies?"

"Goddamn right." Roger folded arms like firehoses across his massive chest. "Do you know what the Russians are?"

Ian frowned. "A bunch of those Russian pussies died for us in Finland, Rog."

"I don't want the goddamn Russian pussies to die for us, Ian. At least not yet." Roger spit on the floor. "I want them to kill for us, and they fucked that up real good."

Ian considered Roger's own inability to kill their little problem in Finland but thought better of it. "Yeah, and at least two I can think of turned on us."

"And that, I am just not prepared to forgive at this juncture." Roger ran his eyes down the rows of his nuclear weapons. He quirked an amused eyebrow. "Ian, you know what Chinese are?"

Ian laughed. "Rog?"

"Yes, Ian?"

"That Shang guy is *not* a pussy."

"No." Roger shook his head slowly. "Most definitely not."

"Well, that's mighty nice of you to admit, Rog."

"A man's got know his limitations, Ian, and frankly, I think we're going to have trouble with that boy, and I am having second thoughts of mixing it up with that son of a bitch."

Ian paused. He had never seen his brother express doubt before. He took comfort in the fact that Roger was still grinning and the look in his eyes was still clearly insane and in command. "But?"

"But I know Shang's limitations."

Ian considered the six-and-a-half-foot tombstone of a human and couldn't imagine what kind of limitations his brother was talking about. "What kind of limitations?"

"Well, for one, I am absolutely positively sure that his fucking skull cannot withstand 5007 foot-pounds of energy." Roger glanced over at the case holding his AI .338 Lapua Super Magnum rifle. "And when the times comes, I'm going to take Old Painless over there and pop that Shang bastard's head like a cyst."

Ian smiled. He was an excellent shot, himself. His brother Roger was simply dog-nuts. His smile faded slightly. "What about our problem in Finland? We took major casualties. If the captain is still alive, they could have your description."

"Yeah, I should have capped his ass back in snow country." Roger shrugged again. "Can't be helped. They got lucky, and the house and the captain got compromised. There's not much they can do with it."

"They can run the records, Rog." Ian's brow bunched. "They can find out who's been using it."

"And prove nothing. Our hands are clean in any court of law, foreign or domestic."

Ian raised an eyebrow slightly. "This guy and his pals don't seem to give much of a shit about foreign laws. The way they come jumping out of helicopters and stealing submarines, I'm wondering if they'll give a crap about our constitutional rights stateside."

"You know, that's a good point, Ian. You're thinking." Roger's eyes went back to his nuclear weapons. "I want you to quadruple security around yourself. I'll have a few of my boys shadow you, as well. Meantime, I'm going to get these here and our people in place."

"What about the Chinese?"

"Give them anything and everything they want. I want their side of the operation to go smooth as silk. We're going to help them fuck themselves, and I want them at tiptop efficiency while they do it."

"Okay." Ian paused. "What about your girlfriend? They have her description, and probably her fingerprints from the hotel room."

"She's never been fingerprinted, she isn't in any police files and our jerkweed, interfering little friends don't associate in the same circles." Roger looked at his brother as if he were a little child. "What the hell do you think they can do?"

New York City, New York

THE EXECUTIONER strode through the pink-marble-walled lobby of the Landau Modeling Agency. However he was armored in ten thousand dollars' worth of Italian wool, leather and silk. The suit had been prepositioned on arrival as well as five suitcases full of accessories. He felt jet-lagged, but at least he looked like a million dollars. Bolan walked up to the desk. A wispy-looking young man sat behind a sweeping arc of marble. The gold nameplate on his desk said Tommy-John.

Tommy-John looked Bolan up and down like a horse breeder appraising a stud. His roving eyes froze as they met Bolan's. He cleared his throat and broke eye contact nervously. "Um...may I help you?"

Bolan relented on the stare-down. "Yes, my name is Belasko. I have 9:30 appointment with Joey Landau."

Tommy-John consulted a leather book. "I'm sorry, you've been bumped. How about we reschedule for, say...two weeks from Thursday?"

Bolan smiled in a friendly fashion. "Absolutely unacceptable."

Tommy-John blinked. "Unacceptable?"

"Absolutely."

"Um..." Tommy-John reached for his phone. "Let me see what I can do, perhaps next week we could—"

Bolan took the phone from Tommy-John and ripped the cord out of the outlet as he hurled it against the pink marble of the walls. Tommy-John went white as a sheet as Bolan examined an immense brass placard on the wall behind the desk that named floors and persons of varying levels of importance. Joey Landau's office was at the top of the list and four floors up. Bolan walked past the reception desk to the elevator. "I'll just show myself the way up, then."

Tommy-John stared frozen while Bolan pushed the button and the brass-doored elevator pinged open. The doors closed behind him as Bolan punched his floor. The elevator began to ascend silently. The door opened, and he found himself in a plushly appointed hall ringed by office suites. The double doors of the one at the end were covered in gigantic gold handwriting proclaiming the name Joey Landau. The doors opened as Bolan walked down the hall. A striking-looking, redheaded woman in her forties regarded Bolan frostily. She was flanked by two young men. One was a platinum blond, the other was black with a shaven head. They looked like a Scotch advertisement. Both men were so handsome they were evil-looking. Both were six feet tall and built like Greek statues beneath their impeccably tailored suits. Their perfectly chiseled faces regarded Bolan with petulant aggression.

Bolan smiled congenially. "Ms. Landau?"

"Yes, and you must be..." She made a show of searching for a name. "Belasko?"

Bolan nodded. "That's me. May I please—"

"Well, this is Marco and this is Buddy." Ms. Landau's face lost all trace of amusement. "And if you don't get your ass out of here, they're going to make a mess out of you."

Marco and Buddy exposed sets of perfect, blindingly white teeth. They stepped in front of Ms. Landau like a human wall of handsomeness.

Bolan sighed. "Ms. Landau, I regret the circumstances, but it is vitally important that you and I talk, today. Now."

"You and I are not going to talk today. Nor are we going to have any future meetings, either." She jerked her head toward Bolan imperiously. "Marco, Buddy."

Marco and Buddy strode forward as if they were on the catwalk at a fashion show. Marco exposed his million-dollar smile again. "I'm a black belt."

Buddy eyed Bolan coolly. "I do three hours of Tae Bo a day, and your ass is—"

Buddy's eyes bugged as Bolan's left hand shot to his throat and closed off his carotid arteries. Both of Buddy's hands instinctively clasped Bolan's wrist. The soldier pistoned his right fist into the point of Buddy's jaw, and his eyes rolled back as he collapsed to the carpet without a sound.

"Ki-yah!" Marco's foot arced up at Bolan's temple in a

credible crescent kick. Bolan blocked the kick with his forearm and Marco showed his lack of combat experience by trying the exact same kick again except even harder and faster. Bolan didn't bother to block. He simply dropped into a low stance beneath it. The Executioner swung a top-fist strike into Marco's ball-sack while he conveniently lifted his leg six feet up in the air.

Marco fell vomiting to the floor.

Bolan stood and gave his most winning smile. "Ms. Landau, I would very much appreciate your giving me just a few moments of your time."

To her credit, Ms. Landau stood her ground. Her blue eyes registered fear but they did not blink. "And if I don't?"

"Then I'm going to pick up Buddy and beat you to death with him."

Ms. Landau blanched.

Bolan smiled. "I'm kidding."

"Um..."

"Why don't you call an ambulance for Marco and Buddy and we'll talk in your office." Bolan turned up the wattage on his smile. "You can call the police, too, if you like."

"The police are already on their way." Joey Landau took out her cell phone and punched a button. "Tommy-John? Yes, call and cancel the police. Yes, that's right. Then have Charles bring the limo around and take Marco and Buddy to the emergency room." She clicked her phone shut. "Come into my office. Let's talk."

Bolan followed her into an office where nearly everything was either black marble or black leather with gold accents. She took a seat behind a massive desk and gestured at a chair for Bolan. She lit a cigarette and stared Bolan up and down frankly. "You walk like a soldier. Hell, you walk like a goddamn army of one, but you don't dress like a soldier."

Bolan accepted the compliment. "You smoke Turkish cigarettes."

Ms. Landau waved the cigarette and rolled her eyes helplessly. "I had just about given up smoking when one of my models got me hooked on them."

"Tereza."

Ms. Landau blinked. "How did you know?"

"She's who I'm here to talk to you about."

Ms. Landau cocked her head. "You're her soldier boyfriend she talks about."

"No, but he did try to kill me."

Ms. Landau blinked.

"He also killed some very good people. Tereza is mixed up with some very bad people, and I need to find out where she is."

Ms. Landau's gaze went out to the hallway. She hadn't bothered to close her door, and Tommy-John and five more handsome-boys were manhandling Marco's and Buddy's moaning and unconscious bodies toward the elevator. "You're not a policeman, are you?"

Bolan shook his head. "No."

"Who are you, then? If I might ask."

"I have a relationship with the United States government."

She looked at Bolan shrewdly. "How do I know you're not the Mafia or not one of these very bad people yourself."

"They wouldn't be making appointments or saying 'may I' and 'please,' and Marco and Buddy don't need body bags."

"Okay..." Ms. Landau seemed to accept Bolan's logic. "But I've met some U.S. government types in my time, and a lot of them don't say 'may I,' 'please' or 'thank you,' either."

"I didn't say I was with the United States government. I said I had a relationship with it."

"You are a very intriguing man."

"You're a strikingly beautiful woman."

Ms. Landau blushed charmingly. She cleared her throat and became serious. "What will happen to Tereza?"

"What I want more than anything is to talk to her. There are other people who will probably consider her a liability very soon and want her dead." Bolan looked at the woman frankly. "I need your help."

"I don't know exactly where she is—" Ms. Landau flipped open the laptop on her desk "—but if she's in the United States and not in New York, I can make some educated guesses."

13

Santa Cruz, California

Gary Manning pointed. "That's the one."

Bolan gazed at the beach house. There were few more beautiful places in the world than the shores of Northern California. The house Manning pointed to was just short of palatial and loomed over a massive jumble of rocks that formed a breakwater above the beach. The late-morning sun shone out of a cloudless sky and turned the waves to jade. A few surfers bobbed out past the breakers as they waited for the big one. Other than a couple of sunbathers, the beach was abandoned. "I'll take the back. Give me ten minutes."

"You got it."

Bolan descended the low cliff to the beach. Golden sand crunched beneath the sport sandals he wore on his feet. He wore khaki shorts and a windbreaker. Sunglasses and a Pittsburgh Steelers baseball cap pulled low over his face concealed most of his features. Beneath the windbreaker he wore Threat Level II soft body armor and carried his Beretta 93-R in a shoulder holster. Joey Landau had been very forthcoming. Tereza Parzilay had a lot of strange friends and liked to party and live on the dangerous side. She had a lot of money, far more money than could be accounted for even by her fairly successful modeling career. The parties she threw at her Santa Cruz beach house—Dionysian

Orgies, as Ms. Landau had referred to them—were things of legend in the modeling community.

Bolan ignored the steep wooden stairs that wound down between the massive boulders and began scrambling up the rocks. He spoke into his throat mike as he clambered up. "Gummer, I am approaching the backyard."

"Roger that, Striker. I am in position on the street. I'll hit the front on your go."

Bolan peered over the top. A long swimming pool with an attached hot tub dominated most of the area between the house and the top of the breakwater. Vast expanses of glass walled the house that faced the beach to give spectacular views from every room. Bolan hopped the fence and padded along the pool deck.

Ninety pounds of Rottweiler came bolting from the side yard.

"Gummer, we've been made."

"Roger, moving in."

Foam flew back from the dog's jaws as it charged in barking. Bolan seized a wrought-iron chair from the deck dining set. As the dog leaped, he brought the chair up in front of him and leaned into the attack. The dog hit him full-force and nearly took him off of his feet. Bolan dug in his heels and pushed forward with all of his strength. The dog hopped on its hind legs and tried to bite him around the chairback. The dog had no leverage in that stance, and Bolan drove the beast backward across the deck. He pushed with all of his strength and toppled the dog into the pool.

Tereza Parzilay stood naked in the glass sliding door, staring in shock at the attack dog paddling in the pool and the man striding across the deck armed with a chair. Her eyes flew wide as she recognized the Executioner. She slammed the sliding-glass door closed so hard it rattled in its tracks. She flipped the lock and bolted further into the house.

Bolan flung the wrought-iron chair through the massive glass door. Six-foot shards of glass fell and shattered on the ground like shrapnel. Glass crunched under Bolan's feet as he entered the violated doorway. People inside were screaming. A naked blond man ran into the room. He took inspiration and picked up a bar stool and hefted it overhead like an oversize club. Bolan thrust out the Beretta 93-R and flicked the selector to 3-round burst. "Sit down!"

The surfer dropped the bar stool and promptly sat on the couch. "Gummer! What have you—"

A shotgun blast roared deafeningly inside the house. "Gummer!"

"I'm all right. I think." Manning groaned across the link. "She did it again."

Bolan ran toward the sound of the shot with his machine pistol in front of him. The front door hung open by one hinge where Manning had kicked it. He was rising to his feet on the front stoop, his Browning Hi-Power in hand. The front of his windbreaker had been shredded by the point-blank blast of buckshot.

"Gummer, which way did she go?"

Manning grimaced and pointed. "Down the hall. Toward the kitchen."

"Cover the dining room!"

Bolan ran toward the smell of coffee as Manning went the other way to cut off the kitchen in a pincer movement. "What have you got, Gummer!"

"Nothing, there's—"

An engine snarled into life. Bolan bolted back down the hall. "She's in the garage!"

The engine was revving up into the redline as Bolan ran out the front door. The house had three garage doors. Tires screamed as the car was shoved into gear. The first garage door flew apart in an explosion of plywood and flying door springs. Bolan hurled himself out of the way as a red Porsche Boxster came howling out of the garage. Tereza Parzilay was in the passenger seat and a large man was driving. A stockless pump shotgun blasted in Tereza's hands and Bolan felt the wind of the buckshot passing over his head. He rolled up as the Porsche fishtailed down the drive and screamed toward the street.

Bolan leaped the hedge and charged across the front lawn to cut it off. He roared into his throat mike. "Get a car, Gummer! A fast one!"

"Affirmative!"

The soldier raced out onto the sidewalk and fired a 3-round burst toward the fleeing Porsche. Parzilay fired back, and the mailbox was blasted off of its post. The Porsche pulled onto the street and began to accelerate away as Bolan ran after it. "Gummer!"

"I'm on it!"

Bolan charged down the road as the Porsche pulled off the residential street and into traffic. The Executioner's lungs burned as he continued on at full sprint. When he hit the street, the Porsche was fifty yards ahead. It was at an intersection, with four cars ahead of it taking up both lanes in front of a red light. The tires squealed as the driver shoved the car into reverse, and the chassis scraped as the vehicle crossed the median into oncoming traffic. Bolan skidded to a halt and took an aimed shot at the back of the driver's head. Cushioning around the built-in roll bar flew. Tires screamed once more as the driver shoved the car back into first. Horns honked and other onrushing cars skidded to the sides as the Porsche moved among them. The vehicle spun into the intersection and peeled back into the correct lane again. The Porsche flew ahead like a bullet.

"Gummer!"

Manning shouted across the link. "On your six!"

Bolan turned. A lowered, jet-black El Camino came thundering down upon him like Judgment Day. The roof had been removed. A chrome air scoop jutted out from a hole in the hood. Chrome lined the wheel farings and every other surface that wasn't painted black. Manning slowed to just less than suicidal speed and Bolan leaped into the empty bed. "Go!"

Bolan was nearly thrown out the back as Manning dropped the hammer on the massive V-8 engine. "Which way!"

The Executioner scanned ahead. He couldn't see the Porsche through traffic, but he could hear the squealing of tires and the honking of horns. A green road sign with an arrow said Highway 880 was dead ahead. "They're going for the freeway!"

Manning took the El Camino over the median and into oncoming traffic. Horns blared and the Santa Cruz prelunch traffic swerved and went up on the sidewalk and the median to get out the way of the rampaging muscle car. Bolan crawled forward out of the bed and jumped into the passenger seat.

Manning grinned. "You like my ride?"

"It's beautiful. Can you take a Porsche in it?"

"I can try!" Manning cut across the next intersection and onto the right side of the road.

"Gimme the wheel!"

Manning shrugged and pulled his knees into his chest. He pushed himself up and over into the truck bed as Bolan slid behind the wheel. The soldier took the wheel in his hand and felt the throb of the massive engine. The sign ahead read Highway 880 North. Bolan was shoved back in his seat as he stepped on the gas. He spied the Porsche up ahead dodging through traffic as it made for the freeway. "Gary! Make a hole!"

Manning slid into the passenger seat and stood. He raised his Hi-Power and started firing into the air. Cars began to swerve crazily to get out of the way of the gun-toting psychotics in the El Camino. The Santa Cruz Mountains loomed dead ahead. A red Porsche squirted out of traffic and flew up the off-ramp.

Manning slid down into the seat and reloaded. "We're losing her!"

"Not yet!" Cars fishtailed and stomped on their brakes as Bolan shot through the last intersection. The on-ramp and the freeway ahead were clear. Bolan dropped the hammer. The El Camino roared like the massive dinosaur it was as the car hurtled forward. Massive redwoods girded both sides of the highway as it wound its way up into the Santa Cruz Mountains. Bolan had been on 880 before. It was regarded as one of the most dangerous highways in North America. Before it had been expanded and a center dividing wall installed, its nickname had been Blood Alley.

Bolan stepped on the gas.

The Boxster up ahead was a midsize engine car, and disabling the engine with 9 mm hollowpoints would be difficult. Bolan also wanted Tereza Parzilay alive for questioning. The El Camino shot up the mountainside and then began to take the long sweeping curves between the peaks. Bolan spied the Porsche up ahead. They were apparently unaware that they were being pursued. That was about to change.

"Gary, I want you to go for the rear tires."

"You've got it." The slide of Manning's Hi-Power shot home on a loaded chamber. The El Camino burned up the road between itself and the Porsche. Tereza Parzilay's head turned. She peered over the rims of her sunglasses and smiled. She reached down and pulled the stockless shotgun from between her knees. Manning raised his pistol. The Porsche jinked lanes and the shotgun roared. Buckshot smeared across the center divider as Bolan hit the brakes. The Porsche shot ahead up the mountain.

Bolan stomped the accelerator into the floor.

The superchargers whined and the engine roared with power. Manning fired another round and the passenger-side mirror smashed away from the Porsche's body. Tereza pumped the shotgun and tried to aim at Bolan's head as he changed lanes. She squeezed the trigger and nothing happened. A feral snarl twisted her beautiful lips and she hurled the shotgun. The shotgun hit the road and walked end over end with unerring accuracy toward the El Camino. The shotgun smashed out a headlight as it hit the grill and came up over the hood.

"Shit!" Manning ducked as the weapon clipped the top of the windshield frame and sent cracks radiating through the windshield.

"The tires!" Bolan reminded him.

"You've got to get me closer!" Manning leaned out over his door as Bolan fought the mountain. He felt the driver's-side tires go light as the car almost lifted up off its chassis. The tires screamed as they tried to hold on to the road. The Porsche whipped through the curve effortlessly and pulled ahead. The road began to straighten out and Bolan saw a sign for the Summit Inn. They would have a few moments without curves.

He dropped the hammer.

The superchargers howled and the engine redlined. The El Camino raced forward over the mountaintop. The Porsche ahead slowed as it met traffic. The El Camino bore down. "Take your best shot!"

Manning took careful aim at the rear tire.

Parzilay turned and stood up in her seat. She held a Glock in either hand. Both pistols erupted into halos of fire as she burned both magazines into the El Camino.

"Shit!" Manning threw himself down behind the dash and Bolan hunched behind the wheel as the windshield spiderwebbed and went opaque with bullet strikes. The supersonic cracks of the bullets passing through the headrests sounded like a swarm of hornets.

The El Camino scraped sparks off the center divider and nearly spun out of control. Bolan kept his grip on the wheel light and tried not to overcorrect the fishtailing muscle car. He popped his head up as the snarl of the machine pistols ceased. Manning lurched up and began kicking out the shattered remains of the windshield. He looked at Bolan. "She's probably reloading, you know!"

Bolan grimaced. He wanted the woman alive. She didn't seem to be burdened with any reciprocal feelings on his behalf.

The Porsche suddenly dropped out of sight as the plateau of the summit ended and the highway fell back down the mountainside. It was here that things got steep and deep.

The El Camino dropped like a stone down the dark side of the Santa Cruz Mountains. The Porsche was whipping through the curves up ahead. Bolan had no illusions. On the hairpin turns of Highway 880 an El Camino, even lowered and supercharged, stood no chance against a Porsche. Bolan couldn't beat the other man's machine. The question was, could he beat the man driving it.

"Hold on, Gary."

Bolan began taking the road. He had no gears to work with. All he had was the accelerator and the brake. He slowed just enough for survival and then accelerated like a slingshot through each curve using both lanes whenever possible. The air blasted across him through the empty windshield frame like a wind tunnel. The speeding Porsche hugged the fast lane and strove to pull ahead. The driver tried to drive as fast as possible and hit his brakes at the last moment. He was actually riding his brakes most of the time. He wasn't a skilled driver.

The El Camino's engine roared and its tires screamed as it bore down on the Porsche.

Manning looked up. "We have company."

Bolan risked taking his eyes off the road and saw the police helicopter paralleling them in the sky. "Check your radio."

Manning flipped the dial on his personal link and shook his head. "We've got Highway Patrol behind us."

A yellow sign flashed by with the black spiral sign of a hairpin turn and a 40 mph speed limit. The Porsche shot the curve with screaming tires. Bolan eased his foot onto his brake. The road curved and curved and kept curving as it fell down the mountain. It was a death spiral at seventy miles per hour. Bolan worked the brakes as he felt the El Camino go light.

"Striker..."

Sparks flew as the car scraped against the concrete divider as the road continued to curve.

"Striker—!"

The El Camino spun out. The Santa Cruz Mountains revolved like a sixty-mile-per-hour kaleidoscope. The front bumper smashed into the center divider, and the car nearly rolled as the rear end swung around for another go-round. Bolan kept his hands loose on the wheel as the car revolved screaming. The crumpled front came in line with the lane marker and Bolan stomped on the gas. The tires shrieked and bit and the El Camino lunged forward. Bolan hit his brakes as they hit the next curve and then shot into a bit of straightaway.

Manning fastened his safety belt. "Jesus."

"What have you got on the radio?"

Manning didn't look happy as he put a finger to his earpiece and listened. "We got about a dozen Highway Patrol units behind us."

Bolan grimaced as he whipped the El Camino around a truck carrying lumber. The traffic on 880 so far had been mercifully light. He was forced to slow as he wove between a minivan and a civilian converted postal jeep. Bolan broke free of traffic just as the Porsche disappeared behind a far curve. The road continued to sweep down the mountainside and then became fairly stable as it swooped through the long curves near the feet of the peaks. The sun played upon the dazzling blue of the reservoir off to Bolan's left. The superchargers whined as he held the accelerator down.

The freeway ahead branched. The off-ramp led to downtown Los Gatos. Highway 880 continued on toward San Francisco. Both the off-ramp and the freeway ahead were blocked off by Highway Patrol and sheriff's cruisers. Officers armed with shotguns and rifles leaned over the hoods and pointed their weapons at the oncoming vehicles. Another helicopter orbited their position. The Porsche's tires screamed as the driver stood on the brakes and then spun as he yanked the wheel and yanked on the parking brake in a bootlegger's turn. The Porsche's tires screamed and burned rubber as the sports car accelerated straight at Bolan.

The Executioner floored it.

The two vehicles roared toward each other in an apocalyptic game of chicken.

"Uh...Striker?"

"He's not our boy. He's hired help. He'll move."

The red Porsche flew at them like an arrow. The engine of the El Camino roared like a beast. Tereza Parzilay's face was an unreadable mask behind her sunglasses. The driver of the Porsche was a large man with almost no neck and a crew cut. His eyes went wide as the crumpled front of the El Camino came on like judgment. His face went white, and he jerked the wheel to get out of the way.

Parzilay's face split into an insane smile as she grabbed the wheel of the Porsche and jerked it back in line.

"Hold on!" Bolan spun the wheel. The El Camino's tires shrieked as the tailgate came around and the Porsche smashed broadside into the El Camino's truck bed. The impact spun the El Camino back around in the opposite direction and sent it into the center divider. The car screamed along and was suddenly riding the top of the center divider in a delicate balancing act. Bolan hooked his feet beneath the accelerator and the brake pedals and yanked his head down below the dash as the car rolled and the world came to an end.

Everything was rending metal and ripping asphalt. Tortured panels screamed as they failed, and the earth became a vast hammer trying to beat Bolan out of position so that his life could be scraped away between the hurtling car and the unyielding concrete. The El Camino rolled four times and finally lay still on its side on the other side of the center divider.

Bolan opened his eyes. "Gary?"

Manning hung by his seat belt above him. The Canadian's face was a mangled mask of blood. One bloodshot eye opened and regarded Bolan bleerily. "Next time...I do the driving."

Bolan took stock. He felt as if he had been trampled by mules. Sirens were wailing. He unbuckled and pushed himself out of the El Camino. He didn't see his Beretta 93-R anywhere. He drew his 9 mm Smith & Wesson Centennial revolver from his pocket and stood.

The crumpled Porsche was twenty yards away on the other

side of the center divide. Tereza Parzilay stepped out of it unsteadily, bleeding copiously from her mouth and nose. Both of the Porsche's airbags had deployed. The driver's head and shoulders lolled out over his door. There was a bullet hole squarely in the middle of his forehead.

Parzilay had killed him so he wouldn't talk.

She held one of her Glock pistols in her hand. She held it with extreme difficulty because the majority of her fingers seemed to be broken. Bolan staggered a step and steadied himself as he raised the Centennial. "Drop it."

Her beautiful eyes stayed fixed as her lips skinned back to reveal bloody teeth. "Fuck you."

"Drop it."

It was startling to see so beautiful a face twisted by insane hatred. "I am going to kill your ass."

Bolan's finger took up slack on the Centennial's trigger. The revolver's hammer clicked onto the half-cock point as Bolan centered his front sight between the woman's eyes.

"Drop it."

"Drop your weapons! Both of you!"

Bolan kept his pistol aimed at Parzilay as police cruisers screeched to halts all around them and the bullhorn blared.

"Drop your weapons!"

Parzilay let her weapon fall from her twisted fingers. Bolan slowly lowered his revolver and let it fall to the pavement. He made no resistance as the armored SWAT team dived into him and took him down. They forced his arms behind his back and then dragged him to his feet once he was shackled. Parzilay was already handcuffed and being shoved toward a car. She smiled at Bolan in passing and spoke loud enough for everyone to hear. "Officer, I believe you should check my identification and passport."

Her smile went feral as she locked eyes with Bolan. "I believe you will find I have diplomatic immunity." The insane lights in her eyes shone like the sun. "I demand to be taken to the Spanish embassy and released into their custody."

14

San Francisco

Bolan was incredulous as he stared at the screen. "She's a member of the Spanish royal family?"

"Yeah," Kurtzman said, "a cousin, apparently. We knew she has Canadian citizenship. She was born there, but the Spanish thing came right out of the blue. Apparently she has dual citizenship."

Bolan felt the noose tightening. He had been exposed to the vagueries of diplomatic immunity too many times before. "So she's going to walk?"

"Apparently so."

"She killed her driver."

"She says you did it, and it's never going to go to court. Her claim of diplomatic immunity is ironclad. Unless she shoots the President, the most that can be done is to throw her out of the country and permanently deny her reentry into the United States. That has to go through State Department channels. Right now the local authorities out there in California seem much more interested in you and Manning."

Bolan leaned back in his chair. His entire body ached. He just wasn't getting any recovery time. He had spent four hours in the Los Gatos City Police lock-up until a phone call from on High had informed the chief of Bolan's own unique and interesting form of immunity. Manning had a broken nose and a concussion. He and Bolan were in a CIA safehouse. A secure doctor was upstairs keeping an eye on the big Canadian's brain. Bolan glared into the middle distance as he considered Tereza Parzilay.

Kurtzman cocked his head as he observed Bolan's expression. "You're thinking about a snatch."

Bolan smiled thinly. "Not exactly."

"Striker, she's in the Spanish embassy. We're talking about a serious international incident. If you do it en route to SFO you'd be going up against U.S. law enforcement escorting her to the airport."

"I was thinking more about having a nice conversation with her in Spain."

"You'll need backup."

"Manning is smashed up pretty good, and like I said, I'm thinking conversation, not snatch."

"Well." Kurtzman punched some keys. "Her flight is going to be leaving in about four hours. She's leaving the United States voluntarily."

"Which way is she headed?"

"S.F. to New York, New York to Barcelona, Barcelona to Ibiza."

"I need someone to lay eyes on her at each stop, and someone to pick up her tail in Ibiza until I can get there. Speaking of which, I need to beat her to the island at all costs."

Bear nodded. "You want a fast mover."

"The faster the better."

Kurtzman pounded more keys. "JG is in Los Angeles. I'll get him down to Miramar and have a two-seat F-18 hot on the runway waiting for you. Barb will see to getting you in-flight refueling. By the time you hit the east coast, we'll have your transatlantic arranged."

"I'm on my way to SFO. I need something fast on the tarmac waiting for me. Preferably a Learjet."

"It'll be ready."

Bolan rose and steadied himself as the room spun for a moment. Kurtzman's brow crumpled in concern. "Striker? Are you all—"

"I'll drop a dime on you when I'm airborne." The laptop's power cut as Bolan flipped the lid closed and disconnected.

Isla Ibiza, Mediterranean

"YOU LOOK LIKE dog dirt." Jack Grimaldi's grin was irritating in the extreme.

Bolan turned red-rimmed eyes upon the Stony Man pilot. "How long have I slept?"

"Four hours, and brother, you needed it. I've kept an eye on the villa. She hasn't left, and nothing has moved."

Bolan glanced at the night sky. He gauged it was just after 4:00 a.m. and checked his watch to find that he was right. A cold wind blew off the Mediterranean Sea across the lime-washed villas. It was off-season in Ibiza. The hordes of Northern European tourists would spend several more months working in their northern climes before descending on the island for days of burning in the all-day sun and dancing in the internationally famous discos at night. For the moment, the island was ruled by fisherman and local businesses independent of foreign tourists. Bolan leaned back in the passenger seat of the rented Ford Falcon, poured some bottled water onto his face and let the cold breeze dry it. "Okay, we're a go."

Grimaldi's grin retained its wattage, but his eyes grew concerned. "Striker?"

"Yeah?"

"You want me to do this?"

"I'd love you to do it." Bolan fixed a small black bag to his raid suit. "But I want you to sit tight and keep the engine running in case I need a fast extraction, and the trunk unlocked in case I need to bring the package with me."

"You sure you're up for this?"

"I'll manage."

Bolan adjusted his com link and slid from the car. He slipped through the shadows of the poorly lit, cobblestone streets. The Spanish-style house sat on a cliff over the dark waters of the Mediterranean. "You read me, Jack?"

"Loud and clear, Striker. I see you by the wall."

"I'm going in." Bolan slid over the wall. He landed with the silenced Beretta in his hand. Grimaldi had done a drive-by during the day and detected no dogs or security cameras. Bolan had done a drive-by in the midevening and seen no infrared beams crisscrossing the grounds. White-barked ornamental willow trees stood like ghosts in the starlight, their drooping limbs shivering like tentacles in the wind off the sea. Bolan moved among them like a shadow among ghosts. A red Alpha-Romeo Spyder convertible was parked on the gravel drive as well as a Vespa scooter. The grounds were well manicured. The Executioner slid around the side of the house and moved to the courtyard in the back. White curtains blew inward at the open windows. Bolan hopped up onto a sill and slid inside the house. "I'm in."

"Affirmative, Striker. I have no movement."

Bolan pulled his night-vision goggles down over his eyes and the light-gathering lenses lit up the inside of the house in grainy blacks, grays and greens. He made a swift circuit of the bottom floor and then moved up the stairs. There was no sound other than the gentle rustle of the wind in the curtains. He came to the landing and moved down the hallway to the open door of the master bedroom. Long lattices of shadow were thrown across the king-size bed from the open balcony doors. Bolan slowly pulled his night-vision goggles away from his eyes.

The blue light of the moon spilled across Tereza Parzilay's naked body. Bolan flicked on the light.

"Striker, I have a light source."

"It's mine." Bolan moved to the corpse. The once-golden skin was ashen. As Bolan rolled the body over, Tereza's flat, dead eyes stared up at him out of a face that had gone fish-belly white and was contorted by agony and horror. The wire of the garrote had cut deeply into the flesh of her throat and stained the bed and the front of her body. Bolan noted the position of the body, stains that weren't blood-related, and the condition of the rest of the bedclothes. The Executioner's eyes narrowed slightly as he surveyed the corpse of a woman he had made love with.

Tereza had been killed during the act of intercourse.

There was no skin or blood beneath her fingernails. The rest of the room was immaculate. There was no other bruising on her body or any signs of force. It had been a consensual act until her partner had upped the ante from sex to assassination.

Grimaldi spoke across the link. "She's dead, isn't she?"

"Yeah." Bolan watched the breeze ruffle her short hair. "She's dead."

"You think the Chinese got her?"

"No. Our friend Shang would have snapped her neck and thrown her into the sea. I think her boyfriend decided to have one last trip down memory lane before he whacked her as a liability."

"And who would her boyfriend be?"

Bolan considered the question. "It's a guess, but I'm betting he's a real big guy who likes real big rifles."

He swiftly cased the house. He found the safe behind a painting and blew it with flexible charge. Inside he found about twenty thousand dollars' worth of U.S. and Spanish notes, an Astra 9 mm pistol and some jewelry. He spent some time getting forensic samples from Parzilay's corpse and stopped a moment as he looked at the book on top of the bureau.

"Striker." Grimaldi's voice rose in slight urgency. "You've been inside an hour and a half. You're pushing your envelope."

"I may have found something."

"What's that?"

Bolan picked up the book. The receipt had been folded in two and inserted as a bookmark. He unfolded the receipt, which was dated two days earlier, from a bookstore in Santa Cruz, California.

The book was a traveler's guide to Iceland.

"Jack?"

"Yeah?"

"We're on a plane."

15

San Francisco, California

Kurtzman was excited. "Striker, I've come up with something. It'll sound crazy, but I'm thinking that I—"

"Iceland."

Kurtzman looked hurt. "Um, yeah. How did you know?"

"Some luck." Bolan peered at the book next to him on the seat. "What did you come up with?"

Kurtzman overcame his momentary disappointment at being trumped and regained his intellectual excitement. "Well, you asked for anything the PRC might be doing in Scandinavia, and after some pretty extensive searching, I could only come up with one thing of any real interest, and that was in the Land of Fire and Ice."

"What are they doing in Iceland, Bear?"

The computer expert punched some keys and began to transmit files. "Geothermal research."

"Really?"

"Yes. Iceland almost completely heats and powers itself with geothermal energy. China is huge, but they never have enough power, and Iceland is on the cutting edge. They've sent some teams over."

"Okay." Bolan glanced out the window of the safehouse. It

was a rare, gorgeous day in San Francisco. "But what does that have to do with tactical nukes?"

"I don't know." Kurtzman punched some keys and brought up a map of Iceland. "But you and I both seem to have a lead that's going in the same direction."

"I'll need a full war load delivered to Reykjavik. Have Barbara set it up, ASAP, plus one for Jack just in case things get hot."

"It's already on the way, though you're going to get there first by a few hours."

"How's the weather up there?"

"The storm is hitting. It's ugly and should be going on horrific within the next seventy-two hours."

"Swell." Bolan didn't relish the idea of chasing Chinese Special Purpose troops through the snow.

"Yeah, you'll have to wear your galoshes when you go out, but we're sending you along full arctic warfare gear and equipment."

Bolan glanced at the files in front of him. One file contained a charcoal sketch of a naked and smiling Tereza Parzilay just before she had shot Manning. Another was a photo from her modeling portfolio. The third was a picture Bolan himself had taken of her dead body on the bed of her house in Spain. "What did you get on Tereza?"

"Akira broke into the Spanish police computer files. The coroner's report coincides with yours. She was showing someone a real good time, and then it got ugly."

Bolan peered at Kurtzman's face on the screen closely. "You have something else."

He grinned slyly. "I do."

Bolan matched his grin. "Orbitech."

"You got it."

"What about it?"

"I have Ian Neville."

Bolan paused. Ian Neville was one of the wealthiest men in the world. He was mentioned in the *Wall Street Journal* just about every day. "How did you get him?"

"It took a lot of digging, and there were a lot of false trails and fronts, but Mr. Neville has controlling interest in Orbitech."

Bolan considered. "Well, that puts the money into the pie, but it still could have come from any of about a thousand other sources. I need something concrete before I go dropping a hammer on a billionaire."

"Oh, absolutely.

"What else have you got?"

"I have a thorough search of Tereza Parzilay's house by the Santa Cruz County Sheriffs and, more importantly, Akira got her credit card and phone records for the last five years."

"And?"

"And there was a lot to wade through, but for one, she's made calls to the Neville family compound in Greenwich, Connecticut."

"We're getting closer."

"It gets better."

"How much better?"

"I've got Ian's brother, Roger." Kurtzman punched keys and an inset popped up the screen. "Will he do for your wannabe Special Forces psycho?"

Bolan punched a key and filled the screen with the image. The man was six feet tall, had the ax handle shoulders and tiny waist of a bodybuilder, and was impossibly muscled. His shoulder-length brown hair was pulled back into a ponytail, and a biker's mustache stopped at his chin. "What's his story?"

"Well, Rog was a United States Marine. As a boot, he was first in his company at Quantico. Broke all the fitness records and was rated as an expert rifleman. Qualified for the Marine sniper school."

Bolan examined the picture. "But our boy wanted to be a Green Beret."

"That's right, and that's when things started turning up on his psyche report."

"Like what?"

"Well, like he's nuts. Doing push-ups and having the DIs screaming at him in boot camp was just a big game to him. Expert ratings with rifle, pistol, submachine, shotgun. He was top dog in hand-to-hand combat training, and qualified as an instructor. Being first in his platoon was easy. But then he had to learn to work together and cooperate in a Green Beret A-Team. Apparently he didn't like the game anymore and he didn't play nice. Apparently there was an altercation involving superior officers. People got hurt. His family connections got the charges dropped and he got an honorable discharge."

"Where is ol' Rog now?"

"No idea. But from what you've told me, I suspect the last place was strangling his girlfriend in Spain."

"How about his brother Ian."

"Him we have pinned down. He's in the family compound in Greenwich."

Bolan considered the quarry. "Greenwich is on the way to Iceland, isn't it?"

"Well—" Kurtzman shrugged "—in a roundabout sort of way."

Bolan punched keys to bring up a photograph of one of the world's wealthiest men. He was grinning confidently into the camera. His wavy hair was slightly gray at the temples, and he had the flat black eyes of a shark. "I think I want to go have a talk with Ian."

"Striker, he's a—"

"Just a friendly little talk. Jack an I are on a plane, but we'll need another plane, something beside a Lear when I get there. And we'll need a helicopter hot on the pad. A Farm special with all the trimmings."

Kurtzman raised an eyebrow. "Anything else?"

"Yeah." Bolan considered the photo of the Neville compound. "I'll e-mail you a list en route."

Above Connecticut, 17,000 feet

"TWO MINUTES, Mack!" Grimaldi soared the Cessna Skymaster across the skies of Connecticut and out over the woods surrounding Greenwich. Bolan checked his chute and equipment a last time and pulled his night-vision goggles down over his eyes.

"Ready."

Grimaldi grinned. "All right. I'm going to dump you and burn back to the airstrip to get to the chopper. It's hot and ready to go. But no matter what I do, there's going to be at least a twenty-minute turnaround time."

"Just sit on the pad and wait for my signal. We don't want to alarm the locals until it's time."

"Okay, we're still talking ten, fifteen minutes from your go. A lot can happen in that amount of time."

"I'll find something to do."

"I'm sure you will." Grimaldi checked his instruments. "We're over the target."

Far below the plane, the woods were dark except for the scattered tiny lights of the mansions of the extremely wealthy. Bolan shot Grimaldi the thumbs-up. "See ya."

Bolan opened his door and rolled out of the plane. He arched hard in the buffeting darkness and brought himself level as he plunged toward the woods below. Bolan checked the compass in his watch and oriented himself north by northeast as he pulled his ripcord. He felt the yank against his harness as the airfoil deployed. Bolan took his toggles and began to steer himself toward his target.

The Neville family was new wealth. The family had been worth millions for two generations, but it was Ian's ruthless corporate raiding in the late 1980s and his uncanny eye for choosing up-and-coming technology stocks that had brought him billionaire status. His compound was newly built, and clashed with the old-style mansions in the surrounding countryside. Ian had built himself a modern castle. The architecture was a vague cross between Spanish hacienda and Norman fortress. Bolan began a slow spiral over the compound, which was ugly. Bolan suspected the neighbors, miles away as they were, hated the sight of it. He suspected Ian was very proud of it. He also suspected Ian felt very secure in it. There was a light on in the great panoramic window of the uppermost level.

Ian was in for a rude awakening.

A helicopter pad was located on top of the five-story main building. It was as good a place as any to land. Bolan had no desire at all to deal with the dogs or the Uzi-armed guards patrolling the outer compound.

The helicopter pad suddenly loomed up, and he flared his chute and stalled it two feet above the ground. Bolan landed as light as a cat and clicked out of his harness. He thought about his entry. The door to the roof stairwell would be wired, and the vast window would leave him silhouetted against the light. Bolan considered the small, darkened window he had seen on his descent and fixed his rope to a ventilation housing. He clicked his rope into the D-ring of his harness and went to the edge of the roof. Positioning himself above the little window, he stepped out onto the wall and walked down until he was straddling the window. The glass was rippled and frosted, and he could see the vague outline of a plant behind it.

Bolan froze as the light within clicked on.

The glass was thick, but moments later he heard the unmistakable sound of a toilet being flushed. The light clicked off again and Bolan took a black box from his web gear. He extended a telescoping probe against the outline of the window and could detect no electrical activity. He glanced around quickly and drew his glass cutter. The thick, rippled glass was an ugly cut, and every crack and pinging noise sounded like Armageddon. Bolan attached the suction cup, pushed the pump button to create a vacuum, grasped the cup as he finished the cut, and the pane came out with a snicking sound. Bolan hung in his harness with his head and one shoulder in the window as he awkwardly lowered the pane of glass into a massive shower stall with four showerheads. He spent longer, even more awkward moments doing slow-motion yoga to worm his body and the gear strapped to him through the two-foot by one-and-a-half-foot window.

Bolan stood in the shower stall and unhooked himself from the harness. The Beretta 93-R came up in his hand as he went to the bathroom door and listened. Drum and bass dance music was playing on the other side. He could distinctly hear women giggling. Bolan pulled his night-vision goggles up on top of his brow and silently eased the door open.

The bedroom was palatial, dominated by a vast round bed in its center. There was a round mirror of exactly the same dimensions fixed to the ceiling above. Erotic woodcuts and paintings decorated the walls. A pair of naked women were on the bed. Both were blond and couldn't have been older than twenty. Their tanned figures were miracles of modern surgery. One girl was doing a line of coke on the other's stomach. The girl sprawled out on the bed couldn't stop giggling and her stomach jumped as the other girl giggled and tried to snort off of the rippling brown flesh.

"Hi."

The two women sat up abruptly. The muzzle of Bolan's silenced pistol precluded any outcry. Black-and-gray combat cosmetics broke up the outlines of Bolan's face so that his startling blue eyes and winning smile seemed to glow from the indistinct field of his camouflage.

"Either one of you seen Ian? I really need to talk to him."

The women stared at Bolan in horror.

"What are your names?"

One girl spoke in a tiny voice. "I'm Kelly. She's Courtney."

"Okay, Kelly. Where's Ian?"

Kelly's eyes went to the door. "He's in his office."

"The one with the big window?"

"Um." Kelly considered this. "Yes."

"What's he doing?"

"He's working."

"He'll be at it all night," Courtney volunteered.

"Is anybody with him?"

"No."

"Just us."

"Okay." Bolan nodded. "I need you both to turn around and lie on your stomachs."

Kelly and Courtney presented their hindquarters and lay on their stomachs unquestioningly. Bolan suspected the girls were used to taking those and other similar frequent kinds of requests. Bolan swiftly hog-tied both girls with plastic riot-cuffs and put a strip of duct tape over their mouths. He went to the bedroom door and listened, but the music interfered with whatever might be going on.

Bolan opened the door.

Ian Neville sat in a bathrobe behind a desk that was a vast arc of polished teak. He was staring intently into a twenty-two-inch monitor. Bolan walked up silently across the carpet. "Hey, Ian."

Ian jumped in his seat and cringed as Bolan loomed over him. "What the—"

"What's Rog doing with a bunch of tactical nukes in Finland?"

Every ounce of blood drained from Ian Neville's face. He looked as if he were about to throw up.

Bolan smiled. "Bingo."

"I…" Ian's face suddenly flushed. "I don't know what

you're—" His hand flashed toward his desk drawer. Bolan let him get his hand half inside before he slammed the drawer shut with his boot. Ian snarled and yanked out his mashed hand.

"Listen, I don't have time to screw around. You're going to tell me everything I want to know. Right now or—"

"Or what?" Ian's face was a mask of rage. "You're going to murder me? You kill me, you don't get shit."

Bolan glanced in the drawer and saw the gleam of a massive revolver. The soldier holstered the Beretta. "Ian—"

Ian Neville lunged up out of his chair and shot a serviceable two-finger strike at Bolan's eyes. The Executioner turned just enough to avoid it, and his own knife-hand chopped into Ian's arm. The blow would have dislocated the elbow, but Bolan threw it into the inside flesh of his adversary's bicep. Ian's face twisted as his femoral artery and nerve were momentarily crushed and the muscle was bruised down to the bone. His arm spasmed with a will of its own as he stumbled backward. He threw a kick at Bolan's groin, but he was already off balance. Bolan caught the leg with one hand and drove his elbow into Ian's thigh. The businessman howled as his quadricep muscles received the charley horse from hell. Bolan seized Ian by both lapels and hurled him across the desk, then walked around the desk and picked him up and threw him back again. Ian flew into a tumbling tangle with his chair and fell in a heap to the floor.

"Ian," Bolan said, his voice as cold as the grave, "I don't have time for sodium pentathol, and I don't have the time or the patience to kidnap you and take you to some experts on extracting information I know. So let's keep it simple. You're going to tell me everything I want to know, or I'm going to beat you until you die."

"Listen..." Ian leaned on a corner of the desk and levered himself up painfully. "You can't—"

Bolan pistoned his thumb into Ian's trachea. "I can and I will."

Ian made a noise like an agonized teakettle and collapsed, wheezing, to the carpet.

"Thirty nukes, Ian." Bolan yanked him up. Ian wobbled on his feet for the half second necessary to deliver a ridge hand strike. The side of the first knuckle on Bolan's forefinger compacted Ian's carotid arteries and nerves. Ian Neville folded and hit the floor again.

Bolan stood over Neville implacably. "Foreplay is over, Ian. The next thing I do, you'll still be feeling ten years from now when it rains."

Ian made a feeble attempt to kick Bolan in the shins, but the soldier stepped back from the blow. The businessman suddenly snarled and kicked toward the underside of his desk. Bolan heard a distinct clicking. An ugly smile split Ian's bleeding face as an alarm began going off throughout the compound. "Fuck you."

Bolan slammed the bottom of his fist onto the top of the billionaire's skull. Ian's eyes fluttered as he fainted and fell backward.

The alarm shrieked on. Ian was the wealthiest man in a filthy-rich community. Police would be immediately responding, but the men in the compound with Uzis and dogs were a much more immediate concern.

Bolan brought a finger to his earpiece. "Jack, I need you."

"Inbound! Ten minutes, Striker!"

Bolan went behind Ian's desk and quickly discovered the security suite. He punched a button and the second monitor on the desk split into ten screens revealing the views of security cameras throughout the house. Several very large and powerful looking men with very large and powerful handguns were charging down a hallway. Bolan rose and went to the twin oak doors to the vast personal office and threw the bolts.

He jumped to one side as bullets began smashing against the doors, went circuitously to the desk and stood on it. If he stood on tiptoe, he could just reach the ceiling. Bolan took out a coil of flexible charge and pulled away the adhesive strip. He pressed the length of triangular charge in a circle in the ceiling and pushed in a detonator pin. He jumped off the desk as bullets began penetrating the beleaguered door and smashed against the vast arc of the glass window.

Bolan took a small black box from his web gear, pushed the arming button and then the detonator. A halo of yellow fire hissed and whip-cracked against the ceiling. Soundproofing and plaster fell in a shower, followed by a circular section of ceiling.

Ian Neville pushed himself up to one knee and reeled like a drunk. "You...son of a—"

"Ian, we'll talk again." Bolan swung the top of his boot into

Ian's jaw. The blow nearly stood the billionaire on his feet only to drop him back down in an unconscious sprawl.

Bolan leaped atop the desk again and jumped upward to grab the heavy reinforcing beams of the main ceiling. He did a pull-up and wedged himself into the crawlspace. He reached awkwardly into his web gear and pressed the other half of his flexible charge in a matching hoop above the first hole.

Beneath him the double doors smashed open and gunfire raked the room. Bolan pushed the detonator and grimaced at the crack of the close-range explosion. The circular section of roofing sagged, and he grabbed a jagged edge and heaved. The section of gravel, tar and wood fell like a collapsing coin into the room below. Gunfire began to rip up into the ceiling a few feet away. The stars shone above the smoking hole Bolan had cut in the roof. The Executioner drew a grenade from his belt and pulled the pin. The safety lever pinged away as he dropped the bomb into the room below. The grenade snapped and broke apart into subbomblets that skipped and skidded across the carpet.

There were several shouts of alarm. "Look out! Gren—" The outcry was cut off by the sudden sound of a bear being impaled. It was joined by a second and a third. Adamsite gas was nasty stuff. It had other more colorful nicknames, like nausea or vomit gas. It affected the eyes and mucus membranes just like tear gas. It also had the more spectacular effect of inducing projectile vomiting and spasms of the bowels.

The gunmen below were violently excreting out of every orifice as if they were the grand finale of a gastrointestinal Fourth of July. Bolan could feel the heat of the room rushing up against his face from the sudden updraft and swiftly clambered up onto the roof.

"Jack?"

"Three minutes!"

Bolan scooped up his chute and rolled it. Below him a crashing noise sounded as a filing cabinet went flying through the vast window. Bolan grimaced. Some brave soul had had the wherewithal to hold his breath and smash out the window to clear the room of gas.

"Jack."

Bolan crouched as automatic weapons snarled into life from the outer compound and began hammering at the edges of the roof.

"One minute!"

"Be advised, LZ is hot. Lighting beacon." Bolan flipped the switch of what looked like an ocean life-vest's strobe. The light began clicking, but to the eye, nothing happened. The Forward Looking Infrared Radar on Grimaldi's Black Hawk helicopter would see flashbulbs going off four times a second in the infrared spectrum.

"I have you, Striker! Affirmative on LZ!"

Rotors hammered the sky in the distance. Bullets ripped up into the sky through the hole in the roof. Bolan pulled a second grenade from his belt and lobbed it into the circle of light he had cut in the ceiling. Thunder boomed and white light erupted upward as the Thunderflash stun grenade sent forth its deafening blast and blinding magnesium flash.

Grimaldi swept down upon the roof like a vengeful black dragonfly. Yellow flashes sparked from the fuselage as bullets struck the armored panels. Bolan broke into a run and leaped through the sliding door of the cabin as JG banked the helicopter. "Hang on!" Grimaldi shouted from the cockpit.

Bolan hung on as the Black Hawk roared into emergency war power and clawed at the sky with its rotors. He held on until the bird was level, then made his way forward to the copilot's seat. Grimaldi grinned as the compound became little more than a splash of light in the distance. "What did you get?"

Bolan remembered the sick look on Ian Neville's face when he had mentioned Ian's brother Roger and the nukes. "I got confirmation."

16

Aboard the Heather

"Rog, we got violated."

Roger looked at his brother's bruised face across the link. Gale force winds hammered the offshore rig. "How bad?"

"He knew about the nukes. He knew about me and you, and Finland."

"Did he mention Iceland?"

"Well...no."

Roger nodded. "So what exactly did you tell him?"

"Nothing. He was beating the crap out me when I hit the alarm."

"How many of them were there?"

Ian's brow furrowed. "Just the one guy who showed up in my bedroom, and at least one guy who had to have been piloting the helicopter." Ian's eyes opened slightly. "What do you think?"

"I think this guy is operating without the consent of the authorities or he's an operator who works only for the highest authority."

"So, what does that mean?"

"How extensive are your injuries, Ian?"

"They hurt like hell, but—"

"But there's barely a mark on you, and no significant damage." Roger shook his head. "It wasn't a snatch, it wasn't even a real interrogation. It was a probe, and he was hoping that with the judicious application of sudden surprise, shock and pain you'd spill something."

"So, we're alright, then."

"No, I think this asshole has had his worst suspicions confirmed." A feral smile split Roger's face. "But remember, Ian. Even if this guy is working for the President of the United States, he still doesn't have anything on us. You've had dinner with the President of the United States. You've contributed a hell of a lot of money to his election campaign, and he's depending on you for the next one, and your current backing of his policies. He won't allow jackshit to happen to you without a concrete proof. The asshole who paid you a visit? He's probably operating in a 'don't ask, don't tell mode,' expendable, and kept at arm's length."

"So what do we do?"

"We finish what we've started."

"And if he shows up in Iceland?"

"Why, we sic Shang on him." Roger's smile turned ugly. "And while those two assholes play King of the Sandbox...you and me? Bro, we take the whole playground."

Keflavik Naval Air Station, Iceland

"JESUS."

Bolan raised an eyebrow. It was unusual to see Jack Grimaldi tense on the stick, but landing the Learjet on the iced-over airfield in the buffeting winds had been a stomach-dropping feat of flying even for the superpilot from Stony Man Farm. It had required special military permission to land at the air base. All other traffic was grounded as the North Sea storm hammered the island nation with arctic fury. The ground controller had been unamused when official sanction to void all safety guidelines had been given to his mysterious visitors. He had followed his orders, but only after radioing them that it was their funeral, and he took no responsibility for their lives or their aircraft.

Grimaldi gave a shaky grin. "That was a fun one."

Bolan forced himself to relax and to let his stomach return to normal as Grimaldi taxied the jet toward the arc of the only open and lit aircraft shelter on the base. A figure wearing the uniform of a naval officer stood inside, flanked by a pair of armed Marines. The officer punched the button on the wall to close the doors as the jet came to rest within. The officer and his Marines took off bright orange ear protectors as the aircraft powered down.

"We're in trouble," Grimaldi commented as he shut off the engine and rose from the cockpit.

He and Bolan clambered out. The officer wore the insignia of a full Navy captain. He was more than likely in command of the entire station. He wasn't smiling. "That was the most damn fool thing I've seen in twenty-five years in the Navy."

Bolan smiled. "Pleased to meet you, Captain, and thank you for allowing us to use your base. Particularly on such short notice and under these conditions."

"Allow has nothing to do with it." The captain was a tall man with a jaw like an anvil. That jaw was thrust out with ill-concealed outrage. "What are you? Spooks? Special Ops?"

"You might say I'm looking into something."

The captain's eyebrows drew down dangerously. "Is this an investigation?"

"Of a sorts." Bolan jerked his head toward Grimaldi. "He does most of the flying."

The captain stared at JG distractedly. "That was an impressive landing...in a psychotic sort of way."

Grimaldi was delighted. "Thanks!"

"Yes. Well." The captain turned back to Bolan. "I'm informed I am to offer you every courtesy and whatever resources you may require." There was a pregnant pause. "So just what is it I can do for you?"

"Well, how about answering a few questions?"

The captain's face turned to stone. "Like what?"

"Where can a guy get decent Chinese takeout around here?"

The Jade Palace Restaurant,
Reykjavik, Iceland

THE MONGOLIAN lamb wasn't bad.

Bolan and Grimaldi sat at a table slurping dan dan mein noodles and drinking Tsing-Tao beer. Bolan had had better in Heilongjiang, but for a noodle house in Iceland, it wasn't bad at all. The restaurant was surprisingly crowded despite the weather, and more tables than not were filled with gigantic Viking descendants awkwardly wielding chopsticks and having passionate conversations over the sound of piped-in bebop jazz. Some U.S. naval pilots were getting drunk and ogling the local talent. Grimaldi sipped his beer and peered at the group of People's Republic of China's geothermal research team members over the rim of his mug. "How do you want to play it? Shall we just show them a picture of Shang and watch their expressions?"

The seven Chinese were sitting at a table by the wall eating and talking quietly among themselves. Bolan's eyes narrowed as he looked at the way they sat and the physiques beneath their sweaters. If at least half of them weren't PRC special purpose troops, Bolan would eat his snow boots. "No. Let's just go introduce ourselves."

"God, I love this stuff." Grimaldi followed as Bolan made his way across the restaurant.

The Chinese looked up from their bowls of noodles at their approach. Bolan waved and smiled. "Hi! I'm Mike Belasko, with the National Geographic Geothermal Survey Project. Mind if I sit down?"

The Chinese stared up at him unblinkingly. They looked at one another silently for a moment, then their spokesman stood slowly from his chair and looked Bolan in the eye.

"Yes."

"Really? Thanks!" Bolan hooked a chair over with his toe and spun it around so that he faced the chairback as he sat down. "Listen, you know there are some absolutely fascinating tectonal amalagous anomalies in the ferrous substratus in the volcanic districts on this island. If you're doing geothermal pre-Babylonian—"

"You must leave." The Chinese hadn't sat down. He blinked once. "Now."

"But the fragometric condensation—"

"Now!" The Chinese around the table rose as a unit.

"Well, there's no need to get sore about it." Bolan rose and stumbled backward with a shocked and hurt look on his face.

Grimaldi patted him on the back as if telling him it was all right. The pilot grinned.

"Pre-Babylonian fragometric condensation?"

Bolan shrugged. "Yeah, well, you know."

"And what did we learn from that little exercise?"

Bolan sat and went back to attacking his noodles and lamb. "You tell me."

"Well, by my count, at least two of those boys were packing substantial heat."

"I counted four. What else?"

"Even assuming a language barrier, those guys aren't scientists. The first thing tech types from Communist countries want to do when they slip the leash and get off the farm is yam with their foreign counterparts."

Bolan nodded.

Grimaldi wolfed down an impossible chopstick load of noodles. "So now what do we do?"

"Now we go pay them a visit."

Mount Hekla, Iceland

BOLAN SHOVED the Sno-Cat up the slope in near-whiteout conditions. The gears ground and the cube-shaped cabin rocked on its chassis as the wind slammed into it and its treads crunched over the ice and lava. Grimaldi surfed the Internet.

"Mack, did you know that Iceland has over two dozen active volcanoes and averages two eruptions per decade?"

"No, I didn't know that."

"It says here that in the eighteenth century Mount Lakagigar blew its top and laid out more than three cubic miles of lava on the ground. Thousands of people and farm animals were gassed to death by the fumes and so much ash was produced that the sky over the island was darkened for a month and the crops all failed. More than a third of Iceland's population died."

Bolan kept one eye on the GPS and one eye on the storm raging outside. "I didn't know that, either."

Grimaldi closed the laptop. "Why do the Chinese want to devastate Iceland?"

"I don't know. The Bear says that using nukes to detonate violent volcanic ejection eruptions is possible."

"Yeah, but so what? Even if you did it there would be massive airlifts of food and supplies in from the rest of the world. It isn't like the Chinese could walk in and buy Iceland like a fire sale."

"No, that's not what they want."

"So, what do they want?"

Bolan checked his GPS one more time and brought the Sno-Cat to a halt. "I'm going to go find out." Bolan pulled his mask and goggles over his face and stepped out into the storm.

17

Mount Hekla Station, Operation Fire God

"The Americans are here."

Shang glanced up as he poured himself a cup of tea and looked over at Communication Specialist Tsen. "How soon?"

"They expect to arrive here at Hekla Station within the hour."

"Very well. Acknowledge and tell them they are expected." Shang sipped tea. Expected, but certainly not wanted. There was no need for them to be here, other than they didn't trust him. Under most circumstances Shang had to admit such suspicion might be well warranted. However, it was most likely that the idiot American wanted to see that their money was being well spent and that his useless brother wanted to stand around and act like a cowboy during the final phase of the operation. Shang focused his breathing in his belly. He had spent a great deal of internal strength generating heat in his body and limbs while he had overseen the final diagnostic checks out in the alternately freezing rain and snow. Now that he was back in the command shack and released the effort, he found himself feeling weak and shaky.

"Possible contact!" Lieutenant Rong Lei looked up from the security suite. Her eyes flicked across her screen intently. Shang glowered at her over his teacup. The storm was playing hell with their security net. The flurrying snow left both the infrared laser net and the infrared imagers next to useless. Worse than useless, because they kept giving off the alarm as the shifting wind and snow threw ghost images across the screens and broke the laser beams of the net. They had been getting phantom contacts nearly every hour on the hour for the past twenty-four hours.

Shang had just managed to get warm. He didn't want to leave his place beside the potbellied stove, and he would be damned if he was going to troop outside again to go looking for the wind in a snowstorm. Rong read Shang's gaze and adjusted her report. "Possible *significant* contact."

Shang considered beating her. "What kind of contact could possibly be significant in this storm?"

"Momentary contact, fleeting." Rong raised an eyebrow. "But on the magnetometers."

Shang lowered his teacup. Unless it was raining iron ingots, which wouldn't have surprised Shang at this point, there was very little way he could see that the storm could give them phantom magnetic metal ground contacts. Shang's eyes hooded like a hawk's. Someone was out there. They had breached the security perimeter, and they were packing.

"Activate the active countermeasure suite." Shang raised his tea again and finished it. "Assemble my team."

SOMEONE WAS OUT THERE.

Bolan knelt behind a sharp blade of lava and peered into the howling white surrounding him. Grimaldi spoke in his earpiece. "What have you got?"

"Possible contact." Bolan slid back along the lava blade and into a cleft in the rocks. A pair of figures seemed to materialize out of the whipping snow. Both wore full arctic suits with goggles and masks. Both appeared to be carrying AK-47 rifles with optical sights. "Definite contact. Two hostiles, armed."

"Okay, I'm going to go requisition a gunship from the nice captain and smoke these guys."

"The captain won't allow it. Neither will the President."

"So we tell the Icelandic government and sic the Vikings on them."

"Iceland has no armed forces, and what they'll mount is an

investigation, not an air strike. The Chinese will stall and clean up the evidence."

"Where the hell can they get rid of thirty tactical and their support equipment on short notice?"

"How many United Nations weapons inspectors do you know who can withstand ten thousand degrees."

"Oh." The line was silent for a moment. "I'd forgotten about the incinerator they're parked next to."

"Yeah, and for that matter we have no proof the nukes are even here yet."

"So what are you going to do?"

Bolan considered. "My contacts aren't moving. It looks like they're throwing a cordon around whatever construction they've been up to on the side of the mountain. I think I've been detected somehow."

"So?"

"So, it looks like they're waiting for me to make an attempt to go look at their grand construction."

"And you're going to?"

Bolan carefully set his SR-25 rifle and his Desert Eagle pistol deeper into a dry part of the cleft. He removed his grenades, combat knife and the smaller knife in his boot, as well. "Nah, rather than making an end run around these guys, I think I'll just go knock on the front door."

LIEUTENANT RONG'S eyes went wide.

The door to the shack had opened unexpectedly. No recognition signal had been given, and the guard at the door wasn't present. An American stood in the door, but he wasn't one of the Americans she was expecting. The man's startling blue eyes stared at her in a friendly fashion. Rong's personal issue AK-47 had been racked by the door. The spoon shape of its black muzzle now stared at her from the big man's hands with much less warmth. As the man stepped into the shack and closed the door behind him, Rong caught a glimpse of the door guard lying in the snow unmoving. The American's eyes flicked up at the window in the far wall of the shack that faced the mount.

"What are you guys doing up there, anyway?"

Rong and Tsen stared at each other a moment in appalled horror.

Bolan looked at Rong. "You speak English?"

Rong simply stared.

He looked at Tsen. "How about you?"

Tsen shook his head slowly.

The soldier flicked off the AK-47's safety and brought the weapon to his shoulder. "Then you two are useless to me."

"We speak English!" Tsen shouted. Rong scowled at his cowardice, but she was secretly relieved.

Bolan kept his eyes on her. "I want you to download every bit of data on the computer over there and give me every disk, zip drive or other storage device you have. Now."

Tsen's hand flashed for the pistol in his desk drawer. The big American was across the shack in a stride. He whipped the AK-47's butt beneath the communication officer's jaw and lifted him out of his chair, dropping him, unconscious, to the floor. Rong's hand had barely touched her own pistol when the cold muzzle of the AK-47 was pressed into her temple. "One last chance. Then I pop your head like a cyst. I really want you to get this right."

Rong tried to stop herself from shaking but couldn't. "The computer is over there."

"Yes," the big man agreed. "It appears to be."

"I need to move to get to it."

The muzzle pressed painfully into her temple. "Go right ahead."

Rong went over to the computer. The muzzle of the AK-47 pressed into the back of her head as she did so. "I do not have all the command codes."

"Okay, who does?"

"Tsen." Rong looked at her unconscious colleague. "And..." Her voice trailed off.

"And Shang?"

Rong's belly clenched as the entire operation unraveled before her eyes.

Bolan's gaze was a force onto itself as his eyes burned into her. "I know you intend to induce an eruption in Mount Hekla, but why do you need thirty nukes to do it?"

Rong's face went blank for a moment before she could regain her composure. "Thirty? I..."

The big man's blue eyes narrowed to slits. Deep in Rong's belly she knew that there was something wrong. Even more horribly wrong than the intruder taking the command shack. "I...I will need to—"

"What the fuck!"

Bolan turned as icy wind blasted into the command shack. Roger Neville's massive physique filled the doorway. He was reaching under his parka. The Executioner brought around the muzzle of the AK-47 and held the trigger down on full auto. The burst walked up Roger's belly and chest and hammered him back out the door. He fell into the men behind him who shouted in alarm and began drawing pistols. Rong stared in shock as he put a burst into them and took himself out of the line of sight of the door. Alarms began going off in the camp. Bolan turned and put a burst through the far window of the shack. Glass shattered and he blurred into a run.

The big man dived through the window and out into the night.

Roger Neville lurched back into the command shack. Five holes had been punched into his parka but other than looking a little pale he seemed all right. He shouted at his men as he drew a pistol. "Sven! You stay with me! The rest of you! Go! Go! Go!" His personal killers dispersed into the night after the stranger. Roger and his bodyguard Sven descended on Rong. "What the hell is happening here!"

Rong couldn't stop shaking. "We had a contact on the security suite. On the perimeter. Near the construction. Shang and a team are investigating. The other man, the man who shot you, he just suddenly appeared."

"What did he want?"

Rong swallowed with difficulty. "I do not understand. He wanted to know what we were doing with thirty tactical weapons." Her brow wrinkled. "But we only have six."

Roger's rage left his face. He stared at her for long moments. "Have you contacted Shang?"

"No, he has probably only just heard the camp alarms."

Roger looked at Tsen as he lay bleeding and unconscious on the floor. "What about him? Did he have any part in the interrogation?"

"No, Tsen went for his pistol. The stranger struck him down with his rifle butt. Then the stranger—"

"Good." Roger flicked the safety off of his .40-caliber Jericho pistol and shot Rong between the eyes. She toppled from her chair as he walked over to the unconscious Tsen. Roger knelt and picked up the spent brass shell casing his gun had ejected and put it into his pocket. "Hey, Sven."

The Norwegian was even more massive than Roger. He surveyed the carnage impassively. *"Ja?"*

"Get Shang on the line. And throw some cold water on this guy."

BOLAN NAVIGATED by instinct as he plunged through the storm. He had shed all of his weapons to get past the magnetometers within the camp. Getting past the wire fence and the guards had been simple after that. However, the equation always remained the same.

Getting in was always easier than getting out.

Bolan tossed away his purloined AK-47 with a slight pang of loss as he spoke into his mask's radio unit. "Jack, we have confirmation of nukes, but not their whereabouts. Contact with Roger Neville. He's down but kill not confirmed. I—" Bolan paused at the sound of shots coming from the command shack and then kept running. "Something's wrong. When I mentioned thirty nukes I got a real funny look. I just heard shots from the shack."

"Funny? Funny how?"

Bolan crouched behind a snow tractor as armed men blundered past toward the shack. "Funny as if the math was wrong."

"What do your instincts tell you?"

"I'm thinking the Neville brothers are running a sweep around the Chinese. I think the Chinese think they're using Roger and Ian as tools, but that it's really the other way around." Bolan rose. He felt as though he was running in slow motion against the wind and the snow. He ran to another snow tractor that was parked near the fence. He leaped onto its treads and clambered up on top of the cab. The wind tried to push him off his perch. Sparks flew as a bullet struck the top of the cab. Bolan went with the wind and leaped over the fence. The porous rock of the lava field reached up and smashed into him as he hit the ground. He rose heavily and kept the snow tractor between himself and the gunman as he plunged on. "They know I've hit the camp, I'm going to double back and—"

"Uh, hold on a minute, Striker." Grimaldi's voice tightened. "I have company."

"SHIT!" Jack Grimaldi rammed the Sno-Cat's left tread into reverse and spun the vehicle around as bullets struck the cab. Men in white arctic suits with rifles were swarming him. "Striker! I've got gunners coming out of the woodwork!"

"Extract!"

"I'm trying!" Grimaldi slammed the Sno-Cat forward and two men with rifles leaped out of the way. They tracked his slow moving vehicle and bullet strikes pocked the windows. The Stony Man pilot's face split into a snarl as cold air poured into the cabin. He was sitting in a glass goldfish bowl, and no one had thought to make the panoramic windows bulletproof. He suddenly found himself confronted by a pair of snowmobiles parked in a vee formation to block the path. He took spiteful pleasure in crushing them beneath the Sno-Cat's treads. A bullet punched through his window and struck his armor, followed by a second.

He kicked out the crumpling glass panel in front of him. Wind and snow blasted into his face. He shoved the throttle full-forward and began spraying the landscape in front of him with bullets from his MAC-10 machine pistol.

"Jack! What is your status?"

"FUBAR!" the pilot roared. He glanced down as something stung him in the leg. There was a ragged hole the size of a dime in the white pant leg of his arctic weather suit. The hole almost instantly turned red and began to stain in a spreading circle.

"I'm hit." Grimaldi burned off the rest of his magazine blindly in the general direction of his assailant.

"I—" Grimaldi started as the chassis rocked and a human appeared on the vehicle's driver's-side stepladder. The massive figure seized the door handle and ripped the door off its hinges. The pilot swung the empty weapon at the masked and hooded figure's head. His assailant caught the weapon and ripped it out of his hands. The figure hung in the door frame and pulled of its mask.

"Jack!" Bolan was shouting across the com link. "Jack!"

Grimaldi stared into the face of Yun Chung Shang, who looked at him unblinkingly. "Stop the vehicle."

Grimaldi considered the spare rifle between the seats. Shang's eyes looked at the weapon, as well. The pilot moved his hand very slowly to the control panel and killed the Sno-Cat's engine.

"You must be Shang."

Shang stared at Grimaldi noncommittally.

Grimaldi's fist was a blur. It gave him immense satisfaction that it buried itself in Shang's trachea before Shang could block. It didn't occur to him that Shang had made no attempt to block. "Striker! I am POW! Consider me compro—"

Jack Grimaldi had no memory of the next thing that happened.

18

"Well, look what the cat dragged in." Roger Neville smiled unpleasantly at Grimaldi as he was dragged into the shack and hurled to the floor by Shang. Neville shook his head. "You are truly fucked."

Shang dispensed the pleasantries. "Stand up."

Grimaldi pushed himself up and tottered on his wounded leg.

"You will tell us everything we wish to know. I will begin with simple blows and progress to nerve strikes. The only way you could possibly hurt me would be with a blow directed to my eyes or my testicles. I will become very angry with you should you attempt such a—"

The Stony Man pilot's good leg blurred upward in savate's "purring kick." It was a nearly perfect attack when delivered by an expert. There was no telegraphing bend of the knee or hip shift. The leg simply swung upward in a straight line. The blow cracked into Shang's jaw and lifted his chin a scant inch. Grimaldi had already recoiled and was sending his foot up between Shang's legs.

Shang caught the pilot's shin in one hand and grabbed the front of his parka with the other. The command shack shook on its foundations as Shang pressed his adversary over his head and hurled him across the room and into the wall. Shang glanced at

Neville. "This one was driving a snow tractor when I caught him. I believe he inserted the one who shot you and was waiting to extract his comrade."

"So we still have at least one unaccounted for." Neville examined the pilot's bloodied, bruised and semiconscious form. "Did this one get off a message?"

Shang scowled. "I believe so."

"Two men, one Sno-Cat. His pal is running around out in the storm. If I were him, I'd double back again. Pick up a weapon and maybe attack the construction site this time."

Shang didn't like to admit it, but the American's sense of strategy agreed with his own. "Yes. That is what I would do. However my men have the site cordoned off. If he attempts to penetrate the perimeter, he will be caught in a crossfire."

"You have some heavy weapons within the site?"

"Yes."

Roger looked at his map. "What if he tried to come down from higher up the mount?"

Shang's eyes slitted. "He would have to negotiate steep cliffs in icy, whiteout conditions. It would be impossible."

Roger grinned. "Could you do it?"

Shang didn't blink. "I could."

Roger's grin widened. "Don't we have the ridgeline rigged in case we need to make an emergency extraction."

"We do."

"Is everything already in place?"

"I had intended to run a final check."

Roger shrugged uncaringly. "Well, it's your call."

Shang turned to Tsen. The communications officer sat holding his swollen jaw. "Tsen."

"Yes, sir?"

"Blow the ridgeline."

Tsen flipped up a plastic shield on the security suite and exposed a red button. He pumped the button eight times, and eight tiny green lights went red.

Roger grinned at Shang as the command shack shuddered with each thunderclap.

BOLAN OPENED his eyes.

He felt warm and knew instinctively that was a bad sign. He was lying facedown in the snow. He remembered working his way up the ridge to get above whatever the enemy had cordoned off and vaguely remembered the world coming to an end. He pushed himself to his hands and knees with a groan. His mask and goggles were gone; his parka and gloves were shredded.

If he didn't start moving, he would freeze to death.

Bolan lurched to his feet, then crouched as he caught movement in the storm. The ghostly silhouette of a man in snow camouflage became more distinct. The man was wearing goggles and carrying an AK-47 with an optical sight. He was walking through the rubble in an obvious search pattern. The explosives used to shatter the ridgeline had incurred some interesting tactical effects. Bolan reached down and wrapped his hand around a ten-inch shard of obsidian. The length of blackish green volcanic glass was vaguely shaped like a teardrop.

Bolan rose as the assassin passed his position and buried the obsidian blade in the side of his neck. The killer jerked and his rifle burned off its magazine on full-auto. The Executioner stabbed the knife downward again and blood spurted from behind the snow mask. The man fell and Bolan stumbled backward. The man was gone. The lava and snow he had been standing on had crumbled, and he had disappeared into an ancient bubble formed by lava. Bolan stared down into the dark hole and mourned the loss of the rifle. He was weaponless, exhausted, Grimaldi was captured, and his communication gear was ruined. Conditions were nearly blind now, come nightfall they'd be lethal. Bolan considered the map of the area he had examined before he and Grimaldi had begun their probe. There was a chance. It was about ten miles away, but there was a chance.

The only way Bolan was getting out of here was to walk.

SHANG DRANK tea. Roger Neville drank Gatorade from his canteen. "It's been hours, Shang. He's buried and dead, and if he's not, he will be by nightfall. He has no shelter, no food, no heat. He's an ice cube."

Shang had to agree. It would be dark soon, and he needed to bring his men in. He turned to Tsen. "Have the men report in."

Tsen began speaking into his microphone in Mandarin. He made a mental tally as each man checked in and reported what little information they had. It was cold. The ridge was gone. There was nothing out there but ice, rubble and the killing wind. Tsen raised an eyebrow as his numbers didn't tally.

Shang read his expression. "What is it?"

"We are missing one." Tsen ran down his checklist. "Erming!" Tsen clicked his send button. "Erming! Report! Erming!"

Shang's massive bulk rose from his chair "Erming is dead."

Roger scowled. "Okay, so the bastard is still out there. It's getting late, he's still dead out there. His only choice is to surrender or try to sneak into the camp. Either way, we own him."

Shang stared into the distance long and hard. The enemy wouldn't be stupid enough to sneak back into the camp. Nor would he be stupid enough to wait around outside and freeze to death in the night. "Tsen, are their any known caves within a dozen kilometers of our position?"

Tsen frowned. "There are many little ones, and hollow lava tubes, but none of them are large or mapped, and I do not believe any of them would provide adequate shelter against the storm without additional equipment and a heat source."

"Hot springs?"

Tsen checked his map. "None that I know of or are mapped."

Shang shook his head. The enemy was out there. He knew it. "Anything?"

Tsen flipped his map over to a larger overview of the Icelandic park area surrounding the volcano. "There is a hunting lodge, but it is roughly fifteen kilometers away. In this weather, in the dark, it would be a death march to—"

Shang's teacup shattered as he closed his fist. "Bring the men in and have them reassemble." The Chinese glared over at Roger. "Get your men ready, as well."

BOLAN'S BLOODY FIST crashed through the glass pane in the door. His hand was a numb lump as he reached in and fumbled for the bolt. It took him several exhausted tries until he finally shot it back and fell into the lodge. The lodge was closed until hunting season and the interior was like an icebox, but at least it was out of the killing wind. Bolan lay in the dark on the frozen carpet and shook for long moments. He had nearly walked past the lodge in the howling darkness. Dead reckoning and dumb luck had been equal partners in allowing him to stumble face-first into the dark bulk of the lodge rather than walk past. Bolan reached into the ragged remains of his web gear and pulled out a lightstick. He snapped it in the middle and cold, greenish-yellow light spilled outward into the lodge.

The interior was roomy with three couches arranged to face a large, stone fireplace. The heads of reindeer and musk ox lined the walls along with framed photos of hundreds of successful hunts. Another wall was dominated by stuffed and posed ptarmigans and ducks. Bolan shambled toward a door and found himself in a kitchen. He closed the door and flicked the light switch, but either the storm had knocked out the power or more likely the generator was turned off. Bolan rummaged through the shelves and found little. He looked in the cupboard and was rewarded with four cans and a bottle of Slivovitz brandy. Bolan tucked the bottle under his arm and examined a can. There was a cartoon of a dog on the label, and Icelandic runes covered the rest of it. Dog food. Bolan turned it over and smiled at what he found. In a gold circle there was a picture of a reindeer and beneath it lettering he understood— 100%! Bolan found a can opener and spent long moments sitting on the floor fumbling with disobedient fingers opening the can.

Bolan closed his eyes in appreciation as he shoved two fingerfulls of Icelandic "100%" pure reindeer meat into his mouth. It was probably "100%" reindeer lips, antlers and intestines and was swimming in its own slimy gravy, but Bolan didn't care. It was meat and it filled his belly. His belly blossomed with warmth as he cracked the bottle and poured back a shot of the dry, fiery liquor. Bolan wolfed dog food and drank plum brandy and felt like the king of the world. He finished the can and shoved the other three into the empty magazine pouches of his web gear. He felt shaky as he stood, but he felt significantly better.

The soldier began systematically ransacking the lodge for anything of use. There was precious little. He liberated a twelve-inch boning knife from the kitchen and abandoned his chunk of obsidian. The polished oak rifle cabinets were lined with green velvet but totally absent of rifles. In a closet he found the bonanza of wool hunting pants, an immensely thick and heavy wool sweater, reindeer gloves lined with fur and a reindeer vest. Bolan found a blue wool cap and pulled it over his head. He put on two shirts and the sweater over it and then strapped on his armor and web gear. He threw away the remnants of his shredded parka and put on a rain slicker, making a poncho out of a wool blanket. For the first time in twelve hours Bolan began to feel warm. He wadded a pair of scarves around his neck and finished his recon. He found the generator in a half basement with two jerricans of gas.

In a back storeroom he found the rifle.

The room was littered with a huge pile of reindeer antlers. There was also a workbench with numerous tools and a saw, and antler horn dust littered the floor. The rifle hung on a wooden rack on the walls. On a little shelf beneath it were a few boxes of ammo. The rifle was a Swedish model 1894 cavalry carbine, and was only an inch over three feet long. Someone had long ago soldered on a makeshift scope mount and a Russian PU 4X scope had been bastarded on top of it. The ancient wood was battered and dinged and came all the way to the muzzle of the rifle. The barrel was a gleaming gunmetal blue that didn't match the bolt. Someone had rebarreled it recently. Bolan took down an ancient-looking cardboard box of ammo and examined a round by his lightstick. Its point gleamed golden in the light. Bolan cocked an eyebrow. The round was Remington bronze-point in 6.5 mm Swedish Mauser.

Bolan gazed long and hard at his new armament. Remington had stopped making bronze-point ammunition forty years ago. The WWII-vintage Russian scope could easily be sixty years old. The rifle itself could well be over a hundred. Bolan eyed the vast tangle of antlers and ox horns filling the back of the storeroom from floor to ceiling.

The ancient cavalry carbine might look like a sad joke, but apparently the old girl could still go.

Bolan examined five large, decrepit-looking crates beneath the table. They were marked Remington 1000. He fumbled through each crate and box after box of spent shell casings. It appeared that someone had bought five thousand rounds decades ago and been working his way through it ever since. Bolan stood and took the two boxes off the shelves. One was empty. One was half full. Thirty rounds. Bolan opened the action, pushed five rounds into the magazine and threw the bolt closed. He went on with his search and found two more gray wool blankets, a pair of old-fashioned, lighter-fluid hand warmers, a lighter and fluid, a flare gun with three shells and an umbrella. Bolan rolled, tied and stashed his supplies about himself swiftly.

The Executioner looked up at the distant sound of engines snarling over the storm. He smiled coldly and ran to the generator room.

19

Shang leveled his Dragunov rifle. Six snowmobiles and three snow tractors ringed the lodge. In the glare of their headlights he could see the black hole in the door where a glass pane had been smashed in. "He's been here."

Roger and Sven stood beside Shang. Roger carried his AI Lapua Super Magnum rifle. Sven carried a Dragunov much like Shang's. Roger stared at the door and the darkened windows of the lodge. "Burn it."

"That might attract attention."

"In forty-eight hours half of Iceland will be burning. No one is going to care about one fucking hunting lo— Jesus!"

A crack sounded above the howl of the storm and Sven sagged and fell against a snowmobile. Roger and Shang dropped. "Goddamn it! Where did he get a rifle?"

Shang rolled his eyes. "It *is* a hunting lodge."

Roger glowered from behind his snow mask. "He shot Sven. Sven's the largest man we have." He looked at Shang meaningfully. "I bet he thought Sven was you."

Shang glared.

Roger scanned the lodge from behind the snowmobile. "So where is he?"

"I saw no muzzle-flash. If he is in the lodge he—"

The rifle cracked again and one of Shang's men crumpled backward from his cover behind the tread of one of the Sno-Cats.

"He can see us because of our headlights!"

"No! All he can see is glare, he— Yes!" Shang rolled around the snowmobile. "He is not in the lodge! He is outside!" Shang roared into his microphone. "Cut all lights! Cut all lights! Cut—"

The rifle cracked again. The head of a man two yards away rocked back as he reached up to kill the lights of his snowmobile. He put a hand to his forehead and then slumped. Steam rose from a hole between his goggles. The lights of the snowmobiles and tractors blinked out and the landscape became one of howling darkness. Shang and Roger tracked their night-vision scopes across the landscape behind them. All was snow-covered humps, blades of rock and broken terrain.

Both men whirled at a thumping noise. Their night-vision scopes nearly went white as a meteor seemed to speed directly at them. They rolled away as the flare bounced off the snowmobile. One of Shang's men rose to shoot and promptly sat back down again as the rifle in the dark fired. A second later he slumped over and lay still.

The flare lay guttering in the snow and went out.

"Fuck him," Roger growled.

Shang lay in the snow with the patience of a stone. The flat trajectory of the flare put the American somewhere in the terrain slightly ahead of their left flank. Shang played his night-vision scope in an arc. "I do not believe he has night-vision equipment or Erming's rifle. I do not recognize the firing signature of his weapon. I believe he has a hunting rifle. He cannot see us, and his next flare will give away his position."

Roger's voice dripped scorn. "So, we just sit out here and freeze our asses off until all of us die? Nice plan."

"No. He cannot see us. We take the lodge."

Roger paused. "The lodge?"

"Yes, the large dwelling over there. We take the distributor caps from our vehicles so he cannot hotwire one. Then we occupy the lodge. He cannot stop us. We stay low to the floor. Inside will be blankets and bedding. We sleep in shifts, in warmth. In the morning, we hunt him. He cannot go far. We will keep snipers in the windows in case he tries to hole up in one of the snow tractor cabins. We will wait out the storm. We will let him wait in it."

Roger wanted to be angry, but he had to admit it was a good plan. He spoke into his radio. "All units, disable your vehicles. We're going to hole up in the lodge for the night." Shang gave similar orders. The vehicles were disabled and the men made their way in twos to the lodge. Shang waited until his last man was inside before he sprinted from cover. He knew his enemy couldn't see him, but it was very likely he might be close enough to have heard them moving. Shang waited for the bullet in his back as he ran. He made it to the house, and one of Neville's men slammed the door shut and bolted it behind him.

Shang spoke in Mandarin. "Quickly, find blankets and bedding! No lights! I want a man in each window with night-vision equipment! See if—"

"Shang."

Shang whirled on Neville. "What!"

Neville tilted his chin and sniffed. "I smell gas."

There was a thump outside, and one of the men by the window began to fire his weapon. The window beside him shattered and sparks scattered as the flare flew in like an incandescent comet. The sparks immediately lit the large puddle of gasoline soaked into the floor and spread up the gasoline staining the wall in a sheet. Shang's rifleman screamed as he leaped from the middle of the flame with his legs burning.

Shang's eyes went wide as the lurid red light lit up a gas can with holes punched in it behind the flaming curtains. There was a pair of empty plastic liquid detergent bottles twisting and blackening beside it. Shang roared. "Down!"

Jets of flame shot out of the can in all directions, and then the can exploded in a hellstorm of homemade napalm. Shang dived behind a couch and sheeting fire slewed across it and clung burning. Heat washed over Shang's face as he cringed and rolled away. Men screamed as the jellied gasoline clung to their flesh. The door was flung open and burning men flung themselves into the snow. Others ran out, firing their weapons. Shang struggled to be heard over the screaming. "No! Wait!"

Outside the rifle in the dark began methodically firing.

Roger Neville snarled from the kitchen doorway. "I want this guy's ass!"

Shang's voice was stone. "Yes."

BOLAN AWOKE, vaguely surprised to be alive. Pearly blue light was filtering in through the tarp he had stretched across the entrance to the lava tube. He had put down his tarp and slept rolled up in his two blankets. He had kept one hand-warmer wedged underneath his sweater above his heart and the other just beneath his belt buckle to keep his inner core warm. Swaddled as he was and out of the wind, he had spent a remarkably comfortable night, all things considered. His ears still rang from the destruction of the ridge, and his body felt as if it had been beaten with a bat. But he was alive, and he was warm.

Bolan celebrated another dawn with a can of dog food and a long pull on the bottle of Slivovitz.

He unwrapped himself and checked the load in the little Mauser. He had five in the magazine and fifteen in a pocket of his web gear. Twenty rounds. Most experts considered the 6.5 mm Swedish round underpowered for both big game and for war, but the little round was flat-shooting, incredibly accurate, and known for its penetration. Bolan hefted the little carbine. It felt like a baton in his hands. It had certainly proved itself the night before. He pulled the tarp aside and examined the day in front of him. The sky was almost black and the wind whistled through the lava fields, but the snow and icing rain had slackened to a freezing drizzle whipped almost to froth by the wind.

Iceland.

It was time to go see what the enemy was up to.

SHANG SUPPRESSED a groan as he stretched out the kinks in his physique. They had spent the night crammed like canned fish in the cabins of the Sno-Cats. The hunting lodge had burned to the ground. In all, ten of his and Neville's men had been killed, and three were too badly burned to continue the hunt. The American commando had stolen a great deal of his face. Shang looked at his men. They looked visibly shaken.

Shang's hand half clenched to form a monkey fist. He imagined in his mind the various strikes he would employ and how the American would scream as his tendons were seized through his flesh and snapped from their insertions. He played the scene over and over with increasing vividness. Shang grimaced. There were higher priorities than face. The American couldn't be allowed to communicate to the authorities. If he had as much pull as it seemed, if he could manage to communicate with the naval air station, American fighter jets could be screaming overhead within the hour. Shang temporarily banished the images of the American's dismemberment at his hands. The mission came first, revenge a close second. Shang's eyes slid over to Neville as he consulted with one of his men.

Shang wouldn't mind warming up on another certain American. He shouted above the sound of the wind in Mandarin. "Form up! Check your personal weapons and break out the heavy weapons. Sweep formation arrow!" Shang was pleased as his men snapped to attention and swiftly equipped themselves. Neville's men stood around carrying a hodgepodge of extremely expensive European assault rifles. Shang had little faith in these men. He eyed Neville and the A1 rifle he carried. He admitted Neville's tactical lethality, the whereabouts of his brain, Shang wasn't so sure about. It was a simple fact that the nations of the West needed reducing. Shang smiled thinly.

Soon. One continent at a time.

Shang's own men were PRC special purpose troops. One of their prime missions was infiltration. A close secondary mission was the capture and killing of enemy infiltrators. He ran his eye across the lunar landscape of lava flows, lichen and rivulets of freezing streams cutting through the rock. His men had the very latest equipment. The enemy had a bolt-action rifle. Shang wasn't a hunter, but many of the men he had worked and trained with in the special purpose forces were hunters from the mountains and plains of northern China. Shang looked at old Kao, his right-hand man. Kao had earned a permit from the government to hunt tigers. Shang knew all too well a good man with a hunting rifle was one of the most dangerous men on Earth. He looked out across the broken terrain of Iceland, and he didn't like it.

Neville seemed to read his thoughts. "We're going to lose some hounds on this hunt."

It took Shang several moments to internalize the metaphor in English. His eyes hooded like a hawk's. "Yes." Shang decided that no matter what transpired, there was one American dog who would die.

Shang raised his voice and shouted in English, "Move out!"

His men moved out in a shallow, V-shaped skirmishing line. Men with grenade launchers were on both flanks, and the light machine gun and the RPG men were in the back like the shaft behind the arrowhead. It was a formation that could easily swing all of its firepower in any direction and put the enemy in a withering cross fire. The next time the American fired, he would be suppressed with firepower while he was flanked, and then grenadiers would pound his position as riflemen moved in on top of him for the kill. But Neville was right, someone would have to be the first to die when the American shot—

A rifle cracked and one of Neville's men with a scoped rifle fell with a hole like a third eye in the middle of his brow. The formation dropped. Men shouted in English and Mandarin.

"Where is he! Where was the shot!"

The shot echoed off the rocks, and the whipping wind seemed to bring the sound from all directions. Shang scanned the area. There was a bit of flat plain with a single rock, and flanking it were two good lines of concealing lava formations. Shang picked the place he would choose and shouted in Mandarin, "Grenadiers! Right rock face! Hit it!"

The grenade launchers thumped, and Neville's men began firing on full-auto into the position. He shouted and grew enraged as the Westerners kept shooting. He realized he was shouting at them in Mandarin. Shang's head snapped around as one of his grenadiers sagged and fell. Shang filled his belly and bellowed.

"Cease fire!"

The firestorm ceased. Shang's rage mounted as he noticed another of the Americans had fallen almost unnoticed during the crescendo. He was one of Neville's men armed with an M-16 with a grenade launcher. With everyone wearing parkas and masks, the American couldn't readily identify Shang or Neville, so he was killing anyone with a heavy weapon or a telescopic sight. The sweep was barely into its first fifteen minutes and three men were already dead.

The American was a ghost.

Shang desperately scanned the terrain and tried to judge the firing angle. He looked at the dead Westerner near Neville and dismissed the right side rock formation. His eyes widened as he examined the lonely rock between them. It was a suicide position, and the American hadn't risen to fire from behind it. Shang looked at the three dead men and his blood went cold. His hand chopped down like an ax. "The rock! Hit the rock!"

Nearly a platoon's worth of rifle power hit the rock. Shang's eyes widened. The rock began to flutter and shake in a most unrocklike manner, then sagged.

"Left flank! Assault!"

Shang's men charged the position, firing from the hip-assault position. Shang lunged upward and charged after them. He couldn't believe his eyes when he reached the position. The rock wasn't a rock. The twisted metal spines of an umbrella poked up through a thoroughly perforated gray blanket. The blanket had been artfully smeared with mud and lichen. Snow and gravel had been packed into its folds. Just behind it was a crevice in the lava as wide as a coffin. Puddled in it were several inches of water. The crevice dipped behind a fold in the ground where water had carved its way through the volcanic rock. The crevice wound behind the fold and led back to the left-hand ridge of rocks. The American had been shooting at them from less than a hundred meters away with nothing but an umbrella to protect him from answering fire.

Shang was appalled.

"Left rock formation! Grenadiers! Everyone else forward!"

He didn't bother to tell the Westerners to stop firing. It didn't matter. He suspected the American was already beyond the formation and settling into a new firing position.

The American was a hungry ghost.

BOLAN ATE dog food. He was down to his last can. He was down to his last ten rounds of ammunition. The enemy was beginning to run him ragged. The warmth and strength of the brandy was mostly illusion, and it was hollow and fleeting, and the bottle was nearly gone.

He considered his scant pocketful of bronze-pointed bullets. He had laid serious hurt upon the enemy, but they were still at about half-platoon strength. He hadn't been able to grab a new rifle. The enemy was stripping their dead, and earlier he had heard the snarl of snowmobiles. The enemy had sent men out in an arc to leapfrog ahead of him. He had been flanked in unfamiliar territory, and there was nothing he could do about it.

He really needed another rifle.

Bolan peered into the sky. It was blackened and bruised, and whistling wind began to turn up to a howl. The slack in the storm was passing and Bolan's instincts told him the island was about to get hammered with an even worse second round. As much as he dreaded slogging through another storm, there could be an advantage to the near-whiteout conditions. It was very doubtful he was going to get out of this alive, but the only way he could stop the nukes and possibly save Grimaldi was to get to one of the men stalking him and to take his communications gear. Bolan took out the twelve-inch carving knife he had liberated from the lodge.

He was going to have to get up real close and personal.

Bolan put the knife back in his belt and finished licking the gravy out of the can. He took up the little rifle and began to move.

To do that he had to survive the next few hours until the storm hit.

ROGER NEVILLE CLICKED OFF his com link. The break in the storm had allowed clear communication through the Orbitech satellite in polar orbit. He and his brother had had a nice little strategy conference, and for once they were in perfect agreement. There was no more time left for dicking around.

The time to strike was now.

Roger rose from behind the blade of lava he had crouched behind to get out of the wind to find Shang staring at him intently.

Roger kept his poker face as Shang eyed him. That was the only real sticking point. Roger Neville had never been afraid of anyone or anything in his life. His fearlessness had started out a byproduct of his mild insanity and was now backed by his considerable physical skills. However, for the first time in his life, Roger was nervous.

Shang made him nervous.

Roger considered how he would kill the man. He cradled his rifle. From a distance would be best. Roger was a black belt in Brazilian jujitsu, but found he had no desire at all to exchange techniques with the stone-faced killer. Shang's men also presented a problem. Despite recent defoliation, Shang's men still outnumbered his. Roger allowed a thought to warm him. He and his men would have total surprise on his side.

"Hey, Shang!"

"What?"

"I have an idea."

Shang blinked. "What is that?"

"I think you should go kill this asshole who's been sniping us."

Shang stared for long moments. "That is what we are attempting to do."

"No, I think you should do it up close and personal. It's going to involve a slight sacrifice, but I think you're going to like it."

THE EXECUTIONER weighed his options very carefully.

The man was almost within reach. He was working his way up a lava ridge. The crown of rock at the top would form a good lookout post. Bolan himself had been using it when he had spied the man working his way toward his position. He examined the man through the ancient carbine's telescopic sight. The man was carrying a Chinese knock off of an AK-47 with an optical sight. His communication rig was strapped to his web gear. He also had a backpack, which probably included food, water, spare socks. Bolan was out of dog food, out of brandy, and down to the four rounds remaining in his rifle's magazine.

He really didn't have any options.

He slung his rifle and drew the twelve-inch carving knife. He waited in a lava fold as the man worked his way up the ridgeline and past his position. Bolan lunged like a fencer and plunged the knife beneath the chin of the killer's snow mask. As the blade sank into the man's throat, Bolan yanked it sideways and arterial blood sprayed out of the hood of the man's parka. Bolan caught him as he fell. The communication equipment was the primary target. He had to get a message out now before—

Bolan leaped away as he caught motion above him. Lava crunched beneath Shang's boots as he leaped monkeylike from the ridgeline fifteen feet above. Bolan spun the carbine around on its sling and swung the muzzle up for a head shot.

Shang's speed was inhuman.

Before Bolan could bring the muzzle online, Shang's left hand swung up in an open-handed slap that lifted the carbine out of the soldier's hands like a magic trick and sent it ten feet over his head and back into the rocks. Shang's right palm came an eye blink later. Bolan hadn't time to dodge or block. The blow struck him in the chest like a freight train and shoved him sprawling ten feet backward. Only the ceramic trauma plate in his frontal body armor had prevented his sternum from being snapped and his heart pulverized. Bolan went with the momentum of the blow and went into a backroll.

Shang paused as Bolan rolled to his feet with the bloody boning knife gleaming in his hand. Shang was larger, stronger, faster and more skilled than he was. Bolan's lips skinned back.

The only option was to attack.

Shang smiled. He dropped into low horse-stance. His hands curled into positions that had been refined over a thousand years of Chinese history for the purpose of dismantling humans.

Bolan put his thumb on the blade of the boning knife and closed.

Both men paused at the sound of the explosion. Orange fire and black smoke erupted in the distance on Mount Hekla. It was instantly followed by rapid bursts of automatic rifle fire much closer to home. Neither man took this eyes off the other. Bolan smiled over the point of his knife.

"You're betrayed, Shang."

The Chinese kept one claw-shaped hand in front of him as he clicked the transmitter clipped to his shoulder strap with the other and spoke in short, sharp Mandarin. The short bursts of rifle fire below ceased as suddenly as they had begun. A few scattered single shots rang out, and then all was silent. They were final kill shots to men who had already been gunned down.

Bolan's blade never wavered. "Neville has killed your men and blown up your station on Mount Hekla. His men are already making double time for the vehicles."

Shang drew a Type 67 silenced pistol. Bolan played his last card as Shang pointed the weapon at his head and flicked off the safety.

"Neville has all thirty weapons now."

Shang's eyes hooded at the number. Bolan knew he had hit paydirt.

"When we attacked the barge on the Saimaa we found casings for thirty tactical weapons." Bolan smiled. "How many did he deliver to you and your team? Five? Six?"

Shang's pistol stayed pointed between Bolan's eyes.

"One or two good, nuclear-induced violent ejection eruptions, and you have crop failures all across Northern Europe and Western Russia as the ash cloud sits over it like a nuclear winter. Crop failures will bring economic failures, and China and the United States move in to all new markets during the fire sale. Was that the plan?"

Shang was a statue.

"But Iceland has over two dozen active volcanoes. What if they all went off at once? Like the earth popping the entire island like a cork. You'd get Northern Europe, all of Russia, hell, if the prevailing winds assisted you..." Bolan locked his gaze with Shang's. "What would happen to China if the entire northern wheat crop failed? You're a northern boy, aren't you, Shang?"

Shang's knuckles were white around the grips of his gun.

"Do the math." Bolan slowly lowered the knife. He also made ready for an underhanded throw at Shang's eyes. "Roger and Ian Neville are supernationalists. They want to leave the United States the only superpower left on the block. All that ash in the atmosphere would affect North America, but we have two oceans buffering us, and we have enough agricultural zones to feed the entire planet if we managed it right, and with nearly the entire continents of Europe and Asia in famine, we could dictate terms. It would be decades before the whole thing was sorted out, and I believe Ian Neville is smart enough to leave a trail pointing to the PRC." Bolan took his last gamble and slowly thrust his knife beneath his belt. "Shang, I think you and I need to pool our resources, and fast."

Shang didn't lower his pistol. "Roger and Ian Neville are dead men. We had thought they might try to betray us, but we did not suspect the scope of it. We will destroy them with one of their own weapons." Shang jerked the pistol down the ridgeline. "I believe I will keep you alive. For the present."

20

The North Sea

Ian Neville was sweating. "Rog, we are in a shitload of trouble."

The storm outside was hitting the platform in full force. Snow and sleet pounded the oil rig like mallets of ice.

Roger's voice came back across the com link. "I'm inbound. What's the problem?"

"That goddamn Chinese sub is a thousand yards east of us, that's the problem. He's surfaced. He's demanding that we stand down. He's demanding the detonation codes for all the weapons we positioned in Iceland. Including the twenty-four he's not supposed to know about. He's demanding our immediate surrender."

"Or what?" Roger's voice was downright jovial. "He and his sailor boys are going to storm the platform with mops?"

"Uh...Rog?" Ian mopped his brow. "He says they've retained one of the nukes. He says he'll blow us to the upside down of Hell, whatever that is, if we don't surrender in thirty seconds."

"Really?" Roger's voice was all smug mirth. "That's awfully one-way of them."

Ian's voice rose toward hysterics. "This is no time for fucking around, Rog!" He desperately tried to keep himself from unraveling with fear. "Are they bluffing? Could they have one of the weapons?"

"Well..." Roger's voice grew thoughtful. "Our engineers estimated it would take five weapons to effectively blow Hekla, Eldfell and Lakagigar. The Chinese insisted they needed six. However, now that I think about it, it's entirely possible that their engineers came up with the exact same number we did, but they decided to keep an extra weapon around as an ace in the hole."

"Jesus! We're fucked!"

"Well, we don't know if they have it or not, and I guess there's really only one way to find out."

"What the hell does that mean!"

Roger's voice modulated to sound soothing. "Ian?"

"What?"

"We put remote detonators in all of the weapons, didn't we?"

"Um..." Ian's fear-frozen mind tried to comprehend where his insane brother was going with this. "Yeah?"

"We put our own remote detonators in the weapons we gave the Chinese, didn't we?"

"Yeah." Ian's eyes flared. "Fucking-A right we did!"

"Now, I could be wrong, but the weapons were numbered, and China is an orderly society. I'm just willing to bet that they planted one through five and kept six as their ace in the hole."

Ian's eyes swept the control panel. "So I should—"

"You should remote detonate weapon number six."

Ian flicked on the satellite link and pushed a button. A little screen told him that the remote detonator in warhead number six was fully functional and receiving his signal.

Ian flipped up the safety shield and entered the command code. The detonator replied that it had received it. His hand hovered over the button.

This would be his first kill.

Roger's voice thundered like a stadium cheer. "Go for it, big bro!"

Ian's finger stabbed the button.

Nothing happened.

Ian's voice grew instantly worried. "Nothing happened."

"Ian." Roger's voice remained as patient as if he were talking to a child. "The weapon was a thousand yards away, inside a sub, in the middle of the worst storm to hit the North Sea in a decade."

"Okay, but—"

"Okay, you hail them, bro, and tell them you surrender."

Ian clicked on the radio. He slowly smiled as he continued to listen.

"So, what are you getting on the horn there, Ian?"

Ian grinned. "The line is dead."

Chinese Embassy, Reykjavik

"THE SUB IS NOT answering." The embassy communications office looked up at Shang nervously. Bolan sat in a chair drinking jasmine tea. Four AK-47 rifles were pointed at him. All of them had their bayonets fixed. Their selector levers were set on full-auto.

Bolan sipped his tea. It was damn good.

"Shang, we need to talk."

"Somehow Roger and Ian Neville have either disabled or destroyed our sub. We have no other warships in the North Sea, nor any that can reach the platform. Any warplanes we send would have to overfly Russia. They would not allow such a thing, even if we were to explain the circumstances, which my government is not willing to do."

Bolan nodded. Shang sure was getting talky. The soldier sipped his tea and waited for Shang to go on.

"I believe Roger Neville is insane. The only viable option is the insertion of a Special Forces team."

Bolan kept his poker face. The only viable option was to have an English attack submarine, of which there had to be at least one patrolling somewhere in the North Sea, go and nuke the platform, without warning, with a sea-skimming cruise missile. However, that would involve the Chinese government explaining to the English government why it was necessary to frag one of their own oil rigs.

That wasn't about to happen.

The PRC seemed ready to risk ecological Armageddon rather than fess up to their misdeeds.

"I agree."

The facial expressions of the Chinese in the room didn't change, but their sense of relief was palpable. Bolan had his own selfish reasons for agreeing. He knew if he made any attempt to communicate or to break free he would be killed, and there would be no chance at all of saving Jack Grimaldi's life.

"How many men can you muster?"

"I have three men on my team who were in the capital rather than at the base. We have several agents here in the embassy, and whatever more we need can be filled out with embassy guards."

"You're suggesting that I join your assault team."

"Yes, our objective is the same now. The Nevilles must be stopped. You have proved your abilities. You have the best grasp of English, particularly if we must negotiate or do quick work on their computers."

"What about our little misunderstanding?"

Shang considered the remark for a moment. "Once the rig has been taken, it and everything on it will be destroyed. Since it is being leased by a cutout company by Ian Neville, all evidence will lead toward him. As for any other matter, with all the weapons accounted for, should you wish to pursue the matter further, it would be a question of your government's word against mine. Since one of your nation's wealthiest capitalist industrialists is involved, I believe that both our governments will find it best to remain forgotten." Shang motioned at the men aiming weapons at Bolan. "If you disagree, then I am afraid I must have you killed, dismembered and distributed throughout the Reykjavik sewer system. Your dismemberment and distribution I shall leave to my men." Shang unfolded his arms from across his chest. His hands clenched into fists by his sides with the sounds of walnuts being crushed underwater. "You, however, I will kill personally."

Bolan nodded. "I believe we have an understanding."

"Good." Shang spoke to his men for a moment and then turned back to Bolan. "We shall proceed to the armory immediately. You may choose any weapons you require. However, you will not be issued them until we are at sea and close to the target."

Aboard the Oil Rig

JACK GRIMALDI LAY on the floor and bled. He was getting rather tired of being beaten on. His ribs were cracked and his vision was skewing. He wondered if he had a concussion. He considered his beatings. Shang had crushed him like a bug, and Grimaldi was man enough to admit to himself that Shang scared the shit out of him. He flinched as a boot thudded into his side. The bastard stomping on him at the moment, however... Him, Grimaldi felt, he stood a good chance of whipping.

If he could just get a hand or foot free.

Unfortunately, Roger Neville had trussed him like a Christmas goose. Neville yanked Grimaldi up by the hair and smashed him back down with the back of his hand. He glanced at his brother. "You want a shot at him, bro?"

Ian looked around himself in mild shock. Roger's mercenaries grinned. Ian looked at the Stony Man pilot where he lay bleeding. "Um, you think I should?"

Roger grinned from ear to ear. "The question is, do you think you'd like to?"

Ian matched his smile. "Stand him up."

Roger dragged Grimaldi to his feet. The pilot tried to pull his knees into his chest for a two-footed mule kick, but all he managed to do was sag. "C'mon!" Roger said encouragingly. "Upsy-daisy!"

Ian pulled back his fist and threw a wild haymaker. Grimaldi's vision tunneled down to a blurry field shot through with purple pinpricks. The pilot didn't feel himself hit the floor. Ian Neville spun around and pumped both fists into the air like Rocky.

"I'm the King of the World!"

Roger threw back his head and laughed. He squatted on his heels and watched blood bubble from between Grimaldi's mashed lips. "Listen, I'm trying to encourage my brother's bloodthirsty side. There really is about to be a new world order, and we all need to get our mantras tight. So, listen, Ian and the boys are going to have some more fun with you. Gonna bust you up like a piñata. You can pipe up anytime and save yourself a world of hurt. We already know you're a tough guy, so like I said, this is just for fun."

Roger nodded at one of his men. "You see that guy over there?"

Grimaldi rolled the one eye that was still open at the man. He was about six feet, two hundred pounds, with black hair and an olive complexion. He had a knife scar on his chin. He held the curved crescent of a Middle Eastern *jambiya* dagger in his hand. He was smiling at the pilot in a disturbingly familiar fashion.

"That's Orhan. I met him in Berlin. He's former Turkish special forces, and that is one crazy, motherfucking outfit, let me tell you. Anyhoo, like I said, this is just for fun. When we get bored with this, you, Orhan, and Orhan's knife are going to have a little talk, and the fun is going to end. You read me?"

Grimaldi rolled his eye upward and saw three Roger Nevilles. He couldn't think of a snappy comeback for any of them, so he lay where he was and continued bleeding. Roger sighed. "Ian, you want me to stand him up for you again?"

"No." Ian Neville had an unhealthy gleam in his eye. "I think I want to stomp him."

Roger nodded at his men proudly and jerked his thumb at Ian. "That's my big bro."

North Sea

BOLAN EXAMINED his armament and his comrades in arms.

People's Republic of China special forces' gear wasn't up to the latest U.S. or Russian standard, and most of Shang's best equipment had been lost when Roger Neville had blown Fire God Station on Mount Hekla. Bolan smiled thinly. Operation Fire God did have a dramatic ring to it. Bolan checked his weapons. They had been forced to loot the Chinese embassy armory, and it was notably lacking in heavy ordnance and much more suited for clandestine activities such as snatches and assassinations than assaults. The entire team was armed with Type 85 silenced submachine guns. Most also carried one or more Chinese copies of Russian Tokarev or Makarov pistols. The submachine guns had no bayonet fittings, and all of the men carried some sort of blade. There was an assortment of daggers. Several men had the short, curved lengths of Chinese broadswords strapped over their shoulders. Shang carried a pair of Kung Fu butterfly knives.

Bolan had found a weapon of interest. The embassy had several Type 80 machine pistols. It was the Chinese update of the antique German Schnellfeuerepistoles. They were bulky, but at point-blank range, in properly trained hands, there was hardly anything more deadly than a machine pistol.

Bolan had a pair of them strapped to his thighs like a gunfighter.

The machine pistols incongruously had fittings for a small bayonet. Bolan had one of the slim blades down his boot and a Butterfly knife thrust through his belt. They all wore antiquated Russian body armor made up of titanium plates sandwiched between fiberglass mesh. All of them wore gray and black face paint, with muted red headscarves tied around their heads. Three of the men were special purpose troops like Shang. The other four were embassy guards. Bolan shook his head. They didn't look like a special forces team.

They looked like pirates of the Sulu Sea.

The little sub continued on, unaffected by the storm raging on the surface a hundred yards overhead. Like much PRC equipment, the minisub was a copy of Russian kit, and it closely resembled the minisub Bolan had taken on his cross-country jaunt in the Lake Saimaa district a few days ago.

Shang turned to Bolan.

"They are not expecting to be assaulted. They have destroyed the one Chinese sub that could destroy them. They know we will not incriminate ourselves by warning any NATO government. If we had, then they would use the threat of carrying out the plan to blackmail their way to safety. The platform is equipped with radar and sonar. They are capable of detecting airplanes, surface ships, and have a good chance of detecting most subs. We, however, are small, and will use the catapillar treads to creep up to the base of the platform. We will then slowly rise. When we surface, the storm will cover any noise of our assault. We will climb the pylons, assault the platform and take control of the weapons. We will attempt to capture one of the Nevilles and keep him alive long enough to extract the command codes to the weapons. Failing that, we will destroy the platform. Do you understand?"

Bolan nodded.

The subdriver spoke softly through the open hatch. Shang translated. "We are nearing our objective. We shall descend to the sea floor now and make our approach to the base of the platform." Shang glanced around at his team meaningfully. "You will always have one or more of my men behind you. Should you attempt to contact the outside, should you attempt to deviate from the plan, should you attempt to disobey or act without orders, should you engage in any anomalous behavior, all of my men have orders to behead you."

Bolan suspected they would just shoot him, but the impressive array of cutlery the Chinese carried did leave them a rather viable decapitation option. He had also noted that unlike the rest of the team, he hadn't been issued a backplate for his armor. The PRC team stared unblinkingly at Bolan, like stone Buddhas. He gazed at Shang steadily. "Our mission objective is the same, Shang. You're in command of this operation, and I understand everything you've told me."

Shang nodded once. "Good."

21

The tiny sub was tossed in the maelstrom like a cork. They had floated upward right beside the drill shaft and had surfaced between the four massive legs of the rig. Rain slashed down through the hatch as it was flung open and freezing air blasted the inside of the compartment. Shang knifed his hand downward, and Bolan slung his submachine gun and rose from his bench with the rest of the team. The Executioner blinked against the sleeting rain as he climbed into the sail. The dark bulk of the platform loomed above them.

There was a small boat dock ten yards away, but Shang didn't want to risk raising an alarm by docking. The Chinese braced himself straddle-legged in the sail and took a coil of knotted rope with a grapnel. He paid out rope and began to whirl the grapnel overhead. His eyes narrowed to slits against the gale and he hurled the grapnel. It dropped over the rail and he yanked it back fast enough so that it hooked fast with barely a clank. He tied off the other end to a cleat in the sail and shouted at one of his men.

The embassy guard went over the sail and began to climb across the rope. The sub bobbed up and down, and the guardsman was repeatedly dunked. Shang shouted encouragement, but his words were cut short as a wave ripped between the massive stilts of the platform and slapped the guardsman from the rope.

The guardsman disappeared in the dark, heaving waters. Several long seconds passed. None of the team had life preservers. All they had was the weight of their titanium armor and the iron and steel they had strapped all over their bodies.

The man didn't reappear.

"You!" Shang's pistol was in his hand and it was pointed at Bolan's head. "Go!"

The soldier flung his submachine gun behind his back and took the rope in both hands. He wasn't wearing arctic warfare gear, and the cold was already cutting through him like a knife. He centered himself and focused on his breathing. Bolan scissored his legs around the rope and began to crawl across like a spider. He felt more like a frozen sloth as the aching cold slowed his movement. He breathed deep into his belly to generate heat and put his mind into moving hand over hand and leg scissors by sliding leg scissors.

Bolan didn't see the wave coming.

It slapped him like a giant iron palm and then closed around him like a freezing fist. The breath was blasted out of his body. His leg-lock failed and his hands burned down the rope until they came to a stop behind a knot. Bolan's muscles contracted like cables across his bones as he put all of his will into his hands, arms and shoulders. The North Atlantic sought to suck him from the rope and pull him down. Bolan's voice burst from his throat in a gurgling roar as he summoned power.

The wave dropped him just as suddenly as it had struck him.

Bolan hung for a moment and then heaved his ankles back up and across the rope. He drove himself to cross with leaden limbs before the next wave hit him. His hand closed around frigid steel and threatened to freeze there as he pulled himself onto the corrugated paneling of the boat dock. Bolan stood and seized the rope to steady it for the next man.

Shang stared at him for one moment and then began his crossing. He flew across the rope in the stone-monkey style that had given him his nickname. One by one, the rest of the crew followed. They were down to seven sodden, freezing men. The sub driver's mate released the rope from the sail and Shang reeled it in. If they didn't get out of the storm soon, they would die of exposure. A screen of storm fencing cut off the boat dock from the gangway that led upward to the rig. It was padlocked and undoubtedly alarmed.

Shang whirled his grapnel, hurling it high. It hooked into the stair landing above, and Shang led as he took the rope and swung out over the heaving sea and began to walk up the side of the storm fencing. One of his men prodded Bolan with his submachine gun. The soldier took the rope, put his boots into the chain link, and heaved himself up one weary step at a time. Shang's hand closed around his wrist like a vise and heaved him up over the landing. The two of them assisted in hauling up the rest of the team.

They stood shivering and exhausted on the exposed landing. Shang led them up the stairs to the doorway beneath the platform. A security camera was mounted above the door. Chang raised his submachine gun and the weapon rattled and chuffed as he put a short burst into the camera. He dropped his weapon on its sling and raised his right palm. He drew it back behind his head in a long, flowing, S-curve and then drove it forward. His palm hit the door like a thundering iron palm. The bolt snapped and the door flung open on its hinges.

A guard with a Heckler & Koch G-36 rifle was rising from his chair. Shang already had his submachine in his hands and put a 3-round burst into the man's face. The team filed into the welcome light and heat of the rig's habitation complex.

GRIMALDI WAS a mess.

"You know something?" Roger Neville said. "You really are one tough son of a bitch. You may have busted one of my brother's knuckles with your face."

Ian Neville stood to one side. Both his hands were covered with blood, and one was obviously swollen. It didn't seem to bother him too much. Ian couldn't remember the last time he'd had so much fun.

He'd been kicking the hell out of helpless adversaries financially for years. Working with flesh was turning out to be a lot more interesting. "Hey, Rog."

Roger looked up at his brother. "Yeah?"

"Didn't you mention something about Orhan going to work?"

Roger rose from his heels. "You know, now that I think about it, I believe you fellas are right. I did say something about Orhan going to work."

The gleaming curve of Orhan's steel came out of the sheath with a ringing rasp.

Roger shook his head at Grimaldi. "Buddy-boy, you are going to suffer."

"Ay, Rog." A big blond merc was holding his radio in his hand.

Roger looked over in annoyance. "What is it, Hans?"

Hans shrugged and spoke in a thick Boer accent. "Rog, I cannot get ahold of Jones."

"Jones is supposed to be on guard duty bottom-side." Roger suddenly glowered. "Hans, you go find that Welshman and if he's whacking off to Internet porn on duty again, you tell him I'm going to kill him."

"*Ja.*" He grinned. "I tell him." Hans turned and left the shack.

Roger turned back to Grimaldi. "Now, where were we? Ah, yes. You, Orhan and Orhan's knife. Oh, yeah, and something about playtime being over."

BOLAN TOOK POINT as they came up the stairs from the bowels of the platform.

He kicked open the first door he came to. Two men were smoking and watching a movie. A pair of Heckler & Koch G-36 rifles leaned against the bunk bed. Bolan walked a burst up both men's chests. Shang had kicked the opposite door in the narrow hall and his weapon chuffed off a short burst.

The next door down opened and a man stepped out with half of his face covered in shaving cream. The shaving cream splattered red as Bolan's burst drew a blood-pocked pattern of holes between his chin and his eyebrows. There was a shout from within but

Shang was already stepping over the faceless corpse, his weapon firing. The shout was cut short, and Shang gave the thumbs-up signal. The team cleared the remaining four dormitory units.

No one else was lounging around off duty.

Shang fell back a few paces and once more Bolan was on point. He was intensely aware of the weapons pointed at his unprotected back. He wished vainly for a bucketful of hand grenades as he took the stairs.

A large blond man carrying a rifle appeared at the top of the landing. The man staggered as Bolan put a burst into his chest. The man flinched and raised his rifle as the Executioner's second burst walked up his armor. The G-36 rifle snarled on full-auto. Sparks shrieked in the metal stairwell, and the sound of automatic rifle fire reverberated off of the metal walls. The autofire cut short as Bolan's third burst tore open the blond man's throat. The gunman sagged, gargling blood, his rifle falling from nerveless fingers. He was dead as he slid to the floor.

The damage was done.

Bolan took the stairs three at a time. The door opened on another narrow corridor. He crouched as alarms began railing harshly throughout the platform. They had lost the element of surprise.

Shang snarled from a few steps down. "Move!"

Bolan moved. He'd been on oil rigs before, and he had a good idea where the command shack would be. He dropped and slid for home base, firing as a pair of rifle-toting men came around the bend. They skidded to a halt just as five submachine guns began filling the narrow hallway with lead from floor to ceiling. The sonic cracks of the mercs' bullets whip-cracked over Bolan's head in response as the two groups exchanged. The pair of gunners shuddered and twisted in the lead hailstorm, then fell to the deck. Bolan ejected his spent magazine and loaded a fresh one.

Another embassy guard had fallen, a bloody third eye centered in his brow. Now the team was six. The look in Shang's eye told Bolan the killer had wished the big American had taken the brunt of the bullets. Bolan released his bolt on a fresh round and stood. He jerked his head toward the stairwell at the end of the corridor. "That way."

Shang motioned one of the guards forward. Bolan fell back slightly as his lead was usurped. Shang was right behind him, and Bolan suspected he had just been designated the man's personal human shield. They approached the stairwell. The embassy guard peered up and was met by a crescendo of rifle fire. He fired back from around the corner and was followed by Bolan and Shang. The soldier flicked his weapon to semiauto and raised his gun to his shoulder as Shang and the guardsman emptied their weapons in fast long bursts up to the stairwell. He stood his ground as two men at the top whipped their rifles around the door frame to return fire.

Bolan took a suicidal second to stand and use his sights. The first man's head became slightly fuzzy as the soldier's front sight became the center of his universe. He squeezed the trigger once and the man's skull seemed to wobble on his shoulders with the head shot. The other man got off a shot. Bolan felt the punch of a round against his armor as he fired. The merc dropped his rifle and fell screaming, clutching his face.

"Move!" Shang shoved Bolan hard. "Move!"

The soldier was getting awfully tired of Shang's command manner. Bolan leaped up the stairs. His blood froze as something bounced onto the landing above and came clattering down the stairs. "Grenade!" Bolan roared.

The cylindrical shape of a Russian-made offensive grenade clanked to a halt by Bolan' boots. The rest of the team was behind him, blocking any cover. He would never make the landing, and his back was unarmored. Bolan went over the side. He dropped down the narrow space between the rail and the stairwell and met the metal floor below with bone-jarring force. The grenade above him detonated with a crack, and men screamed in the stairwell. Grenades threw their fragments in spheres, and the steel steps above protected Bolan from fragments flying directly downward. The ricochets and concussion, on the other hand, were spectacular in the narrow stairwell, and sparks screamed off the walls as thunder rolled in a hot wave.

Bolan rose shakily. His ears were ringing, but he found he wasn't bleeding. He and Shang were pointing their weapons at each other. Another embassy guard and one of Shang's personal men lay sprawled in the stairs like bloody dolls.

Now they were four.

Shang lowered his weapon and jerked his head for Bolan to come up the stairs. He said something to the remaining embassy guard. The guard didn't look pleased to being assigned point. So far, only the big American seemed to be surviving the experience.

The guard took point.

Another grenade came bouncing onto the landing as he reached it. The guard roared out something in Mandarin and hurled himself upon the grenade selflessly. His body shuddered as it detonated. Shang had already run up the stairs and was firing down another hall even as the heroic guardsman trembled and smoldered. Rifle fire from somewhere was answering back. Bolan paused at the top and rolled the man over. Blood leaked out of his mouth and smoke oozed from his stomach. The Russian offensive grenades packed much more explosive than U.S. and NATO weapons. By lying on top of it, the man had taken the entire blast. A hole had been ripped in his stomach armor a person could put a fist into.

Shang snarled something over his shoulder. One of his men lowered the muzzle of his weapon and shot the wounded guardsman in the head. Shang's hooded eyes met Bolan's as he crouched back around the corner to avoid the rifle fire from down the hall. He looked at the dead guard and grunted a single word. "Merciful."

Bolan eyed the killer. The words "cannon fodder" and "no witnesses" came more to his mind. The PRC wanted no one to know of the atrocity they had planned in Iceland. Embassy guards weren't part of the inner circle of the operation. There was a mercy round waiting for Bolan before the op was over.

But the Executioner had known that from the start.

"Yeah." Bolan kept a straight face as he closed the dead hero's eyes and mentally thanked him for his sacrifice. "Merciful."

Shang nodded. "Lead."

Bolan rose and went around the corner firing. Another bullet struck his armor, and his answering burst tore out the throat of the man who had shot him. The hallway was much shorter and ended at a set of steps that led to the command shack. The door was open and men were firing from cover. Bolan emptied his weapon on full-auto and kicked a door in the hallway. He lunged into the cover of a maintenance closet as light machine gun fire ripped downward from the command shack into the hall.

Shang shouted as bullets filled the corridor. "Lead!"

"You lead!" Bolan shouted back. "Or walk your ass down here and cut off my head!"

Shang snarled something unpleasant in Mandarin.

The machine gun fire ceased. Roger Neville shouted down jovially. "Hey! Guys! If you don't back off, I start the next ice age! Understand?"

"You're going to do that anyway, Rog!" Bolan dropped the silenced submachine gun he carried and loosened his machine pistols in their holsters. "Tell you what. You surrender, right now, and I'll give you over to the United Nations."

"Hmm. Wait a minute. Let me think about that." Roger paused a sarcastic second. "Nope. Don't like it. Don't like them. Never have. Don't think much of the deal."

"It's a great deal, Rog. United Nations tribunals don't have the death penalty." Bolan paused significantly. "Shang on the other hand, is talking about beheading both you and your brother, and that's after he demonstrates tendon tearing techniques on both of your narrow asses, extensively."

There was nothing sarcastic in the new silence down the hall. The Neville brothers both knew the absolute validity of the threat.

"C'mon, Rog!" Bolan called encouragingly. "With me you get to hire a lawyer, and your brother can afford a good one I'm thinking. But you make us come up there, with Shang, all you get to do is scream."

"I have your little buddy." Roger's voice was no longer jovial. "You want to hear some real screaming?"

The enemy had heavy weapons, the high ground and a hostage. Bolan wouldn't back off to save Grimaldi's life. They were both expendable, and they both knew it. But Roger Neville was about to pull the sniper's draw. You wound a man and leave him screaming, then you keep wounding him until his buddies can't stand it anymore and break cover to rescue him. Bolan took a long breath. He had no idea if he could prevent himself from charging down the guns if Jack Grimaldi started screaming.

Bolan stared out the doorway of the closet to the opposite wall. A huge red-iron reel was coiled with the brown canvas of a firehose. The brass nozzle shone. Above it, Warning, Extreme High Pressure was painted in big red letters on the wall. Bolan glanced around and found a clipboard with a maintenance checklist. He turned it over and scrawled a quick note: *Shang, I am going for the fire hose. Cover me and then charge.*

Bolan hoped Shang's English comprehension was enough to cover all the bases. He crumpled the paper into a ball and judged his shot. He stood just inside the doorway and threw. The paper wad flew diagonally down the hall, bounced off the far wall and back into the stairwell. Bolan picked up his submachine gun.

Roger's voice sang out. "Last chance before we start carving!"

"Fuck him!" Bolan lunged from the closet.

He fired the submachine gun on full-auto and burned the entire magazine. He dropped the weapon as he reached the wall, seized the red-iron wheel of the pressure valve and spun it. Rifle fire erupted, and one bullet and then another hammered into Bolan's armor. Something stung his calf, and he almost buckled as he spun the valve to full open. The silenced weapons were chuffing and hissing from the stairwell. Bolan ripped the hose free of the reel, and the heavy flaccid canvas suddenly went taut as it came alive in his hands. Bolan turned.

The machine gun in the command shack opened up.

The .30-caliber bullets hammered into the frontal arc of Bolan's armor and smashed him off his feet.

Shang and his men stood stoically, firing their weapons. The machine gun ripped one of Shang's men from his crotch to the top of his skull. Bolan sat up. The firehose throbbed like a boa constrictor in his hands. He shoved the brass lever forward full and leaned all of his weight back.

Water erupted like a white lightning bolt from the massive brass nozzle. The hose was meant to fight an internal fire on an oil rig. Bolan laid his body back on the hose to try to control the intense pressure. The torrent smashed into the doorway of the command shack and took one of the riflemen in the face. His head whipped about and he fell screaming, clutching his eyes. Bolan lowered his aim and drove the man flopping backward into the stream of the light machine gun. The autofire halted for a moment and Bolan snarled behind him, "Shang! The hose!"

Bolan rose, trying to control the force writhing in his hands. He could see the machine gun as he stood and the man trying to bring the muzzle over the body of the dead, eyeless corpse blocking him. The hose suddenly felt lighter in Bolan's hands as Shang grabbed a section from behind. The soldier turned the high-pressure jet on the prone machine gunner and swept him and his weapon out of the line of sight.

A grenade lobbed into the corridor from within the shack.

Bolan said a microsecond prayer to the Universe for Grimaldi and blasted the grenade back the way it had come. The bomb disappeared in the jet, and a second later it detonated in a yellow flash within the command shack. Bolan and Shang advanced. They were the only two left. They stepped into the command shack with the firehose like men with a flame-thrower clearing a bunker. A soaked, dark-complexioned man rose into view with a rifle and Bolan hosed the weapon from his hands and the man off his feet.

A figure stepped into Bolan's peripheral vision. He struggled to bring the writhing hose around as the shotgun roared and knocked him backward. The nozzle whipped free. Shang had dropped his weapon to support the hose, and he let go of the whipping hose as Ian Neville pointed the shotgun at his head.

Grimaldi popped up like a bruised and bloodied jumping jack.

His hands were manacled and his feet shackled. He flew upward and turned in midair as he drew his knees into his chest. He exploded both feet into the back of Ian Neville's skull. The shotgun blasted and sent a pattern of buckshot into the wall over Shang's head. Gravity overcame the Stony Man pilot, and he fell to the floor like a battered sack of potatoes. Ian staggered forward with the momentum of the blow, directly toward Shang. The Chinese killer drove his palm into Ian's heart with the sound of a cast-iron skillet swatting a side of beef. Blood burst from the businessman's ears, eyes, nose and mouth.

The richest man on Earth fell dead without a sound.

The firehose whipped around the room like a berserk and beheaded sea serpent in its death throes. The brass nozzle crashed against the walls and smashed equipment. Bolan rose. His foot slipped in the frigid seawater and his bloodied calf buckled. The dark-complexioned man dodged the flailing hose and vaulted the counter. The soldier recognized Turkish words as the man screamed insults. He raised a dagger and went for Shang. The Chinese assassin's twin butterfly knives came free in his hands.

The fourteen-inch blades blurred into quick-silver steel fans that wove a deadly web in front of him.

The Turk blinked as his dagger and the hand holding it flew across the room. He had only a split second to stare in shock at the stump before Shang's second blade sheared his neck.

The Turk fell one way, his head fell the other.

Grimaldi shouted feebly from the floor. "Mack!"

Bolan turned. Roger Neville stood in a side doorway that led to an office in the command shack. A pair of Heckler & Koch Personal Defensive Weapons filled his hands. Bolan turned as his two Type 80 machine pistols cleared leather.

Bolan and Neville stood ten feet apart, automatic weapons filling their hands. They stood and exchanged fire like Wyatt Earp and Ike Clanton at the OK Corral.

Roger Neville had the drop, his H & K PDWs hissing out two streams of fire. The guns fired armor-piercing rounds, and the needle-shaped bullets could whisper through woven Kevlar and penetrate NATO-standard steel targets.

But Bolan wasn't wearing NATO armor.

The Russian military was nearly bankrupt, and they couldn't afford Kevlar armor, ceramic laminate inserts, or the latest, experimental carbon composites. The Russians had fallen back on a tactic that had served them well for over a century. When technological subtlety couldn't be achieved, apply brute force.

Russia was one of the biggest producers of titanium in the world.

Roger Neville screamed wordlessly as his Heckler & Koch PDWs drew smoking lines up Bolan's chest. The woven fiberglass parted like tissue but the needle-shaped projectiles bent or broke apart against the overlapping titanium plates of Bolan's frontal armor and failed to penetrate.

Bolan held down his triggers. The machine pistols in his hands were based on a seventy-year-old design. The Chinese used the 7.62 mm round primarily in their submachine guns, and they hotted it up for their shoulder-fired weapons. The .30-caliber bullets came screaming out the five-inch barrels at over 1500 feet per second, and the Chinese armor-piercing rounds were steel-cored, steel-jacketed and shaped like the nose cone of a rocket. The machine pistols were totally uncontrollable on full-auto. Bolan had aimed low, and he let both weapons buck and climb as they willed.

Balls of fire blasted from his muzzles in a deafening crescendo. His 20-round magazines expended themselves in exactly one second. They stitched two lines up Roger Neville's Kevlar armor, plunged straight through the woven fiber armor, tore through his torso and drew matching lines on the wall behind him.

Both men's weapons clacked open on empty chambers.

Roger Neville's jaw worked but no sound came out. Blood leaked across his lips as his face went fish-belly white. Roger sank to his knees and fell facefirst into the inch of standing water on the floor of the command shack. Bolan took a shaky breath and turned.

The firehose had managed to flip back upon itself to wedge into the doorway of the command shack. A great loop was trapped in the doorway in a swollen, throbbing kink, the nozzle straining against the top of the door. Shang stood over Ian Neville, the butterfly knives back in his hands. Bolan stood with his two smoking, empty pistols.

Shang glanced at Bolan's calf, his eyes unreadable. "You are wounded."

Bolan considered the pair of spare magazines for the machine pistols in his belt. He would never live to reach them. Much less reload. "You going to be merciful, Shang?"

The smile that spread across Shang's face was horrible to behold.

Bolan flung the pistol in his right hand at Shang's face. The Chinese killer knocked it aside with one of his blades as he closed. The soldier flung the pistol in his left underhanded and Shang swatted it away like an insect. He ripped free the butterfly knife he had taken from the Chinese embassy, feinting at Shang's leg. The Chinese lowered his guard slightly, but he was in no danger.

None that he knew of. Shang wasn't Bolan's target.

The Executioner swung up the fourteen-inch blade and sliced it down across the throbbing loop of hose straining in the doorway.

The hose exploded.

Bolan's jaw was nearly dislocated as a section of the canvass whipped across the side of his face. He lurched to his feet and fell back against the wall as he saw stars and the command shack skewed in his vision. He put a hand to the wall to steady himself and brought up the butterfly knife in a high guard.

Shang stood in the same spot. He had dropped one of his knives, and his left hand covered half of his face. He slowly lowered his hand. Shang had taken the brunt of the water pressure right in the face. His left cheek had been ripped open to his ear as the high-pressure torrent had torn past his lips and violently expanded in his mouth. His nose was spread in a flattened mass from one cheekbone to the other. His left eye had been smeared to bloody pulp in its socket.

Bolan bent and drew the little machine pistol bayonet he had tucked in his boot.

Shang's right eye regarded Bolan with stone-cold murder as he stalked forward.

The Executioner threw the bayonet in his hand shovel style in an underhanded toss at Shang's blind eye socket. The blade went low and sank two inches into Shang's neck. Bolan backed up as his adversary reached to pull the knife free. He had either missed the artery or Shang was somehow controlling the bleeding with internal strength. Shang bent and picked up his fallen butterfly knife.

Bolan lunged. His knife hissed through the air and met one of Shang's with a clang. Their guards grated, and Shang suddenly hooked the weapon out of Bolan's hands. The man's second weapon whipped upward. Bolan heaved himself backward, and the blade ripped a furrow in the fiberglass of his armor and grated on the titanium plate beneath. His calf nearly collapsed on him as he hopped backward. Bolan abandoned his balance and rolled backward across the command shack control panel. One of Shang's blades chopped down through a computer monitor next to where the soldier's head had been a moment before. Bolan toppled across the table awkwardly but landed on his feet. He kept the table between himself and Shang as he inched backward. His eyes flicked across the floor for a fallen rifle.

Bolan lunged for a G-36.

Shang flung his knife. The blade bounced off Bolan's armor and sent him tottering on his injured leg. He reeled and ducked as the second weapon scythed an inch past his face. Only the wall kept Bolan from falling. Shang bent his knees and exploded into the air. He cleared the table and the control panels on top of it in a single standing leap. Bolan leaned against the wall. There was nowhere to retreat and no weapons within reach. His hands stiffened into blunt spears.

Shang's ruined face smiled like a jack-o'-lantern as his hands curled into tiger claws. His English was slurred as he spoke past the flapping shreds of his left cheek. "I believe you mentioned a demonstration of tendon tearing techniques."

"Shang!" Jack Grimaldi popped up off the floor in a repeat performance of his bound-and-shackled, jumping-jack maneuver. Bolan's eyes flared. A six-foot length of the exploded hose lay flopped across the end of the control panel. At the end of it, the nozzle lay half submerged in the water. Grimaldi hurtled through the air in a flying mule kick. However, Shang had seen the manuever before and Grimaldi had gone to the well one too many times.

Shang caught Grimaldi by his crotch and his collar and pressed him overhead, then hurled him through the window of the shack. The Stony Man pilot flew into the gale in a shower of shattered glass. Arctic air and freezing rain blasted into the shack. Shang turned to finish Bolan.

The brass nozzle swung around at his head. His blind left eye prevented him from seeing it a split second too late. He threw up his arm to block, but the canvas hose curled around his forearm and only speeded the arc of the nozzle. The five pounds of brass collided with the side of Shang's head. He staggered backward.

Bolan yanked his weapon back, took a second to steady himself on his good leg, then whirled a six-foot length of flexible weapon in both hands. The left side of Shang's head was bleeding a river. His right eye was unfocused. He reeled, stunned, and put up his hands awkwardly to cover his head.

Bolan swung the hose down and around in an underhand blow. The brass nozzle hurtled up crushingly between Shang's legs.

The Chinese assassin's hands dropped as he faltered.

The soldier yanked the weapon back and whirled it around his head like an Olympic hammer thrower. The blood-drenched brass whipped around in a horrible arc and collided with Shang's skull.

The man fell backward across the control panel.

Bolan took the slippery brass weight of the nozzle in both hands, raised it overhead and brought it down onto his adversary's head. Bones splintered. The five-pound brass nozzle rose and fell a second and third time. Bolan staggered back, gasping for breath. The length of hose fell from his hands.

Bolan toppled forward again and caught himself on the control panel. The interior of the shack howled like a wind tunnel, and he could feel the water and blood covering him freeze. He struggled to pull the freezing air into his burning lungs. Bolan let his breath normalize, but he couldn't stop shaking. He ignored it as he went to the far door of the shack. The gale assaulted him as he opened the door to the observation deck.

It took all of his will to heave Jack Grimaldi's beaten body over his shoulder. He half hopped, half staggered back into the shack. Bolan tottered into the side office and dropped Grimaldi into the chair behind the desk, then slammed the office door shut against the cold and cranked up the thermostat. Bolan leaned against the wall, then slid down as his knees buckled.

"You got Shang," Grimaldi croaked.

"Yeah," Bolan wheezed back.

"How'd you manage that?"

Bolan closed his eyes and leaned his head back. "I beat him to death with a firehose."

"Nice." Grimaldi closed his eyes. "I really hated that guy."

"Yeah, me, too."

The two men spent long moments just breathing. The frozen blood that covered them was thawing in the heat of the office. Fresh blood was beginning to seep out of each of them with renewed vigor. Bolan examined his friend. He looked as if he'd gone a full fifteen rounds out of his weight class.

He looked horrible.

Grimaldi groaned. "So what happens?"

"I don't know. I don't think the government will risk the crisis of exposing the Chinese. The President will probably hold it over their head as one hell of a bargaining chip during any high-level negotiations for the rest of his term."

"Typical. What about the nukes?"

"Hal can worry about them."

"Yeah." Grimaldi was silent for long moments except for the labor of his breathing. Bolan almost thought he had passed out until he spoke again. "So what do you wanna do?"

"I don't know. The command shack is smashed to hell. It's also flooded and freezing over. There's a Chinese minisub parked below, but I don't think they'll be happy to see just you and me." Bolan peered at the shelf beside Grimaldi. "There's a bottle of Scotch over there. I suppose we could just wait out the storm and see what happens."

Grimaldi sighed happily at the bottle of single malt. "I wonder if these assholes have cable."

James Axler
Outlanders®

MAD GOD'S WRATH

The survivors of the oldest moon colony have been revived from cryostasis and brought to Cerberus Redoubt, leaving behind an enemy in deep, frozen sleep. But betrayal and treachery bring the rebel stronghold under seige by the resurrected demon king of a lost world. With a prize hostage in tow to lure Kane and his fellow warriors, he retreats to the uncharted planet of mystery and impossibility for a final act of madness.

Available February 2004 at your favorite retail outlet.

Or order your copy now by sending your name, address, zip or postal code, along with a check or money order (please do not send cash) for $6.50 for each book ordered ($7.99 in Canada), plus 75¢ postage and handling ($1.00 in Canada), payable to Gold Eagle Books, to:

In the U.S.	In Canada
Gold Eagle Books	Gold Eagle Books
3010 Walden Avenue	P.O. Box 636
P.O. Box 9077	Fort Erie, Ontario
Buffalo, NY 14269-9077	L2A 5X3

Please specify book title with your order.
Canadian residents add applicable federal and provincial taxes.

GOUT28

DEATH LANDS.

Hellbenders

*Available in March 2004
at your favorite retail outlet.*

Emerging from a gateway into a redoubt filled with preDark technology, Ryan and his band hope to unlock some of the secrets of post-nuclear America. But the fortified redoubt is under the control of a half-mad former sec man hell-bent on vengeance, who orders Ryan and the others to jump-start his private war against two local barons. Under the harsh and pitiless glare of the rad-blasted desert sun, the companions fight to see another day, whatever it brings....